Kept to the Shadows

By Lisa J. Comstock

2018

Second printing: 2014, 2018

This is a work of fiction. Names, characters, businesses, places, events and incidents are either products of the author's imagination or used in a fictitious manner. Any resemblance to actual persons, living or dead, or actual events is purely coincidental.

.

Enclave Productions, LLC has allowed this work to remain exactly as the author intended, verbatim, with limited editorial input.

Softcover ISBN: **978-0578414690**
PUBLISHED BY ENCLAVE PRODUCTIONS, LLC
USA

Printed in the United States of America

Keep an eye out for all the books from
Lisa J. Comstock:

If you don't find them in your local book store –
ask them to order them for you!

This book is dedicated to:
my sister and best friend, Nina Liv Witham
Thank you for all your help making it perfect!

I want to thank so many people for helping me see my books in print, but I want to give special thanks to:

My husband, Steve Comstock, for understanding my need to visit with my characters so often.

My mom, Jane Witham, who has always encouraged my imagination.

My dad, Royce Witham, who is smiling down on me from heaven. I miss you so much!

And, my little sister, best friend, and fellow author, Nina Liv Witham for being there in all things, not the least of which has been acting as sounding board and proofreader!

I wouldn't be here without all of you, I love you all!

1

Labor Pains

The physician from Arrachsnow finally arrived with the potion to ease the queen's pain and induce labor.

The king and queen had been trying for years to give the kingdom an heir and had been overjoyed when her cycle stopped nine months before. It had been a hard pregnancy, plagued by complications since the first month so no one was surprised when it seemed the child didn't want to cooperate and enter the world unassisted.

She had been in labor for nearly thirty-six hours now; the midwives didn't know what they could do for her. She wasn't fully breach; the child just didn't want to come out. The head midwife was working as hard as she could to get the baby to turn but it was refusing to.

The queen was barely cognizant when the physician poured the thick liquid down her throat but she unconsciously swallowed it. It took effect on her quickly, lucky for her; she couldn't have bled anymore without risking her life.

The queen screamed out as the child came into the world moments later.

The head midwife quickly cut the umbilical cord and took the wet baby to the waiting physician to check it for any defects.

The man submerged the squirming child in the bucket of waiting water, to wash off the blood, then laid it on a clean linen sheet and began to look it over. Meanwhile all but the queen, who was still unconscious, waited in anticipation. Finally the man stepped back and said, quite proudly, "He is perfect." He wrapped the boy up in the sheet and held him up in the light streaming through the window.

As soon as they heard this the other two midwives began to clean the queen up to prepare her so the physician could stitch up her torn opening. They jumped back when she let out another blood curdling scream. Her womb suddenly contracted again and they saw another head begin to come out. Their hands went to their mouths in horror as they backed away, calling for the head mid-wife and physician, unsure what to do.

The physician, still holding the first child, and the head midwife looked at the priest, who had been standing silent in the corner, for direction. He jumped as another scream ripped from the queen.

Father Anaith motioned for them to act, grabbing a blanket from the trunk beside him as the queen screamed out again. He went to the bed, held out the blanket, took the bundle from the frightened woman's arms, closed the blanket over it and held it at arm's length. "This thing did not happen, do you understand me?"

he said pointedly, looking at each in turn, "Swear, on your lives, this day will never be spoken of," not moving his eyes until each nodded. Without another word he left the room through the side door, to a set of stairs that would lead out to the courtyard.

The physician called the lower midwives away from the queen and instructed them to get the prince made presentable to his father then went to work on the queen, who had fallen into a coma. He stitched her up and called for the pig's bladder of blood to replenish her body of what it had lost. He didn't relax until she had begun to breathe easier and fell into a deep sleep.

He stepped away and told the midwives she would be weak for a few days but she would live as he went to the bowl of water and began to clean himself up.

The priest reentered the room just in time to hear the happy news. His chest hitched as he looked at the queen, who had been his friend for more than ten years. He said, "Please forgive me," under his breath.

****

King Vianor and his advisor, Dulmuth, were pacing back and forth outside the queen's chamber. The midwives wouldn't allow them into the room no matter how much he swore and threatened their lives.

Each scream that ripped from the queen's chamber ripped through each man's heart like a dull sword.

Vianor wasn't sure what he should do, what if he lost the queen, what if the child was stillborn? He was sure this was his punishment.

Another scream, this one lasting quite a while, came from the chamber then, stopping his heart. He couldn't take any more. He had just reached the handle when the door opened to the smiling face of a midwife. She had a bundle in her arms, which she held out to him. The king hesitated then took it and jumped, it was alive and squirming.

"You have a son, your majesty."

The king looked down at the small baby in his arms, his son. He had two eyes, which were bluish looking when he opened them, wisps of dark hair on his round head, a nose, a tiny mouth with tiny lips, and ten perfectly formed fingers and toes. He smiled then looked at the midwife and asked about his wife.

She only shrugged then turned away from him and went back into the room.

He started to follow but again the door was closed in his face. He looked from it, to his new son then to his advisor, who was smiling at the boy, and sank to the bench.

2

Harsh Measures

Life in Glochester County had never been easy but the drought of 925 had made it worse and the Populace Edict enacted to counter the effects had made it worse still. Many of the lower classes, those lacking the education to know better, thought the gods had forsaken them for some unknown sin and began to worship emphatically, others swore off them entirely, sure they had done nothing to possibly anger them, which made the former even more fanatical, trying to appease those gods the latter were further angering.

Either way, the drought wouldn't end.

The first droughts were only days, then they lasted months, then they didn't stop.

When Auldenway Council met to enact the law that was now haunting them, they were two years into the most recent drought. This one was only now, seventeen years later, considered to be over. The damage it caused was enormous and was only now being remedied.

Despite popular opinion they hadn't done this to be cruel, they had done it for the people.

Crops in the fields had withered before they even sprouted, what did manage to survive was all stunted and tasteless. Because there wasn't enough water to spare the livestock pastures weren't maintained, so most of the herds of cattle, goats and sheep had to be slaughtered or sold to neighboring counties, leaving few to feed the people. The huge storage coffers, that once held a surplus thought to last five years, had long since been drained and there wasn't any to replace the stores with. Hunger, sickness and death were all each new morning seemed to bring.

It had taken most of the last four years for these issues to even begin to be reversed.

Though the famine brought on by the drought had killed thousands, the population was still too great. The few farm fields that had managed to remain fertile could not support that still increasing population. Measures had to be taken – harsh measures.

The edict was cruel and had made many hate the king but he had no choice. Even he'd had to abide by it, having to take measures to prevent his queen from conceiving a second time.

The law stated no couple was allowed more than one child living with them at a time. If a woman became pregnant while she had a child under the age of sixteen living at home the child would be destroyed in her womb. If it was unsafe to do this it would be destroyed upon its birth.

If the mother died during childbirth and the father couldn't, or did not want to, raise the child, it would be put into an orphanage. Multiple births, luckily, were rare; in these cases, if the firstborn appeared healthy, then the second, and any that followed, would be destroyed.

Because of the sickness caused by the drought the orphanages were overflowing. Some of the larger cities of Glochester County had only one, the capital city, Ghorst, had three. Largest of them was Abbeydrew, which could hold fifty safely, the smaller two, Coatstair and Joyate, were meant to accommodate only twenty five each, this year, 940, all were far over full capacity.

Something had to be done – harsh measures.

****

King Vianor paced before the assembly in the great hall. The Auldenway Council had met every month since time and memoriam, this time it was to reevaluate the populace edict. The council was split on whether it should be ended. The king was trying to stay open-minded as he listened to their arguments.

"We will know what to do now if another drought hits us. The edict was needed when it was upon us but it is done now," said Lord Durbaith of Arrachsnow.

"If we allow them free reign the serfs will be unstoppable. They have no comprehension of the need for not allowing this to happen again. They do not understand abstinence; they will not stop themselves and we will soon have too many again," spat Lord Felwaith of Doveslade.

"We can educate them. If they understand the need to keep the population down…" said Father Anaith.

Many didn't believe a priest had any right to be on the council but one had always been. Father Anaith himself had been for the whole time of the edict and had always felt it was very inhumane. Slowly, he was turning some to his way of thinking but this made others nervous.

"The serfs are already causing strains on the coffers. The turnout tomorrow is going to increase the numbers too much too quickly. We must leave it a few more years at least," spat Lord Anyach of Cuttersville. "To insure that increase doesn't put us back in a deficit."

"Enough! I will be making my yearly rounds with Prince Acthiel end of the month. We will see what effects it has had and consider it then," said the king as he poured himself some more wine.

"What!?" squawked the young prince, jumping to attention.

Acthiel couldn't understand why he needed to be at these inane meetings at all, he had a hundred things he would rather be doing and secretly hated his father for making him have to sit in on these. He had been sitting in the corner through the entire meeting, as he did every meeting, one leg over the arm of the chair, pouting. He had been unconsciously picking apart a loaf of bread and dropping the crumbs on the floor at his feet. He dropped his leg to the floor and the last bit of that loaf dropped from his hand.

King Vianor shot his son a look telling him to be quiet then looked back at the other men and added, "I will be evaluating the impact of the restrictions on the counties as well this trip. When we meet next month I will give report and we will make a final decision then. You may all retire to your chambers until dinner." No one argued with him. They all respected him and his thoughts more than any other.

The council members each came forward, bowed to the king and prince, kissed the kings rings and left the main hall, leaving only the king and prince in the hall.

The prince was still standing in the middle of the crumbs he had been dropping on the floor with the same look of disbelief and shock on his face. He was staring hard at his father, expecting him to tell him he had only made the threat to appease the council, not really meaning it. He could see by the stern look the man had that he did.

"Very adult, Acthiel," said Vianor, indicating the floor at his son's feet with irritation. "I do not ask much of you, Boy, the least you can do is show the council the respect they deserve when in their presence."

The prince would be turning sixteen in three months and wasn't expected to take rule for many years to come but the king wanted him included in as many aspects of it as he could be, so he would be ready if, the gods forbid, something unexpected happened.

Acthiel rolled his eyes, "They don't respect me; how am I to respect them?" He brushed at the crumbs with his feet then and added, "and I wouldn't want the staff to think we don't need them anymore. Haven't you been trying to teach me that a serf is human as well?"

Vianor had never once lifted his hand to his son, something he was now regretting. He clenched his hands into fists and took a deep breath; trying to calm himself before that was no longer a regret.

He had tried to be a just king, he didn't believe in ruling by force but he had been forced to make some hard choices for his people. He wanted Acthiel to understand why he'd had to do this. It wasn't to punish the people or force his wishes on them; it had been for the good of them all. He hoped, if the prince could see this firsthand, see how the people had suffered, he would understand why and could prevent any further harm to them. Most weren't allowed to speak for themselves so they had to. Unlike many of the nobles, he didn't see serfs as insects.

"Would you like me to get on the floor and clean them all up, Father?" asked Acthiel irreverently.

Prince Acthiel was much harder than his father, partly because he had grown up through the whole of the proclamation. He was born the year it was instituted so he didn't know a time when life was easy. As prince he had a far easier life than most would have had though so in all sense he would never truly know it either way.

Vianor had given his son a parcel of land, a small keep with a farm and about fifteen serfs to handle any way he saw fit, in an attempt to show him what it truly meant to rule people without using force. If anything, it only made him harder. He'd had more than one serf punished for little or no reason. If the king hadn't taken the lands back he would have done more and risked being hated.

"That's enough, Acthiel," snapped the king. "You can stomp around here, shred as many loaves of bread you like, pout and act as childish as you like, you *will* be going with me."

They would be leaving for the annual visit of the counties in only a few days. This time the king was going to allow many of the serfs to speak on their own behalf. He hoped what he heard from them would allow him to rescind, or at least change parts of the edict and he hoped his son might finally find some connection to their people.

"Why can't I stay here?" whined the prince. He was at the age where he questioned every rule, seeing what ones he could get away with bending and which could be broken entirely. He found this easier to do with his mother but he still tried occasionally with his father.

This was to be his first trip with his father so he had new rules he had to test.

"You must see your people and be seen by them, Acthiel. Being a ruler is more than just living in a castle and having servants to wait on you hand and foot," said the king, tired of having to fight everything with his son.

"I can see them just as easily from the balcony on market day or when they come for the audiences, father... Why can't they come to us?"

The queen came into the room as the prince said this. Seeing the look of anger on both of their faces, she knew it was only going to get more heated. "Why are you two fighting now?" she asked. She loved both men but was always softer with the prince.

This was a fact that irritated the king to no end. He wondered if she was again going to take his son's side, which would cause the two of them to fight in turn.

"Mother, tell him I don't have to go. Remember, Princess Anya will be arriving later this month. Shouldn't I stay here to welcome her? Wouldn't it be rude of me not to be here when she arrives?"

"She will need time to get herself situated, Acthiel. You will be back well enough in time for the reception," said Vianor.

"But…"

"Acthiel, your father is right this time. You are a man now; you cannot hide from your duties any longer."

The prince looked at his mother as if she had just slapped his face. "I am not considered a man until I am eighteen!" he said as he kicked the piece of loaf on the floor in front of his foot. He knew this was a bad argument even as it was coming from his mouth, considering the council had just decided a male orphan of fifteen was now an adult to free up the overcrowded wards. Still, he waited for his mother to back down and tell his father to leave him be, as she had every other time before. The look on her face told him that this time she wasn't going to. He huffed out an indignant breath, stamped his foot and left the room, slamming the door loudly behind him.

The queen jumped and gasped then started to go after her upset son.

The king stopped her with a hand on her arm. The first time the two had touched in close to a week. "Leave him be."

"I should not have been so harsh with him," said Queen Vela.

She had never fully recovered from the boy's birth; her physical weakness had caused her to be mentally weak as well. She had never felt connected to the boy. Perhaps knowing she had almost died giving birth to him made her fear him in some way.

"You should have been harsher with him. You coddle him too much, Vela, you always have. He will grow to be a weak man if he does not learn his place now," spat the king as he walked over to the table and poured two chalices of wine. He drank from one and held the other out to the queen.

She didn't take it. "There are other ways for him to learn to be a man, Vianor."

Vianor would never admit it aloud to anyone but he resented his son. The boy had taken away the queen's spirit and no matter how hard the king tried to make the boy learn he tried to break his father's.

The King slammed the chalice he'd been holding out to his wife down on the table, spilling half its contents and making the wine carafe jump, and said, "He will go with me if I have to tie him up and throw him over his horse."

"I will not fight you on this, Vianor," said the queen, putting her hands to her temples and rubbing at them roughly. "I am very tired now, I am going to bed."

He watched her leave the room then walked to the window and looked out it, the sun wasn't even beginning to set and she had barely been up a few hours. He closed his eyes, shook his head, sighed and thought the same thing he had nearly every day since his son had come into the harsh world, *this is my punishment.*

Kept to the Shadows

3

Kept to the Shadows

Four people slowly walked down the shadowy alley. The one in the lead put his hand up, halting the other three in a tight line. He waited for a light in the window opposite them to go out then counted to ten before motioning the one behind him to step out.

The second in line took the signal and slowly crept toward the side of the house opposite them. Since they had done this nearly nightly for a week, their eyes had grown accustomed to the dark; the boy could make out the sack at the bottom of the steps without trying. He slowly crept across the street and lifted the brown cloth sack sitting at the base. He was pleased with the weight of it, much larger than the others they had collected this night. He threw it onto his back and slowly rejoined the group.

They made one more stop like this before making their way to the warehouse district.

The warehouse district ran along the sea side of Ghorst. Here the buildings crowded the streets and went up several floors. Most were made of brick and didn't have many windows. There were no street lamps along the street since no one had ever needed to be in the district after dark so it was darker than the others.

Once they had been a bustle of activity during the day, workers loading and unloading merchandise off ships and packing up that merchandise to be taken by cart to the inland cities. They all stood abandoned now, and had been ever since the last drought had struck. They were now home to serfs that didn't want to work at legal jobs, didn't meet the requirements of work visas or were too young for hospice and too old for the orphanage. Most of the building's occupants now were thieves by trade.

The four reached a two-story silo at the end of the row and ducked inside. They could see a fire burning in a fire pit that was cobbled together in the corner, which was where Sabban and Beau were waiting for them.

"A good gathering!" said Sabban happily, seeing five bags. He and the other boy behind him began to move toward the four eagerly. "Empty the bags and I will sort through it." He saw the two tallest tensing up and knew they were about to protest. He knew this lesson would have to be taught quickly; with a flick of the wrist Beau stepped forward and the grumbles subsided.

Sabban and Beau were completely opposite.

Beau was Sabban's muscle, all strength and no brain. He was stalky but tall, at about six feet, had straggly black hair and didn't seem to be able to grow more than the patchy stubble he always had on his square jaw. Whenever Sabban needed someone *pushed* Beau was ready, able and eager.

Sabban barely stood five feet tall. He was only nineteen but he was already balding, what was once bright red hair was disappearing quickly, mostly in a ring around his head. He always had a sunburn on his face and the bald part of his head and always wore nice, whole, clothing, partly because he always kept the best of his workers finds for himself.

He had been in the Coatstair home on the east side of town; he had been turned out three years before and had been living, as he called it, since shortly after. The things he had learned to stay alive since could be essential to the four if they were going to survive.

He had been through the system and been spit out, which had hardened him. He was placed at a farm in Lichland for employ upon his release but the treatment there was worse even than he had received at the orphanage. It had given him more than one of the many scars he had. He was beaten on a daily basis and expected to do anything the hateful farmer and his wife expected of him without complaint. His work habits didn't meet with their expectations and they had accused him of having sticky fingers – which he did have.

He had been taking in other orphans being turned out and training them to his life for many years now; he had nearly thirty workers in Ghorst and neighboring towns now, all giving him a percentage of their finds, and had some acting as bodyguards or as muscle to force local merchants to pay for protection. Now he had these *new* recruits ripe for the life but he had to push his authority on them before they left the building.

Wayde, Dell, Kyi and Cameron had been in the west side home, Abbeydrew, since birth. This home was considered wealthier than the other two, partly because it was closest to the castle so they got the better handouts. Sabban knew it tended to turn out orphans that held themselves in higher esteem than the others as well. The housemother there was much more caring than the others; she treated her wards with caring and respect, this in turn made them have more self-esteem and self-worth than most orphans. They could still be made to work for him but it would make them harder to mold. He needed to do it quickly.

He knew the thought of leaving their home was one of the most frightening things they could likely imagine, shadowed only by thoughts of being separated from each other maybe. He knew meeting him would seem a godsend to the frightened wards; so he had the advantage. He had shown them the people and places they could get help from, now they were going to be learning what he wanted in exchange for his information.

He wasn't worried about Kyi or Cami, they were followers no matter who was the leader; Wayde and Dell were the strong-willed ones. They had a friendship that would make it hard to keep them separated, and they both protected Cami and Kyi above all else.

That was why he had Beau with him.

"Now, you all can sort through the rest," he said after he had removed about half the pile, leaving a few good pieces this time to make them think he was a generous person. He watched them while they took turns taking pieces from the leftovers, smiling to himself.

Cami went first, partly because she was a girl, Kyi next, then Dell and finally Wayde.

The thug studied each, looking for the best way to work them. The order of their mini class seemed to be Wayde, Dell, Cami and Kyi, which had been a little unexpected.

Kyi was small for his age of fifteen and very shy. He had brown hair, cut in a pageboy fashion, it made him look silly and weak but the boy liked it. His eyes rarely looked up so Sabban wasn't sure if they were green or brown. He always looked to either Wayde or Dell before anything he did. He would be the easiest to mold – he only needed to make him to worship him as he did his friends.

Cameron would be a beautiful woman when she had a few more years on her. At sixteen she was already quite striking. Long blonde hair fell in waves of curls to her waist and her eyes were the deepest blue he had ever seen. Her skin was fair and unblemished and looked delicious. She always wore loose fitting clothing so he couldn't get a good idea of just how well turned she was but he knew men who would like her either way. The twinkle in her eyes told him that she likely would enjoy the work very much. He would enjoy training her very much, though he had little doubt he wouldn't be the first. She would prove a little tougher to break than Kyi but still not impossible. She too valued Wayde and Dell's opinions but she seemed drawn more to Wayde. Sabban found this interesting since Dell would seem to be the one woman would flock to and looked more the leader type.

Dell was almost too pretty to be male. His long, wildly curly, brownish black hair framed his well-shaped face perfectly and his teeth were all but perfect. His light blue eyes penetrated to one's very soul; those eyes could make men or women do just what the boy wanted them to. His build was nearly equal to Beau's. He had helped rebuild more than one part of the orphanage over his years there, lifting and carrying the heavy timbers had built him up some fine muscles. What showed through his gauzy tunic told how the work had changed his sixteen year old frame. His delicate features looked to be of noble blood. Sabban wondered if this were so, if he perhaps he could find out who his parents had been and use this to his advantage.

For all Dell's perfection made Sabban nervous, even he looked to the last for guidance.

Wayde was good looking as well but in a more rugged sort of way. He was solid for his age as well but his presence of mind was more a worry than his physical strength. He had spirit that came from deep inside and he seemed able to find calm in any situation. He too was sixteen but he seemed much wiser and seemed to know his place in the world. His eyes were blue-gray and quite bright, considering he likely had never gotten a lot of health care. He had good teeth, a well-shaped smile and strong, well-defined, features but wasn't overly large for his build. His blondish brown hair was left long in the front to hide a scar on his forehead, not because he was ashamed of it but because of the odd reactions people had when they saw it. He said that their housemother told him it was likely made by a tool used during his birth, which implied it had been rough. It had likely been him that had killed his mother leaving him in an orphanage. Sabban couldn't find any way to use this bit of information without creating a formidable enemy though.

Wayde would be considered attractive to members of either sex for his presence as much as his handsome features. Sabban had little doubt the boy would learn to use this to his advantage as time went by but he wanted to find a way to force him to use it to his advantage. He had many ideas for the boy but he doubted he would get a chance to see any of them to fruition; Wayde was simply too strong-willed. No, it would be far better to take him out of the picture entirely.

Sabban waited until they were finished dividing up the last of the lot before he spoke, "Tomorrow you will be out of the home, have you decided to join us?"

Wayde looked to the others to be sure nothing had changed before he answered. Speaking quietly but surely, he said, "We appreciate the lessons you have taught us, Sabban, no doubt they will be lifelong, but we have decided we are going to see what the council can offer us for work first."

Sabban had partly expected that so he had an answer already ready for them, "You won't like being forced to do for others. You do know that you'll have even less freedom than you did at the home and will likely not be placed near each other?"

"Still, we will try," said Dell, standing up behind his friend, though he wasn't any wider he was a good head taller than Wayde so the impression this made was strong.

The bully shuddered briefly before saying, "Very well. I'll give you a month. If you don't return to me before you will not be welcomed so quickly."

"We need to get back before we are missed," said Wayde as he stood and motioned for the others to go.

The other two stood right behind him, bundled up their finds and followed Dell out of the building.

None of them even questioned Wayde; this further proved to Sabban who was their leader.

The boy didn't immediately follow, instead he waited until his friends were well out of earshot and said, "I don't take well to threats, Sabban, nor do I take well to having my friends threatened. I will tell you, right here and now, anything happens to any of them and I learn you were any part of it..." His finger came forward then to set the point.

This Sabban didn't have an answer to.

The thug let the words linger as he watched Wayde jogging to catch up to his friends, he turned to Beau and said, "I think I must speak to my friend on the council before morning."

4

Abbeydrew

Fifteen years of overflowing orphanages had taken their toll on the county's finances, the council didn't like it but they had to do something, they had no choice. They would remedy the situation by turning out any that were physically able to be out on their own. Normally, a child would remain a ward of the homes until they reached eighteen but the council was forced to change the age to fifteen for boys and sixteen for girls.

The exodus had been held off until the warmer months at least, to allow them to procure employment on a farm, take an apprenticeship or some such. The king had appointed the local bailiffs to assist in finding the wards adequate placements in hopes of making the transition as smooth and painless as possible.

Although life at Abbeydrew was tough it was heaven compared to the other orphanages. The keepers at this one treated them as people; the others were often treated as criminals, there the keepers often used *turning them out* as a threat to keep them in line.

Life for the wards under ten years old in Abbeydrew was spent playing most of the day. The only chores they were expected to do was to make their beds in the mornings and take their dishes into the kitchen to be washed after each meal. Once they reached ten that changed, then they had school to attend and their list of chores increased exponentially. Like the younger wards they were expected to make their beds and take their dishes to the kitchen but they also had to wash those dishes, as well as the younger children's, help cook and serve the meals, wash floors and windows, do laundry, dust and help maintain the buildings; though much of these were tied in with their schooling.

Girls were taught sewing and embroidery, cooking, housekeeping, and how to handle a house's finances. Some of the boys also learned cooking and handling finances but most were taught carpentry by helping out with repairs to the facilities buildings, farming on the parcel of land the king had allotted each home for their use, how to handle the livestock the homes kept for milking and slaughter, and, for the ones who wished it, swordplay.

Boys and girls both were encouraged to learn reading, writing and basic math skills.

Schooling took up eight hours of each day and the chores took up much of the rest. They had only four hours each day to pursue their own interests, two hours at midday and two hours before lights out.

Working in an orphanage was never easy. Very few could stomach the conditions or bring themselves to care for the unwanted. The ones that did were saints. Sister Jessa had been the housemother of Abbeydrew, in the west side of Ghorst, for about five years. She had started as a scullery maid in the kitchen nearly fifteen years before, just as the orphanages were reaching full capacity. The turnover of workers at the orphanages was high – few lasted more than a year. Her longevity had meant that she had worked her way up quickly to her current position. It was one she had enjoyed, for the most part. Today, she hated it.

As it was now, her facility had seventy-five wards, almost twice what it should have, far more than their coffers could afford. She hated what the council was ordering them to do but she too knew they couldn't continue with so many.

She opened the door of the first ward slowly, walked the length of cots, turned when she reached the end of the row and walked back to the doors. She did this for a number of reasons but mostly counting the heads to be sure all were where they should be and were well, or as well as could be expected in their overcrowded conditions.

A few stirred as she started out of the room; she stopped and waited for them to fall back into their fitful sleep. A few coughs broke the silence but no one got up so she allowed herself to breathe again – so often, one moving would wake them all.

The children in this wing of the building were safe from tomorrow's proceedings, the oldest was barely nine, but many would be moving into the next room after tomorrow. Some were reaching the age when they should no longer share quarters with the opposite sex. She said a quiet prayer for good dreams and closed the door.

The next room would likely be losing five or six but more than half would be moving to the last room. Now that they would have the space to do as the wardrooms were intended, girls over eight would be in one wardroom and boys over eight in the other.

She peered through the crude window before entering this room. Lights out was at four until midnight for these wards but since it was just about midnight they should all be long since off to dreamland. She could see no movement so she started into the room. As with the previous room, she walked the length, again counting heads, then turned and walked back out.

This room was more crowded than the first. The youngest was eleven, the oldest fifteen. There were three boys that would be leaving her from this room. She felt they were too young to be out on their own but she had no choice. Like the first, this room was overcrowded and had mixed sexes, not a good idea during the pre-adolescent years of discoveries. Part of the Populace Edict was that all children born had to be educated on all parts of the edict and of the need for abstinence when they became adults but it was easier said than done when the children were forced to live in such close quarters with members of the opposite sex.

They had never had any wards become pregnant while she was housemother but they had had troubles in the past. And hopefully, after tomorrow, it never would happen. Tomorrow they could move the girls to the last room.

The last room of wards would be empty at this time tomorrow evening. Jessa stood outside this room and listened. She heard nothing from inside but snores and loud breathing so she opened the door.

The children in this room were considered adults due to the council's decree. The youngest was fifteen, the oldest just turning seventeen. These were the children conceived during the worst of the drought. It sickened her to think they were being punished a second time for nothing they had done.

Pain clutched her chest at the thought of sending them out into the harsh unfair world. They had been sheltered, fed, clothed and cared for their entire lives by others, now they were being forced to fend for themselves. She knew some of them might not live long after.

Some would be placed in local noble households as servants, some would be put to work on one of the farms, and some would be offered apprenticeships with a local tradesman but few would stay. As with others that had left the homes, many would leave the county entirely, would become bandits and thieves or would be dead in a matter of months.

Jessa began to walk the length of this room, as she had the other two, again counting heads. This time she stopped at the third bed in. That one and the next three were empty, the sheets on each still made up from the morning chore. Panic gripped her heart and she started to bolt from the room then she stopped.

Normally, her immediate response would have been to sound the alarm. An instinct she had to fight now. This night she would let the absences go. The four would not be there this time tomorrow so it would do no good to raise the alarm tonight. She crossed herself and kissed the silver cross she wore on a chain hanging between her breasts, praying they were alright; those four were her favorite, albeit most troublesome, wards. She finished her check and left as she had the two before. Wiping a tear from her cheek, she headed for her office at the end of the hall.

5

Harsh Reality

Wayde stayed three to four steps behind the others as they made their way back to what had been their home for as long as they could remember but would be off limits to them within a few hours; then they would learn to what new world they would be sent. He was still angry at what Sabban had said, partly because he had a feeling it was more true than he wanted to admit.

The other three wouldn't hear his warnings about the thugs or about their future. They were naïve enough to think they would get placed together. He knew the chances of this was slim at best, even before Sabban had voiced this same sentiment. None of them had been considered especially lucky.

Meeting Sabban had seemed such a godsend at first. Having no one to answer to but one's self after having curfews and chores and schedules seemed like near heaven. The older boy had shown them places and people they could get help from without the danger of getting in trouble. Wayde knew that knowledge came with a price, one he wasn't keen on them having to pay. Dell was careful with how friendly he got with the older boys, seeing how nervous Wayde was, but Cami and Kyi were immediately taken with the seemingly easy life Sabban was offering, not seeing anything bad in it.

Placement could mean a more reliable roof over their heads and more regular food in their stomachs or it may not – they had been told horror stories by the thug of what some of the turn-outs he had helped had found themselves faced with in their placements – even Wayde would admit living under the thumb of the thug was better than that.

Choosing Sabban's way of life would have its drawbacks too. They would be considered lower even than the workers if they refused the offer of placement. They would only be able to come out at night and they would have to move often – the castle guards raided the hovels on a regular basis – rounding up any they found and forcing them into servitude on one of the local farms or factories. Was it better to conform now or be forced to do it later?

Wayde had not liked the threat he heard behind Sabban's words – guessing he had plans for them he was not divulging and none of them would like all that much. Plans that might be worse even than the possibility of getting placed in situations far away from each other. His threat to the thugs had been mostly only words. Although his outward appearance would suggest otherwise he really didn't like to fight. He fully intended to stand by his friends and he would fight to his death if the man tried to corrupt or harm them in any way. He had little doubt the world they were about to enter would do that well enough all by itself.

****

Thanks to the older boy they now knew the side streets and alleyways by heart so it took them little time to get back to the home. The first time they had snuck out they had almost been caught because it took them almost the whole night to find their way back, not realizing how far from it they had wandered.

They heard the bell in the church tower on the other side of town ring just once, telling them it was almost two hours later than they had intended to be. They stood in the shadows of the street across from the home and just watched it. There would have been lights on and lots of activity if Sister Jessa had sounded the alarm, that silence was a good sign. They didn't want to take any chance that the woman might change her mind. Wayde motioned Kyi and Cami to cross the street then he and Dell hitched the bags they were carrying higher up on their shoulders and followed.

The side door to the home's inner yard was still unlatched, telling them either it had not been found or Sister Jessa never went looking. They opened it just wide enough to slip through and did so, one at a time. They stayed flat against the wall until they were all in then they slunk along that wall, staying in the shadows, until they were below the window to the storeroom. It too was still unlatched.

Dell, being the tallest, pushed it open then pulled himself up onto the ledge and dropped inside first, moments later he put his hand down to pull up Kyi up.

Wayde stayed on the ground, as always, and helped lift the other two up then passed Dell the two bags and grabbed his hand and let him haul him up. The door to the storeroom was also still unlatched.

Wayde opened it a crack and glanced down the hallway; everyone, including Sister Jessa, should have long since gone to their beds but a light was still burning inside the housemother's office. He felt a twinge of panic and guilt. He knew she had to know they had gone out and knew she was likely beside herself with worry of what they'd gotten themselves into but... it couldn't be helped. He put his finger to his lips and pointed up the hall to let them know she was still up so they had to stay quiet, then motioned Kyi to step out.

The smallest of them did so, being surprisingly quiet considering he seemed somehow to always find anything that could possibly make a peep without trying.

Dell went next, for all his large size he *could* be quiet without hardly even trying. There really wasn't much he couldn't do.

Cami stepped up behind Wayde then but she didn't immediately leave the darkness of the storeroom.

He turned to her, put his hands on her hips and pulled her into a kiss.

One she happily returned.

So far kissing and some mild fondling was all they had done; mostly only because they hadn't wanted to get caught and be separated.

It took all their efforts to stop themselves this night, knowing they would be able to get away with it this night because they were being turned out tomorrow so there was nothing they could really threaten them with for punishment. They stopped themselves this night only out of respect for Sister Jessa and all she had done, and was continuing to do, for them, by not sounding the alarm on them this night.

Cami's blood was pumping erratically from the kiss of moments before as she stepped out and made her way back to the room she shared with Wayde, and twenty-four other wards.

Once she was safely inside it, Wayde stepped out and stood looking at the door to Sister Jessa's office for a moment. He could see her silhouette moving in the flickering candlelight and knew she was pacing in worry. He knew she was likely going to be making another bed check soon, hoping to find them safely returned, so he made his way back to their room, wanting to be there long before she did.

Kept to the Shadows

6

Turning Out

Sister Jessa sat behind her large desk looking at the list of names of the wards that would be leaving her care today. She also had a list of jobs available. She was trying to place each ward in the position that would best suit them and give them the best chance of a happy life. Some she didn't know well enough herself, those she would seek help for, but the ones she did were easy.

She made selections for her four favorite wards first, hoping to get them the best placement and keep them together if possible.

Kyi loved horses; he had a way of making even the most spirited of beasts eat out of his hands and had trained many of their draft horses so that now a simple verbal command was all that was needed to get them to respond. He wasn't so good at the farm chores though; he didn't like getting up early. He didn't have the stomach for any other animal and he wasn't the most ambitious with a pitchfork so farming was out of the question. She had two choices for him; the stables in town and the castle stables each had one open position. She wrote down castle stable hand for him. The stable master was not the nicest man but she had little doubt kyi would conform well enough to the man's rules for him to find few if any reason to find ilk in him enough to do him harm.

She would have preferred a more glamorous position for the beautiful Cameron but she, herself, had started as a scullery maid here at this orphanage and she knew, like her, Cami would take pride in whatever job she was given. She would likely be made a permanent member of the cleaning staff within weeks and as higher positions opened would no doubt move up the ranks quickly. She marked her suggestion for the girl as castle scullery maid.

Dell was an easy match to a soldier. He had taken very quickly to swordplay, learning the various parries, thrusts and swings with ease. He was very strong in mind as well, which would serve him well if he was ever in a situation where he needed to know whether to use force of will or steel. He preferred discipline and followed orders far better than he gave them. She had little doubt his presence and pride would bring him to the king's attention very quick. She would very much like to see him win the man's favor and become a knight.

She was very pleased with those three placements but she was frustrated with what to do with the fourth, and her favorite of the four. Wayde really didn't fit into any of the positions at the castle but she wanted to keep him close to the other three. She knew he wouldn't be happy unless he was and she knew the other three needed him close by to feel safe enough to let themselves be happy. He had become their protector almost as soon as the four met. Dell was the stronger of the two, physically, but bullies at the home were more intimidated by Wayde's quiet poise. They all quickly learned better than to try anything on the other three as long as he was around.

She knew he wasn't afraid of hard work, quite the contrary, but he would be best matched to something that would allow him to use his mind, which was sharp as a whip. The local bailiff was looking for an assistant but would the upright and always-moral boy be able to handle the man's corruption? Likely he would try to change him, and this might create issues, but it would have to do.

The position wasn't actually at the castle, the bailiff's office was in town, but he made regular enough trips to speak with the castle hands. Most of those trips would likely be handled by an assistant, since he was known to think of himself as better than that, so Wayde should get to see the other three often enough and she might get to see him once a month on Alms Day.

She wiped a tear from her cheek; she was really going to miss those four, for all her life would be a lot less hassled for having them gone.

****

It took Sister Jessa close to three hours to recommend places for all twenty-eight wards that were leaving them. She felt drained and lifeless as she stood to leave her office. The wards would be heading for their lunch and then would be on their own for a few hours before the placements. She wouldn't be able to see them all before then but she wanted to see as many of them as she could, beginning with the four mentioned above.

She slowly walked to the cafeteria, which was noisier than usual, because the older wards were trying to guess where they were going to be placed. She normally would have called them down but this time she only smiled at how excited they all sounded. She hoped they wouldn't be disappointed.

She looked over the screaming and excited faces and found the four she wanted sitting in the far corner; their heads together, as usual. She spoke with, and exchanged hugs and kisses with, several of the wards on her way across the room and was close to tears again by the time she made it to the table that was her intended destination.

Jessa saw Dell notice her first and watched him tap Wayde on the shoulder quickly, to let him know. This told her they were likely discussing whatever they had been up to last night, likely thinking she was going to be upset with them for it. "What, pray tell, are you four up to now?" asked the ward mother in the voice that was supposed to sound accusatory and upset but this day was more in teasing.

"Nothin', Sister Jessa, we swear," said Dell quickly.

Wayde gave him a hard look to say that was telling her exactly what they were up to but he softened it when his eyes met hers. "Just the same as all the others, Sister Jessa. Hoping you have recommended places so we will all be near each other."

"I have tried my best to. I cannot promise you will get the positions I have listed, it will be decided by the representative for the council. If... if you all present yourselves well..."

"We promise to be on our best behavior, Sister Jessa," said Wayde, smiling at her.

She so loved to see him smile, especially when it was heartfelt. His whole face changed, softening, and he had a twinkle in his blue eyes then that was completely mesmerizing. Dell was considered more classically handsome but she thought that Wayde would grow into an equally impressive man. "Where were you all last night?" she asked with far less teasing.

Cami and Kyi quickly looked away, both blushing.

Dell tried to put an innocent look on his face.

Wayde still had the confident look on his, the one that said he knew they'd done nothing wrong, the one that had always made it so hard to punish them even when she knew they had. "We wanted to wait 'til after your rounds but... It was such a pretty night," said Wayde.

Jessa wanted to be angry with them for worrying her but she couldn't be. "I just... you know I am going to miss you four, even though I swear my hair would still be blonde if not for you."

"It's more beautiful as it is now, Sister Jessa, it sets your eyes off better," said Dell.

He was definitely the charmer of the group.

"Just promise me to keep yourselves safe, no matter what?"

Cami jumped off her bench and threw herself at the woman who'd essentially been their mother. "I'm gonna miss you, Sister Jessa," she said through sobs.

Jessa wasn't able to stop her own tears now, "And I you, Child. All of you."

Kyi stepped forward then and joined the two in their hug.

Dell shrugged and came up beside the boy moments later, wrapping his long arms around them all.

Wayde did not join in. He turned away from them so they wouldn't see his eyes getting red, not wanting them to see him that way. His pride went deep.

Jessa finally pushed the three off her and said, "Please be in the inner courtyard promptly at four after noon," as she was wiping away the tears and rubbing her eyes.

"We will be, Sister Jessa," said Wayde, wiping a tear from the corner of his eye quickly then scratching his cheek as if that was what he had actually been doing.

****

The courtyard was a bustle of activity as the children, whom were now all considered adults but had no idea what that meant, were chasing each other around. They were being unusually silly because normally they would all be hard at work preparing the evenings meal at this point.

All but four of them.

Wayde took his promise to Sister Jessa quite seriously so he was leaning on the large oak tree in the corner of the yard with his arms crossed over his already well-muscled chest, acting very much like the adult they were now considered.

Dell was beside him, one hand perched against the trunk, the other on his hip, looking nearly as stoic as Wayde, taking a cue from him to be restrained.

Cami was sitting across from them, in the cool grass, staring up at Wayde. They had been planning to consummate their relationship the day they got out of the home so thoughts of what this meant and how it would feel were rushing through her mind, warming her blood, making her equally excited and frightened.

Kyi was trying hard to be as restrained as his three companions but he wanted bad to join in the games going on around him. He was just about to ask Wayde if he could when

Sister Jessa and a man none of them had ever seen before stepped from the door.

Wayde didn't like the looks of this man, or how interested in the girls he seemed to be. He knew he was a representative of the council, which meant he was a member of the king's court, which meant he was an authority figure, which meant he had to be obeyed. This was the man that would be deciding to what fate they went so they had to be on their best behavior for him if no one else. "Kyi," Wayde said quietly, pulling the boy to his side, "Cameron." The girl stood quickly and went to his other side. "You heard Sister Jessa; we need this man to find us all responsible."

Kyi and Cami looked like they weren't sure what he meant but they both nodded.

Sister Jessa began to call out the names of the wards before her, asking them to come forward and speak to the representative. She was doing it in alphabetical order so Cami was called before the others.

Wayde and Dell strained to hear what the man said to her.

The representative was also the county's bailiff, Felbyr. He smiled wickedly as the beautiful young woman stepped up to him.

She curtsied and said, "I am Cameron, my lord."

"Very proper, she is," he said smiling up at Sister Jessa. He brought his eyes back to the girl, looking her up and down slowly. "She looks clean enough and well kept. Show me your teeth, Child."

Cami looked at Jessa, unsure why he would need to see her teeth.

Jessa smiled reassuringly at her and nodded quickly.

Cami opened her mouth then and spread her lips.

"Look good enough. I am sure the head maid can provide her with some peroxide to get them whiter."

Cami wasn't sure what this meant so she made no real reaction.

Jessa smile grew larger then, that meant Cami was to be placed at the castle.

"I am placing you at Auldenway Castle, Child. This will be a temporary position, if the queen is pleased with your work she may decide to keep you on… She is not the easiest woman to please. You would be a scullery maid; this is the lowest rank of the servants, Child, you'll be the assistant to the kitchen maid. Your duties may include cleaning floors, stoves, sinks, pots and dishes. You'll also likely be expected to wait on other staff in the servant's hall and you may be required to empty and clean their chamber pots. Does this sound like something you're able?"

Considering she'd had to do all except the last since she was ten she could honestly nod to this. She didn't relish the idea of the hard work continuing but she wasn't naïve enough to think she was going to get a gravy job either.

"Very well, then. You are to report to the castle's outer bailey door this evening at six. You will be given a tour of the grounds and castle, told your full duties and shown where you will sleep. You will not leave the castle grounds until you are given leave by the kitchen maid to do so."

Cami looked over at Wayde at hearing this, that meant their night of being together was at risk. She looked back at Jessa then and saw her looking hard at her, obviously expecting her to respond.

Her heart in her shoes, she nodded again and said, "Thank you, my lord."

Wayde's heart was in his throat as he watched the man before Cami.

He watched him eye her over and didn't like the way his eyes lingered. She was wearing one of her loosest tunics but her well-formed breasts were still peeking out as tiny bumps. He half expected the man to reach out and touch them with the way his eyes were glued on them. He started to step forward, ready to tell the man to back off but Dell's hand on his arm stopped him.

Moments later Cami came over and showed them the signed writ saying she was now the temporary property of the castle's kitchen.

Kyi and Dell both congratulated her.

She accepted them with smiles and hugs for both but it wasn't their approval she wanted. She looked at Wayde and said sadly, "I'm to report tonight and I cannot leave the grounds again without permission."

Wayde had half expected it, knowing it was going to be even harder for them to find time together now; it twisted his heart up as well. He did hug her and wished her well, like the other two, but he didn't kiss her like he wanted to.

He suspected that Dell had figured out they were in love but he doubted Kyi had and he certainly didn't want the rest of the orphanage to know.

"It will all work out, you'll see," he said into her ear before he pulled away.

It was about another ten minutes and three other wards before Dell was called forward. He smiled at his friends and jogged over, eager to hear where he was to be.

The bailiff had been looking around the yard, trying to figure out who his next was to be, he was a little shocked when this almost beautiful young man waved and came jaunting over with a very warm smile on his face. He looked at the suggestion the housemother had made and then back at the ward, he certainly looked brawny enough to be a soldier.

"Says here you are good with a sword. Ever killed anyone?"

Both Dell and Jessa jumped at that.

"No, sir, I have not, but I have little doubt I could hold my own if the situation of needing to should arise."

Both the bailiff and Jessa looked impressed with his answer.

"You are well spoken. Tell me, do you know who your parents were?" asked the bailiff. He doubted a low born or serf could have had such a beautiful child, which would mean he was possibly from a noble family.

Dell looked at Jessa before answering. That was something even she, though she said she wished it were otherwise, couldn't tell him. "No, sir."

"Well, it matters not, really. I have little doubt myself that you will be a fine enough soldier. The barracks master will be expecting you this evening at seven. You will be given a set of trials to see how well you do with a sword then placed accordingly in the ranks. This is a temporary position to start. You learn quick enough and can follow orders well enough you will likely be given a commission," said the man as he stamped the letter before him and passed it to Dell.

"Thank you, my lord."

"If you serve well, there is every possibility you could one day even become a knight and command your own brigade. I hope you appreciate this opportunity, Boy."

"I do, my lord," said Dell. He whispered a thank you to Sister Jessa, who he saw had a tear in her eye, and bowed to the bailiff.

He was smiling brightly, truly happy with his placement, as he started back to his friends. He had planned to act anything but pleased, just to tease them, but he knew Wayde wasn't in the mood for the joke this day. He handed his friend the writ as he reached up, snapped a twig from the tree branch over his head and began to pretend to be in a sword battle.

"A soldier, ay? Just be sure you don not fall on that sword," said Wayde, trying to sound as if he thought Dell was being foolish. He could not think of a better place for his friend and knew he would be just as loyal to the king – whom he hoped would come to know he couldn't have a better man at his side.

It took close to half an hour before they reached the letter K, Kyi being the only ward with a name beginning with the letter. He looked nervously at Wayde and Dell before he slowly walked over to stand before the table.

"Says here you are good with animals," said the bailiff.

"Horses," said the boy.

"What?" asked the bailiff grumpily, he was getting sick of dealing with the wards at this point, and he had a headache. He began to rub at his temples as he said, "We have several open positions at the farms of Lichland," looking over the long list of them.

Both Jessa and Kyi got stiff; neither wanted him to go to one of them.

"He is good specifically with horses, my lord," said Jessa.

"Horses, you say? I see that there are two positions open, one here in town, the other is at the castle... I suppose... Sister Jessa has recommended the castle stable. You do realize they are far stricter than the town stable is, yes?"

Jessa was about to speak but held her tongue.

"I do not mind taking orders, my lord," said the boy.

"Well then... I suppose... There are not many positions open at the castle, they may think I am showing favoritism if I send all wards from your home to fill them, Sister Jessa," said the man, looking at the woman strongly.

Kyi was now looking close to tears.

"Well, it is well known the queen favors this home, being so close to the castle, and since this was the first place I came it will not be so hard a thing to explain... The town stable has fine quality horses as well though, Boy, would you mind it so terribly?"

Jessa stiffened again, not liking him pulling their strings like this.

"I will be happy in either location, sir, but I have always wanted to train horses for knights," said Kyi, being unusually forward and brave.

Felbyr couldn't hide how impressed he was; he had figured that the small boy would fold quickly and take anything he was given. "Very well, Boy. If you don't work out it will likely be one of the farms you will be sent to, in any case."

Kyi looked like he wasn't quite sure where the man had just said he was sending him. The bailiff stamped the paper before him and passed it to the boy. Kyi looked at it and smiled when he saw the words Auldenway stables written on the top. "Thank you, my lord."

The bailiff only waved the boy away.

Like Dell, Kyi was happy in his placement, unlike Dell, he didn't have a teasing bone in his body so he was nothing but forward with where he was being placed. "I will be at the castle also, training horses for you, my lord, Sir Dell," he said pretending to be bowing before the soon to be knight.

Dell made as if motioning him to stand then held his hand out for the boy to kiss.

Wayde had to wait close to twenty more minutes for his interview. He had never been afraid to face anything down in his sixteen years up to now but it took all his strength to make his legs move and take him to the table. All his dire warnings to his friends to be ready for them all to be sent to opposite ends of the world had seemed unwarranted for his friends; he was now praying it was as unwarranted for him. He wasn't sure their luck was good enough to hope for that, which meant...

He knew Sister Jessa would have recommended something at the castle for him as well but he had no idea what it could possibly be. He wasn't a soldier; for all he could wield a sword well enough, he had no desire to be one. He had no report with animals like Kyi, so the stables were out. He knew Jessa would never request he be placed as a simple kitchen worker – she was always adamant that he should do something with his keen mind. What was there at the castle that would allow him that? There was only one way to find out.

Wayde stiffened up his shoulders and nodded to Dell, who balled his fist up and held it up to show support. He patted Kyi on the shoulders and touched Cami's hand then walked proudly to the table before Jessa and the bailiff.

"Wayde?" asked the bailiff.

"Yes, my lord," said the boy, trying very hard to be respectful as he had promised Jessa he would be.

"Sister Jessa has listed here that you like to work with your mind?"

Wayde wasn't sure he liked the undertone he was detecting in the man's voice but he said nothing.

"You do not seem terribly convinced of this."

"He has a good mind for directives and is very good at keeping books," said Jessa, trying to help.

"Keeping finances is woman's work," spat the bailiff under his breath. The fact that he actually had to keep the books in his own position apparently played no part in this. "You are good with math as well, I take it?"

"I am," said Wayde plainly. He added a quick, "my lord," after for good measure.

"Yes, well… Sister Jessa has offered suggestion of you as my assistant. This position is one that will obviously be working very closely with me. I want whomever I choose to be someone I trust. I am sorry but I do not feel you and I would work all that well together."

Jessa tensed up.

"I think, from your body type, you would actually do much better in a more physical position," said the bailiff.

Wayde got stiff now.

"I have an opening in Arrachsnow. The blacksmith there is in need of a new apprentice. I think you would better serve society in this position. What say you to this?"

Wayde's heart had stopped beating and his face was feeling very cold and flushed, he wasn't sure how he was even still standing, his legs felt like rubber. He could see the man was waiting for a response but he couldn't make his mouth work.

"Sir, I can understand it if you do not wish him to be your assistant but surely there is something in Ghorst that you can offer?" asked Jessa, knowing that her speaking out like this would show that she had more than a professional desire in this ward.

Felbyr looked at the housemother, having realized this himself. He looked back at the boy, wondering what their relationship was to have made the woman so staunch a supporter. "I am pleased to see that the boy here is so good an asset in your eyes, Sister Jessa, however, I do not feel that there is any position in Ghorst that would suit him as well. If he does not wish to learn the smithing trade then perhaps he could work in the mi…"

Wayde knew Sister Jessa was about to say there was no way she would allow him to be sent to the mines, and likely get herself punished, and he certainly didn't want that fate, so he quickly said, "My lord, Bailiff, it would please me to accept the position of apprentice blacksmith in Arrachsnow, thank you." He didn't want to be that far from Ghorst and his friends but he wanted to get Sister Jessa into trouble even less. At least the others would all still be close together.

The bailiff looked back at the boy, unsure now that he wanted him there either. He could tell this one was and likely would be trouble. Part of him was tempted instead to send him out of the county entirely, to the mines in the south in fact, but he guessed, if the housemother was this involved in this boy's life he would have a hard time doing it.

He stamped the paper before him quickly and said, "Very good. The master smith will meet you at the coach station tomorrow morning at seven. If you are not there he will report to me and I will have you hunted down and brought to justice. Do you understand me?"

"I do, my lord," said Wayde, not liking the way he was looking at him.

"Good day to you then."

Wayde looked at Jessa and tried to relay to her that he was okay with this. He wasn't sure he had because he wasn't sure that he was. He was being sent miles away from Dell, Cami and Kyi. He stumbled back to his friends trying to put a smile on his face for their benefit.

"So?" asked Dell.

"I am to be a blacksmith's apprentice," Wayde said dryly.

"The smith in town serves the castle so I will likely see you often when I bring the horses to be shoed then," said Kyi, smiling brightly.

"And I will no doubt need your help to make me a sword worthy of my rank and position since I intend to be a knight and command my own brigade within five years," said Dell, as he swung the thin branch he had been stripping as he waited for Wayde to get his assignment.

Cami wasn't sure how she would find a way to get to see him in her position but she had no doubt he would find a way, knowing him.

Wayde only shook his head to them.

Dell picked up on his meaning before the others, lowering his pretend weapon, "Not the smith in town?"

"No," said Wayde.

"Where then?"

Wayde handed him the writ.

"Arrachsnow!?" asked Dell. "Not seriously! they cannot send you that far away."

"How far away is Arrachsnow?" asked Kyi, he had never been good at geography.

"It's a full day journey by carriage," said Wayde.

"But..." said Cami, realizing then that meant even if she could get permission to leave the castle she wouldn't be able to see him. "When?" she asked, her voice cracking.

"I am to meet the smith in the morning," said Wayde, ramming his fist into the tree.

Kyi looked at his writ again and said, "I must be at the outer bailey door at six."

"As do I," said Cami, having a hard time keeping herself from crying now.

"You had better start in that direction then," said Wayde very plainly, looking down at his bloodied knuckles because he didn't want to look at them.

"But..." started Cami.

Wayde knew the tone of her voice was the defiant one. He gave her a hard look, one to say he would not be the reason for her to get into trouble, but he could see she wasn't going to back down.

Dell motioned Kyi to step away with him, knowing that Cami and Wayde needed time together.

The younger boy looked uncertain but did so; he would never question either Dell or Wayde.

Wayde realized what his friend was doing immediately. He looked around quickly and took Cami's hand, leading her to the backside of the storage wing, under the window they used to make their nightly escapes from, away from the eyes of everyone else.

"I don't want to be that far away from you, Wayde," said Cami, not able to hold back the tears now.

"I don't want to be that far away either... Once we are established in our positions we will be able to... Maybe... I will find a way to come back to Ghorst, Cameron, this I promise you," he said as he took her face in his hands, wiped her tears off her cheeks and kissed her.

"I am scared, Wayde."

"I know; so am I," he said taking her in his arms and holding her tight. "Work as best you can. Do whatever they ask of you, alright? Eventually we will be given some free time. I will find a way to get here to you for mine."

"Alright, I will do this for you," said Cami.

"For us," said Wayde.

"For us," said Cami, sniffling and hugging him tight again.

"I will send you dispatches by messenger as often as I can, and you can write me back as often as you can, alright?"

"It will not be enough," said Cami, "I cannot hug or kiss a dispatch... I cannot make love to a piece of parchment."

"I know... We *will* make love, Cami, I promise, just not tonight."

"I will wait for you," said Cami.

"And, I promise I will wait for you," said Wayde back, kissing her again. "Now, you get yourself and Kyi to the castle. Promise me you will stay close to him and try to get together with Dell as often as you can."

Cami didn't want to leave his arms but she knew he was right, if she and Kyi were late they would be punished and she didn't want to know where that might mean they would be sent. It took all her strength to step back into the yard where she found Dell and Kyi waiting. She could see Dell was worried about

Wayde as well. She tried to relay her own fear to him and could see he had gotten it by the look that came to his face, worriedly looking at the wall beyond which Wayde was still.

"We will see you around the castle, right, Dell?" asked the girl as she hugged him tight.

"We will," said Dell.

"We need to go now, Kyi," said Cameron, fighting back a fresh round of tears.

"Where is Wayde?" asked the boy.

"He said he would catch you later," said Dell; knowing Wayde was in no shape to see or be seen by anyone right then.

"Okay," said Kyi, smiling a little stupidly. "See ya later, Dell?"

"Of course, Kid," said Dell, playfully punching the boy's shoulder and pushing him away.

Cami and Kyi made their way across the courtyard then to say goodbye to Sister Jessa.

Wayde stayed leaned against the wall with his head back, listening to his friends saying their good-byes, trying to stop the tears that were trying very hard to escape.

He didn't want to let anyone see him this way; he didn't want to leave Ghorst, it was the only place he'd ever known; he didn't want to leave Dell, though he knew his best friend could more than take care of himself; he didn't want to leave Kyi, though knowing he would be close to Dell and Cami helped; but most of all, Cami. He couldn't imagine not seeing her every day. How could they hope to be together now?

The tears broke through his tight lids then and began to march down his cheeks. He heard a twig snap and lowered his wet eyes to find Dell half around the corner, trying to let him know he was there without it being too obvious.

Dell knew how proud Wayde was so he stayed hidden. When he saw he'd been noticed him he stepped around the corner and asked, "You okay?"

Wayde only nodded, now fighting to keep from vomiting. He used his sleeves to wipe the tears from his face, angry at their betrayal.

"Maybe you can change to the smith here in town after a couple weeks?"

"Yeah, right," said Wayde, trying to sound like he might believe that.

"I do not... What else can we do?" asked Dell, now having a hard time keeping himself from crying.

"There is not anything. Sister Jessa tried... if she could not... Promise me... promise you will look after them, Dell? And... Promise you will do good yourself; be the best soldier you can be," said Wayde.

"I will, Wayde. Promise you will write to us?" said Dell as he stepped forward and the two stepped into a tight hug.

"I promise."

"I will try to get assigned to a troop that has rounds near Arrachsnow," said Dell, for all he knew the chances of him getting to choose where he was assigned would be slim to none.

"You had better going now too," said Wayde, swallowing down the lump in his throat.

"Alright," said Dell as he and his best friend embraced tightly again.

****

Felbyr was slowly walking up the street intending to make a stop at his office before he went on to his next appointment, at the Joyate home. He was about two doors from it when he heard his name called from the alley across the street – from the side for the serfs. He looked up and down the street before he crossed then followed the man standing in the shadows further in.

"Any news?" asked Sabban.

"The darker boy says he does not know who his parents were, neither did the blond one, nor did the housemother," said the bailiff as his hand came out.

"Dammit. Will take some more digging then," said the thug looking a little angrily at the outstretched hand, "There was more to our bargain."

"The blond boy was sent to Arrachsnow," said the bailiff, not moving his hand.

"That wasn't our agreement, he was to be sent to the mines," snapped Sabban.

"You didn't tell me he was the housemother's favorite. There was no way I could send him further away without her having a fit. Neither of us need the attention brought to us," said Felbyr. "Now, my payment, if you please?"

Sabban slammed the bag of coins into the man's open hand then started to say he would be speaking to him again soon when the man turned and left. He thought about calling him back but decided he would let the man's insult go this time.

Kept to the Shadows

7

Indentured Arrangement

Cami, Kyi and four wards from other houses were standing outside the outer bailey door when the church bell rang six chimes. Kyi and the others all looked excited.

Cami tried to put a smile on her face but couldn't quite. She jumped when she heard the latch of the door rattle telling her it was about to open, it took all her fortitude not to run back to Abbeydrew. She was scared that if she went through this door she would never see Wayde again. She jumped again when she felt something touch her arm; she looked down to find Kyi smiling at her. "Yes, Kyi?" she asked.

"Don't worry about Wayde, Cameron, he knows how to take care of himself. It will do him good not to have to worry about anyone but himself for a while."

Cami couldn't help but smile to this, the boy acted very silly and stupid most of the time but he really saw more than he let on. She could see he was excited about what was to come for him but then he was getting the position of his dreams. She really was glad he was happy. "Yes, it will."

The door opened then, drawing their attention forward. A woman that looked like she had a very rough life, with wrinkles on top of wrinkles and dark eyes, peered out. The sour looking smirk on her face told Cami she didn't particularly like them being there or likely children in general.

"I am Clara, which one you all from?" she barked.

"Coatstair," said the one closest to her, a boy that said his name was Samuel; he had been assigned to the kitchens as well.

"I hear the sisters there are kind," she said dryly.

"They are," said Samuel.

"I am from Coatstair as well," said a heavier girl.

"We are from Joyate," said a tall thin boy, standing beside one who was quite portly. They were both to be chimney sweeps. The older woman snorted at this, the taller one would likely work well in the position but the fat one would find the tight shafts interesting. She motioned them through the door quickly, directing them away. Her eyes then fell on the final two.

"Kyi and I are from Abbeydrew," said Cami proudly.

Clara knew that home well, "Yes, well, you can just forget that fine treatment, you hear? We expect you to do as told, no questioning, understand?"

This snapped even Kyi to attention.

"You were each given writs, get them out now," snapped the woman. She grabbed them forcefully from their hands and looked each over closely, as if suspected they were forgeries.

She handed Kyi back his and said, "You need to go into the castle grounds. You should see the barn and stables no problem but if not just follow your nose to the smell of horse dung. Go straight there, do not to dawdle," she added with a sharp finger only inches from his nose.

Kyi kind of whimpered a, "Yes ma'am," then moved past the woman, not even stopping to hug Cami good-bye as he had intended to.

The woman then looked back at what she was left with. The other three writs she put into a scrip at her side and put her hands on her hips.

A boy and two girls were left standing before her.

The boy, the one who had so enthusiastically told her what orphanage he was from was to be the smokehouse boy. "You will be reporting to the chef, boy. Get your ass to the gray building beside the privy right quick," she said, pushing him through the door in the direction she had just pointed.

The two girls were to be her new scullery maids. She looked them each over with barely any sign of emotion.

Clara didn't like children but she disliked slackers more. She wondered if these were two more. One was stout and looked strong, her dark hair was pulled up in a tight bun and her harsh looking face looked like she'd already been working in the kitchens, a younger version of Clara herself. She looked like she could pull her weight well enough. "What's your name?" she barked.

"Gerti," said the girl.

The woman nodded and looked at the other. This one looked like she could be trouble. She was beautiful and, for all she was dressed in loose fitting clothing, was obviously nicely turned. She would have to keep a tight rein on this one. Girls with looks like those and that type of body always got into trouble, especially when there were handsome young guards around. That and the prince liked to take his pick of the new serfs and she was just his type.

He had gotten too many of her girls with child, a thing made even worse with the decree his father had put into place. Many of them had claimed they hadn't wanted nor had asked for his advances, implying he had forced himself on them, a thing the queen wouldn't hear and certainly wouldn't prosecute. She was certain the queen would insist anyone on the staff that got pregnant out of wedlock, no matter whom was the father, be tossed out because it would give the castle a bad name – though she had never brought any of them before the queen to know for certain. Clara was a firm believer in *spare the rod, spoil the child.*

She really could not care less whom the prince touched; she just didn't want to be without the girl, even if she didn't pull her weight. It was because it would be another year before she would get a replacement. She would still do enough to be worth having around. She would just have to see what she could do to make her less attractive. "Your name?"

"Cami," said the girl proudly.

"*Cami?*" the woman mimicked, obviously thinking it was a silly name.

"It's short for Cameron, ma'am," she said.

"I don't like smart mouths, Cameron," snapped the woman.

Cami started to say something smart back but remembered her promise to Wayde. She looked down and said, as humbly as she could muster, "Sorry, ma'am."

"Right then. Come with me." She took each girl by the shoulder, holding Cami's tighter, and directed them along the side of the bailey to the back of the kitchen.

Clara saw the pretty girl looking around them, likely looking for ways to get herself into trouble already, and snapped harshly, "What you looking for, Cameron?"

"What? Oh… just a couple friends assigned here as well."

"This is not a social gathering place, Girl, this is work. You have no friends here," the woman snapped as she pushed the door before them open and pushed her roughly inside.

The door opened to the pantry, which had barrels and canisters of all different shapes and sizes on one side and mugs, bowls, trays, utensils and other preparation items on the other. "This is the pantry. The outer and inner doors are locked at all times and I'm the only one with a key to either of them. I ever find it open whoever was last in the room will be beaten. I personally inventory the stores before and after each meal, anything turns up missing you'll lose one pent from your earnings for each item missing and you will get a whip with a lash for each item. It happens more than ten times and you are out. Understand?" She didn't continue until both nodded.

She motioned them on, and shoved Cami, through the door at the other end. Beyond this door was the kitchen. It was a room nearly the size of Abbeydrew's whole cafeteria. It had three stoves, three stone dry sinks, two hand operated pumps and a wall of iceboxes. In the center of the room was a huge wooden table made from strips of wood glued together, like a butcher's block. It acted as cutting board as well as counter top. Hanging from the roof rafters in the center, around the table, was several different sized cast iron pots.

"This room is to stay in the condition you now see it in at all times. We never know when her highness, Queen Vela, will choose to make an inspection. She doesn't take kindly to messes. If

I ever hear a bad word from her I will be looking for who caused it, and I assure you, you will know the back of my hand when I am finished with you, do I make myself clear?"

"Yes, ma'am," both girls said quickly.

"I'm putting you on the bread line, Gerti. Arms like that look good for kneading dough," said the woman as she handed the girl two gray frocks and a white apron. "We do laundry daily so be sure one of these is always clean. Keep them like they are your Sunday best, understand?"

"Yes, ma'am," said Gerti, taking them.

Clara looked hard at Cami then and said, "You, I think, will begin by being a busser."

"A busser?" asked Cami, never having heard the term before.

"Means you clean up the messes," said the woman as she grabbed one of the girl's hands and held it up to the light. "You can say goodbye to these pretty nails, Girl, they don't last long when they get wet and caked with grime." She then grabbed a handful of Cami's full hair and added, "And, enjoy this for the night 'cause it's coming off in the morning. Any of the nobles finds a hair in their food I will personally skin you," she said, smiling wickedly.

Cami jumped, hoping the woman was only making an idol threat. She loved her hair, and so did Wayde, he loved to bury his face in it and run his fingers through it.

Clara didn't seem to notice, or more like didn't care, that she had just frightened the girl as she handed her two gray frocks and a white apron as well and told her the same thing she had Gerti then pushed them on down a tight corridor to a dark and narrow set of stone stairs that led upward into an even deeper darkness.

At the top of these stairs was a door, which the woman pushed open with her foot. It was a long thin room with five cots on each side and a thin pathway up the middle. The wardroom Cami had grown up in was cramped, having twice the number of wards in it than it should have, but it was a dancehall compared to this. There was barely elbow room between the cots and it was obvious all but two of them were already taken, the two open ones being theirs; one was at the farthest end of the room, the other was two beds in on the right side.

Clara looked hard at Cami as she said the next, "Girl's *only* in this room. The boys' room is downstairs and is kept locked at night. You can have the one back there, *Cameron*," she added, pointing at the one on the back wall.

It was right under a window, meaning it would be drafty, and because it was the farthest in, if she needed to get up in the night, to use the privy, she would have to walk the full length of the room, twice, which meant likely waking the others.

"The others don't take kindly to their sleep being messed with none, either," snapped the woman.

Cami jumped then, unsure if she had actually read her thoughts.

Clara was pleased with the reaction this got her. "To show you I'm not all rusty nails, I'm giving you this night to get yourselves settled."

"Thank you, ma'am," both girls said, almost in unison.

"You ain't to leave this room once lights out is called, unless it's for the privy. My room is next door, you will wake me and let me know you have left and let me know when you return.

It takes you more than ten minutes I will send the dogs to find you."

"Yes, ma'am," the two said quickly.

"The others will be up in a couple hours, lights out is at four until midnight and we get up when the rooster calls. Understand?"

"We got to be up until two until midnight at the home, Miss Clara," said Gerti.

Cami cringed, expecting the statement to get the girl a slap.

"Well, we ain't the home, Gerti," snapped the woman as she turned and slammed the door shut on them.

"You really think she will cut off your hair?" asked Gerti when she was sure the woman wasn't going to come back. She was running her fat fingers through her own greasy and thin hair as she said this, looking very envious of Cami's beautiful locks and glad hers weren't as nice at the same time.

Cami shrugged, she hoped it was just a threat to frighten her into serving willingly. She had a sinking feeling the woman didn't make idle threats.

"This ain't so bad," said Gerti as she went to her cot and began to go through the bag she had brought with her.

Cami couldn't even muster a comment. She knew if she opened her mouth it wouldn't be a pleasant one, anyway. She stumbled to the cot pointed out for her, at the end of the row, all but in tears. She was holding them back as best she could; a little afraid Clara might come back in and catch her. She could feel the cool night air already starting to creep through the thin glass panes of the window and got a chill.

She sat down on the thin mattress pad, which made the one she had thought was thin at the home feel like a cloud, and pulled her bag of belongings to her. She opened it and took out a glass heart Wayde had made her. She set it on the edge of the window casing, where it caught the light from the lamppost below and threw it around the ceiling in rainbows, and stared into it, wishing she were with him now. She stuffed the bag with her other belongings, mostly clothing, under the bed and sat back, with her back against the cold wall. She pulled her knees to her chest and started to rock back and forth. She could feel the tears she had been fighting starting to flow.

****

Kyi walked slowly to the big barn that was to be his place of employ at the castle.

He could smell the pungent stench of horse manure almost immediately but to him it was like a fine perfume. He could hear the horses neighing and snorting inside as he stepped around to the front of the building and smiled. He was very happy that he was going to get to work with the majestic animals – this was practically a dream come true for him. He wondered how he might find a way to thank Sister Jessa for getting him placed here.

Feeling quite giddy, he stepped up and knocked on the regular-size door cut into one of the larger barn doors. It was several minutes before it opened to a burly looking fellow in gray coveralls, holding a pitchfork that was coated in horse manure and straw.

"Yeah, what?" barked the man, looking down at the scrawny boy before him as if he was a pile of the previous waiting to be tossed out.

Kyi held the writ up in front of him.

The man propped the fork against the door casing and looked at the paper. He squinted his eyes and scrunched up his face, then he looked back at the boy and said, "What is this?"

"It is a writ from the bailiff."

"Is it? I dunno how to read," said the man. He didn't sound ashamed of this, more like that he didn't see as a person in his position should be required to know how.

"I am one of the turnouts. It says I am your new stable hand."

"Says who?"

"Says the bailiff and Sister Jessa."

"Who is Sister Jessa?"

"She is housemother of Abbeydrew orphanage."

"Abbeydrew? I told that idiot, Felbyr, I wanted one of them from Joyate. They raise 'em tough over there."

"I am tough, sir," said Kyi, trying to push out his chest.

The man lunged forward, snarling. He began to laugh when the boy before him fell back and got a look on his face like he was going to cry. "Tough, my arse. Well... guess ya can muck as well as any other. We will just have to put some meat on your bones... I do not like weaklings. I hear you whine, even once, about what I gives ya to do and I send your arse packing, got that?"

"Yes, stable master, sir," said Kyi, still shaking a little.

"Alright then. I ain't your master and I do not like being called sir. I am Galin, got that?"

"Yes, sir... Galin. I am Kyi."

"Well, get in here, then," he said as he stepped aside and motioned Kyi in.

He led him through the center of the stable, which had thirty stalls, each with a single horse, a wall of various tools and racks of saddles, bridles and horse whips to a door in the back.

Behind this door was a small room with two bunks. One was obviously being used, the sheets were half off it; the other was a straw filled mattress with a pile of what was likely another set of sheets lying on top of it.

"That one there is yours. We bunk down only when all the work is done, not before," he said then he grabbed the bag from out of Kyi's hand and tossed it on this second bed. Before the boy could say or do anything, the man grabbed a pitchfork, only a little cleaner than the one he was still holding, and pushed it into the boy's now empty hands. He pointed back into the stable and said, "We got three more stalls to muck then the barrow there needs to be taken to the back privy yard, emptied and cleaned up enough to be able to be eaten off by the king himself."

****

Dell walked through the main gate into the castle's inner bailey and looked around. He saw smoke rising from a massive chimney to his right and guessed that was the kitchens, where Cami was. The stable, where Kyi was, was directly in front of him. At least he could keep an eye on the two of them as he had promised Wayde.

It was going to be strange not wishing them all good eve before going to sleep and not seeing them when he woke up, or had to be awakened by Wayde, as was most often the case, in the morning. His heart twisted as he wondered what his friend would do until morning, when he was to be picked up by the smith of Arrachsnow.

He looked to his left and saw the long thin barracks that would house his bunk and started in that direction. The bells in the tower of the church on the square were just ringing out a seventh chime as Dell reached the door. He knocked loudly and waited. It opened moments later to a man in a chain mail vest with a coverlet showing the king's crest – a profile of a dragon rearing before a cobra.

"I have been assigned here by the bailiff in the turnout," Dell said, holding the writ up to the man.

"So you are, yeah?" asked the man, taking the parchment sternly and tossing it behind him, not even bothering to look at it. "I am the sergeant at arms, Sir Alyn, and you be?"

"Dell, sir."

Alyn looked the boy over and said, "You're a bit scrawny for a soldier but a high protein diet will put some muscle on you."

Dell had no response to this. He was, in fact, equally as toned as the man before him.

"It's too late in the day to run you through a field test now, have to wait 'til morning. You done any sword fighting before?"

"Yes, sir, I was champion of my ward," said Dell.

"What does that mean?" asked the man.

"Each of the wards competed against the others. I was champion of Abbeydrew," said Dell, just as proudly.

"Well, you will not be fighting no other babies here. We use real swords here and draw real blood here, Kid."

Dell swallowed hard but said nothing.

"You will start out as infantry, Boy. Once I get an idea of your worth we will see about something higher."

Dell again said nothing.

The man stepped aside then and motioned the boy, who was a head taller and a shoulder wider than him into the barracks and led him to where his bunk was.

****

Wayde was sitting under the same tree he had been standing under with his friends only a few hours ago in the courtyard of the orphanage as the sun started to go down. He had the twig Dell had broken off a branch above him only a few hours ago and had been pretending was a sword in his hands. He was running his fingers up and down its length, wishing, at that moment, it was a real sword so he could use it to end his misery. He was no longer trying to stop the tears now, frightened for his friends, and himself.

He didn't know what to do or where to go, he wasn't being picked up until early the next morning, no one had thought to tell him what to do until then. He guessed he would sleep where he was and hope he woke up in time to make it to the coach station in the morning.

He listened to the church bell toll ten times, and was surprised by how much he was going to miss hearing it. He thought how this night he would have gladly climbed into the hard cot in their room and not even considered going out, as he and his friends had done every night previous of this week, if he had been able to.

He was just wiping a fresh batch of tears from his cheeks when he heard the door across from him open. He sniffed the loose mucus from his nose and started to get up. He was intending to hide beside the storage shed, not wanting to get caught. He stopped when he saw who it was.

"Who is there?" asked Sister Jessa's soft voice, holding the candle she had in her hand up before her face.

He had forgotten she always started her nightly rounds by checking all the outside areas. He thought again about hiding, not wanting her to see him this way or get her in trouble, now that he was no longer a ward he shouldn't be on the grounds, but he couldn't do that to her, she had been so nice to them all. "It is only me," he said, trying to keep his voice steady.

"Wayde?" asked Jessa. She saw a form stand up from in front of the oak tree and stepped closer; the handsome boy's face was now spotlighted by the tiny candle's ring of light.

"Yeah."

Jessa could hear the emotion in the simple word and felt her heart clench. "What are you doing out here?"

"I do not get picked up until morning… I… I did not have anywhere else to go."

"Oh my goodness, I never even… Come inside, Child, you can stay here for the night."

"I do not want to get you in trouble, Sister Jessa."

"Do not be silly, Wayde. As you are not being picked up until morning, you are still my ward," she said as she placed her hand on his cheek and rubbed away the tears he had missed with his sleeve.

"I am sorry, I…" he said. He pulled his face out of her hand and wiping it with his sleeve again.

"Do not be, Wayde. I know how much you care about Dell, Kyi and Cameron, and I know how hard it will be for you to leave Ghorst. You have no need to act so tough for me."

Wayde shrugged and nodded, halfheartedly.

"I am sorry I could not get you placed in Ghorst. I will try to find something... get you changed over to... but I am afraid, to begin with at least, you will have to go to Arrachsnow."

"I know," said Wayde.

Kept to the Shadows

8

Forging Zeal

Morning came fast for Wayde, leaving him feeling less than rested. He had nightmares of all three of his friends, of what they faced, and, as if that wasn't bad enough, of Sabban making a move on them now that he wasn't there to protect them. Dell he wasn't worried about, in fact he had kicked Sabban's ass in the dream, but Kyi and Cami…

He shook himself fully awake just as the sun began to peek in through the curtain and hit his eyes. He listened to the world coming awake outside and wondered how it could sound so happy about it. It was only moments before he heard the church bell tolling. He counted them, praying it wasn't seven in the morning yet, and that it was at the same time. He was actually thinking maybe he *would* take Sabban up on his offer of assistance, so he wouldn't have to leave Ghorst. They only rang six times.

He was just pulling his shirt over his chest as a soft knock rattled the door and it opened to Sister Jessa.

She looked at the floor when she saw he wasn't fully dressed and said, "I am having some eggs and toast brought to my office, when you are ready come and eat then I will take you to the coach station, alright?"

"Thank you, Sister Jessa," said Wayde.

She nodded and closed the door.

The room Wayde was in was the same storage room he and his three friends always used to sneak in and out of the home from. There was some spare mattress pads in the corner which Jessa had helped him set up to sleep on. He hadn't realized they were there, which was just as well. He and Cami would have used them if he had known they were there. If they had and had been caught they would have been separated. But then, they *were* being separated, weren't they?

He quickly buried the thought deep, partly because it hurt to think about what they hadn't gotten to do together and partly because it made him want to run to the castle, get her and take her with him. He finished getting dressed and peeked out the door, just as he had each time he and his friends returned from their nightly outings. When he saw no one was about he stepped out and walked to the closed door of the housemother's office.

The light from a candle flickering inside told him she was waiting inside as she said she would be and the smell of the breakfast she promised was lingering in the hallway making his stomach growl.

Neither Wayde nor Sister Jessa said anything the short ride to the coach station, because neither knew what to say.

As the covered structure neared Jessa looked over at the boy that had been her ward for sixteen years and said, "I know that you're frightened, Wayde, but you are strong… You are the strongest of all my wards, ever. It will be hard for you the first couple weeks, but once you get into the routine…"

Wayde only nodded, he knew she was only trying to help.

"Dell, Cami and Kyi will all be alright, as well. They are strong as well; they only never really had to be as long as they had you there to watch them. They will be alright as well."

Wayde had a feeling this was said for herself as much as for him.

"You need to put yourself first now, Wayde. I have tried to prepare you all for the real world… It is not the easiest or nicest place… there are people who will try to take advantage… Promise me you will think before you act, in any manner… Think of the consequences?"

"I will," said Wayde.

He knew she was worried that the four of them had found it so simple to slip out of a tightly run place like the orphanage that he might think he could get away with it wherever he was. He didn't want her to know he had thought this very thing and had been running ways to sneak away and get back to Ghorst through his mind himself since they left the home.

Jessa pulled on the reins to stop the mule pulling the home's small carriage and stepped down. She waited for Wayde to get his bag then moved to the end of the ramp with him.

"You do not have to wait here with me, Sister Jessa, I promise not to sneak off now," said Wayde, a little teasingly.

Jessa started to giggle at how easily he could seem at ease and said, "I really do not mind waiting; I would like to see the man that will be your master."

Part of him wanted her to stay, not wanting to be alone, but part of him didn't want her to see the man, in case he looked especially cruel. He knew she would have a hard time letting him leave with him then. He knew that he and his three friends had been her favorites, for all she had sworn she had none, so he knew it was like she was sending her own child away.

He didn't have time to tell her he would rather she go. A carriage that most certainly must belong to a blacksmith, by the fancy scrolling wrought iron railings along its sides, came rolling to a stop before them before he could.

The man in the driver seat looked twice as big and tall as Wayde in the seat but when he climbed down he was closer to the same size, though his arms were far more muscled. His skin was deep bronze colored, likely from working so close to the hot ovens all the time, and his head was bald. Later he would explain that it was better not to have long hair around furnaces. He had a lot of burns and scars, showing through his thin tunic, and his right hand was missing the last two fingers. He apparently wasn't ashamed of the injury either as he thrust it out to take Wayde's equally as large hand.

"I am the blacksmith from Arrachsnow. Are you the one assigned to me as apprentice, Boy?"

"I am, sir. My name is Wayde."

"Wayde? A good, strong sounding name," said the man as he looked the boy over. He reached out and took hold of his arms, feeling his muscles. He lifting them up, patted his chest and grabbed him pointedly in the groin, taking hold of it all firmly.

This made Wayde jump and gasp, for obvious reasons. It also surprised Jessa, who looked ready to slap the man for fondling the boy in that manner.

"I see you are all real. So many I get have padded themselves up with thick clothing to add bulk then they find out what the job is all about and go running to the hills with their tails between their legs," said the man. He was eyeing Sister Jessa now like he might inspect her body in the same manner.

"I am real and I will put my tail between my legs for no one," snapped Wayde indignantly, stepping in front of Jessa to break the man's stare.

The man had a strange smile on his face as he asked, "You a virgin, Boy?"

"What business is that of yours," snapped Jessa.

The man looked at her again then and said, "And who might you be? The assignment is for the boy not the boy and a wet nurse."

Wayde could see Sister Jessa winding up to give the man a tough lecture, like the ones she had given him a few times over the years, when she got mad enough to forget how much she liked him, and quickly said, "No, it is just me. Sister Jessa was my housemother at the orphanage, she gave me a ride over only."

"Yes, well, you ain't one of her wards no more, you are mine now, *if I accept you*," said the man, implying he might change his mind.

Wayde turned to Jessa then and said softly, "Thank you for all that you have done for me, Sister Jessa."

Jessa knew he was telling her he wanted her to leave him now and she knew she should but she couldn't get her heart to agree to it. She had hoped she would be able to give him a hug goodbye but didn't want to do it in front of this man so she only nodded and said, barely over a whisper, "If you ever need anything."

"Thank you," said Wayde. He watched her walk away, knowing how hard it was for her.

When she was well enough off the stage to not hear his answer he turned back to the man and said, "In answer to your question; no, I am not a virgin."

He couldn't imagine why the man needed to know this but the man was higher blood than him so he technically had to answer him. He wasn't ashamed of the fact but he was ashamed of how he wasn't. He had promised Cami, when they first admitted their attraction to each other, that he would wait for her but one night when they had fought, over making love actually, he had snuck out of the ward room and run into a girl named Sara. He was attracted to her and she had never hidden her desire for him. She was more than willing to let him take his anger and frustration out on her.

"Good, I don't need anyone who is frustrated working the forge," said the man bluntly. "I am not condoning the use of a whore or nothing, I am only saying, if that is what you choose to spend your stipend on, who am I to judge?"

Wayde got an impudent look on his face then crossed his arms over his almost as large a chest and said, "I will never bed a whore, sir."

"Yes, well… no need to take that attitude, I hear even the prince has before… Ain't no harm, nor shame, in it. Ain't nothing wrong with it."

"I am not the prince," snapped Wayde.

Stories of Prince Acthiel were prevalent. He had never come to Abbeydrew but wards at other homes told stories of how he frequented the female ward's rooms there and had his way with any of them he wanted. He seemed to frequent Joyate the most. Wayde had sworn he would slit the prince's throat if he ever saw him at his home; especially if he ever eyed Cami with that in mind.

"You are about as arrogant as he is though, or so I hear. I ain't never yet met the boy."

Wayde only got an even deeper impudent look.

The man before him began to laugh then. "I'm just joshing with ya, Boy. I just wanted to test your zeal is all. We smiths got to be able to deal with heat to be around them furnaces all the time, hot as the hinges on the gates of hell, they are," said the man as he pulled the left side of his tunic open to show a nasty burn along his right breast.

"Long as that is not some kind of initiation ritual," said Wayde. His perfect skin was one of the few things he could truly say was his own by right.

"You will likely get yourself a fair few times but I do not brand you or nothing," said the man. "There are a lot of lords who do though. My Name is Hithal," he said as proudly as Wayde had said his. He stepped aside then and motioned the boy to get into the carriage. "I started out as an orphan as well, though mine was long before the decree. My parents already had eight mouths to feed and did not want to even try with another. So, you see, you will not likely always be a serf. You can be free if you have the desire to be."

"You are accepting me then?"

"For now. I ain't got time to see the bailiff about another right now. I will give ya a few days anyway. Stow your stuff in the back."

"Thank you, sir... ah, how would you like to be addressed?" asked Wayde as he tossed his moth eaten bag into the back and climbed into the seat beside the man.

"I don't expect you to call me master or nothing, just Hithal is fine. I do expect you to work though. I pay ya ten pents a week. Lot higher than most but the work is a lot harder too. I do not expect ya to pay me nothing for your freedom, if ya want it. I will grant it to ya after your third year; same as my master did with me. I will expect you to work six outta seven days – full days' work each – to earn it though.

"We have a good bit of business, keeps steady even through the colder months. Them is the times you won't mind being 'round the fires. The customer is always right, no arguing with them. No matter who you belong to a fancy blood decides they don't like the looks of ya you can be hanged. Leave any arguing to me. I don't want to hear nothin' 'bout a customer not getting his goods when he was promised neither. I don't like to hit no one, got plenty of it myself, but I will give your arse a good tannin' if I got to," said the man. "The first weeks you will be my shadow – you eat when I do, sleep when I do, shit and piss when I do, got it?"

Wayde only nodded.

"Seeing as you are intending to be a monk, though, I won't expect you to bed no one when I do," he added, laughing heartily.

Wayde tried to laugh with him but could only manage a slight smile.

Hithal didn't seem bothered by his lack of enthusiasm. He reached back and pulled a bag he had in the carriage forward and handed it to Wayde. "These are yours now."

Wayde opened the bag and found a thin pillow, a wool blanket, a flint box and a heavy metal hammer with a regular head on one side and a ball on the other.

"That was my last apprentice's. He is now running his own forge, down south. It should work well enough for you. If you find you like the work you can purchase yourself a better one."

"Thank you," said Wayde as he tested the weight of the tool. It was heavier on the head end, as was expected, but fit his large hand well. He couldn't say he liked the idea of being so far away from Ghorst and his friends but he had to admit, the thought of learning a new trade was exciting.

9

Life as a Scullery Maid

Cami woke with a start. She knew where she was but she wished she didn't. She lay still in the bed trying to get her heart to slow its erratic pace, wishing she had awakened anywhere else – wishing she had awakened in Wayde's arms as they had planned to.

She had fallen asleep before the others came into the room, apparently exhausted since their entrance hadn't awakened her. She sat up slowly and looked down the length of the room. She saw nine other bodies in the cots. Most were sleeping quietly but one was talking in her sleep, mumbling incoherently, and one was snoring rather harshly, Gerti she guessed. She wasn't especially shy but she had grown up beside all the wards she shared a room with at the home so she didn't need to wonder how they would treat her.

She looked at the glass heart on the windowsill and thought about Wayde. She wondered where he had found to spend the night. She felt tears welling up in her eyes again. She wrapped her arms around herself and tried to imagine it was his arms. A girl beside her began to stir then. Moments later others did as well. She closed her eyes and pretended she was still asleep, not wanting them angry because she had awakened them.

The loud crowing of the rooster Clara had said was their wake up call sounded from the yard below seconds later. Within moments all the girls were awake. Some were stretching and yawning, some were rubbing their eyes and moaning and some seemed well rested. Gerti was one of the latter group. Cami sat up slowly and looked at each, hoping they would all be friendly.

"That is right, we got two new ones last night, didn't we?" said the girl sitting in the bed to the right of Gerti. She looked to be a tall thin girl with blonde hair in braids. "I am Kathy," she said, looking from the heavy girl beside her to Cami.

"Gerti," said the girl beside her happily.

"I am Cameron but most call me Cami."

"You are a looker though," said the girl beside her. She had a dark complexion and dark hair that was cut similar to Kyi's style. "I am Maria. You might want to do something to make yourself look plainer," she added as she stood and started to get herself dressed in the same gray frock Clara had given Cami and Gerti the night before.

"What do you mean?" asked Cami.

"You do not need to frighten her none, Maria," said the one across from her. She was almost a spitting image of Kathy. "I am Sally, Kathy's sister," said the girl.

"How was it meant to frighten me?" asked Cami.

"Nothing… just… Prince Acthiel always likes to meet the new girls on the staff is all… He likes your kind."

"My kind?"

"Pretty," said the one diagonally from her. "I am Abigail. I been with him a few times. He ain't that bad, mostly."

"Been with him?" asked Cami, hoping she meant it different than it sounded.

"You know, like man with woman? You still a virgin?"

"Yes," snapped Cami. "And I will not be with anyone but Wayde."

"Who is Wayde?" asked the one closest to the door. She had blonde hair as well but it was thin and very greasy looking and she had dull gray eyes, made even more so by the gray frock she put on then.

"He is... he is a friend... We are promised to each other."

"You from the same home?" asked the last girl, Dora.

"Yes. Abbeydrew." Cami took the glass heart from the sill and held it to her own.

"He make that for you?" asked Maria.

"Yes," said Cami happily.

"You will not be wanting Clara to see it; she does not like trinkets," said Kathy.

"I would suggest you keep it under your mattress," said her sister, Sally.

It took close to ten minutes for the girls to get dressed, the tight confines making it hard to maneuver. Cami felt a little gross, not having bathed before she got dressed but none of the others seemed to think this unusual.

As they started to leave the room she whispered in Sally's ear, "When do we get a bath?"

"We get one twice a week for free. Last one was yesterday, next is Thursday. Any more than that you have to pay for. Two pents for ten minutes."

"I… I have no money… I have to wait four more days?" asked Cami, sadly.

"If Clara says it is alright I can loan you the two pents; if you promise to pay me back," said the girl.

"Please," said Cami.

"We will ask her," said Sally. "I am a busser," said the girl, "My sister is one of the bakers."

"Clara said I am to be a busser as well," said Cami.

"I will show you the job then," said Sally.

"Thank you, Sally." Cami found herself breathing a little easier then.

Clara was waiting for them when they reached the bottom of the stairs. A thick wooden spoon was in her hand, the bowl end of it resting on her shoulder. She was dressed in a frock like theirs but hers was brown. "Kathy, take Gerti and show her the steps of making the breakfast bread."

"Yes, Miss Clara," said Kathy, motioning the new girl away with her.

Clara turned her eyes to the girl's sister and Cami then and said "Sally is a busser as well, she ain't the best one but she will show you what is expected of you here."

"Yes, Miss Clara," said Sally, then she added, almost whispering, "Cami has asked that she be allowed a bath, Ma'am."

"She missed bath day," said Clara sternly. She looked the girl over, and scrunched her eyes.

"She has asked if she can borrow two pents to pay for a bath this evening," said Sally, looking over and smiling at Cami.

Clara was staring hard at Cami. She was positive this one was going to prove a problem now. She tried hard to find a reason to deny the request but she couldn't come up with anything so she barked, "What you do with the pents you earn is your own affair, Child. Do not come to me crying your eyes out if she does not pay you back."

Sally looked at Cami then.

Cami nodded and said, "I will, I swear."

The girl smiled and said, "Then I wish to loan Cami two pents."

Clara snorted. She reached into her pocket and pulled two coins out of it. She held them up to Cami but she didn't offer them to her. "You'll get ten minutes at the end of the work day. After all your chores are done and not before. I'll be waiting for you here at six this evening. I expect you to be dirty enough to be *needing* a bath by then."

Sally nudged Cami then and gave her a hard look.

"Th... thank you, Miss Clara," she said a little shyly.

Clara snorted again and said, smiling wickedly, "First, we need to do something about your hair."

Cami jumped at that. She had hoped the woman would forget her threat in the night. "I can I put it up, or maybe braid it?"

"We will let the queen decide," said the woman. "The tapestries in the great hall need a beating today, Sally, that is as good as any job to be the first to show the girl," she said as she took Cami under the arm and began to drag her from the room.

****

Queen Vela was pacing the back of the great hall, waiting for her husband and son to come down for their breakfast. She was anxious because the two of them had done nothing but fight, not that they did much else anyway, since the prince was told he was going on the tour with his father in two weeks. She was about ready to pull her hair out.

She started to her chair when the doors of the room opened and the woman who led her kitchen staff and two of the scullery maids came through them. One was familiar to her, though she didn't know the girl's name. She went to the tapestry on the east wall and began to pull it from its hooks, apparently intending to take it in the yard to be cleaned. Her head kitchen maid was dragging the other girl forcefully toward her.

She straightened her shoulders and turned to face the woman, wondering why she felt the need to be seeing her in this manner. She got a good look at the girl as she came closer and was a little surprised. She was beautiful, unlike the usual staff. She guessed she was one of the new ones assigned her from the turnout. She tensed, wondering if her son had used her as a plaything. She was frightened that the girl was about to claim she was carrying his child, or thought she should get something in return.

Clara stopped several feet from the queen. She pushed the girl to her knees then went down on her own quickly, "Begging you pardon, your grace."

"Speak," said the queen.

"I got two new ones last night. One is gonna work well in the baking line, I think. This one … I wished to ask your thoughts on."

"Rise, Child," the queen said to Cami.

Cami was afraid to; afraid that she might decide she needed to lose more than just her hair. She knew she had no choice. To not do as the queen commanded was certain death. She did stand up, slowly, keeping her head bowed.

"Look at me," said the queen.

Cami did then.

"What home did she come from?" the queen asked the head maid.

"Abbeydrew," said Clara quickly, her dislike of the place showed clearly on her face.

"Yes, you would have been." This made her relax a little. She knew their housemother had never allowed her son in her wards. "What is your name, Child?"

"Ca... Cameron, your grace," she said. She wasn't sure what the proper address for the woman was so she repeated the one she had heard Clara use.

"You have lovely hair, Child."

"Thank you," Cami said quickly.

"I was wondering what we should do about it, your grace," said Clara. "I do not want none to be getting into any of the food or nothing."

"Yes, you have a valid point, Clara," said the queen as she walked around the girl. She lifted some of the waves up as she did. She wished her hair was as lovely, it was about the same color as hers but much thicker.

"Cut it to her shoulders, Clara."

Cami jumped at this.

"I am not ordering this to be cruel, Child, it will make it easier for you to work without the bulk of it."

"But..."

Vela didn't wait for a response, she had made her decision and it was final. She stepped away from them and went to her chair as she had intended on their entry.

"Do not, ever, question the queen's wishes, Girl," snapped Clara boldly. She'd hoped the queen would say even shorter but she would obey.

"Please do not cut my hair," begged Cami.

Clara took the girl under the arm again and dragged her from the room.

****

Vela watched the girl and her head kitchen maid go. She wished she hadn't had to be so harsh, she could see how upset the girl was at this order but it really was for her own good. Hair like that was too much of a beacon of trouble.

She didn't like her son's blatant use of the servants as playthings any more than his use of the orphan girls but she would rather he be with them than the whores that worked the streets and would bed anyone with a few pents. She wouldn't discourage Acthiel from being with this girl if he wished to be but she didn't want to encourage him either. If the girl was kept hidden for the next few weeks the prince might not even notice her, his mind being on other things.

****

Cami was fighting tears as the woman took her through the kitchen. All the girls, moving about preparing the royal families breakfast, stopped to see what was happening, some looking like they knew, others like they wished they could watch.

Clara stopped only long enough to grab a pair of shears from the shelf above the sinks. They were used for cutting the bones of the meat portions they got from the butchers. They weren't the cleanest things or the sharpest anymore but they serve the needs of the head servant.

She dragged the girl to the door of the pantry.

"Please, Miss Clara, I will promise to always wear it up," cried Cami.

Clara paid her pleas no attention as she threw the door open.

Cami was pushed inside the small room then through the outer door to an area where bed sheets were hanging from lines. She had no idea what was going to happen next or how to stop it.

Clara released the girl's arm then and told her not to move as she reached for a bucket set against the wall to dry out. She set it upside down on the ground and said, "Sit on this and don't move."

Cami did have a brief moment where she thought to move. She wanted desperately to run away but she was afraid of what Clara might do to her if she did. She jumped and whimpered when she saw the dirty scissors coming at her. She hung onto the edge of the bucket tightly, like she might lose herself if she let go. She closed her eyes as the woman began to grab handfuls of her beautiful locks and began to cut them away. She could feel the pieces hitting her shoulders, tears from her eyes were falling with them.

Kept to the Shadows

10

Life as a Stable Hand

Kyi was beyond sore when he awoke; the rooster in the barnyard was what had done it. He remembered again then why he hated all other animals.

He rolled over, planning to ignore it and go back to sleep. He jumped when the blankets he had just pulled up over his head were suddenly yanked from his body. The cold morning air rushed in to take their place. "Hey," he shouted.

"Up, Boy, we got things to do," said Galin gruffly.

Kyi remembered where he was then. He opened his eyes to the unkempt face of his new master and wasn't sure whether to laugh or cry. He did neither, only sat up and began to pull on his clothing.

"First we need to feed and water all them horses, then we get ourselves some grub."

"Yes, sir... Galin," said Kyi as he started out of the small room that was their bunkhouse.

The boy stumbled to the door he had come in with a bucket in each hand; Galin said he would find a clean shovel by the side of the silo he could use to fill them with the oats and grain mixture they fed the horses. He did. He placed one of the buckets under the small grain door and opened it then took the shovel and pulled out enough to fill it, moved it and filled the second.

The now full buckets weren't heavy but he wasn't used to doing anything so strenuous first thing in the morning so he groaned the whole way back. He had to make six trips to get enough to feed all of the horses. While he did this Galin was doing much the same with buckets of water he was filling the troughs on the side of the barn with.

They both finished about the same time.

Kyi used his sleeve to wipe the sweat from his forehead as he waited for Galin's next instructions.

The man pointed at the side of the barn and said, "Fetch some bales of hay and put some into each stall," then he started walking toward the kitchens.

Kyi watched the man's back for several second, wondering if he might see Cami while he was there. He wondered how she had faired. He hoped she had slept better than he had. His head turned to the right then as he heard the distinct sound of metal hitting metal and the grunts of someone trying to put force behind their swings. He wondered if that was Dell being tested for his position on the king's guard. He longed to run over and watch but he didn't dare – not knowing what Galin would do to him for leaving the barn. His mind went to Wayde then and his heart clenched, remembering he was going to his new home this morning. He wondered if the man that was his master was nicer than his own.

Knowing none of this was going to do him any good, the boy walked over, grabbed a hay bale that was almost as big as he was and began to inch it to the barn.

Kept to the Shadows

11

Life as a Soldier

A large hand shaking his shoulder, quite forcefully, awakened Dell. "What!?" he barked, thinking it was Wayde, who'd had to do this so many times in his first sixteen years. Dell didn't like to get up in the morning.

"Is this how you got to be so pretty, Boy?" asked a grizzly voice.

"What?" asked Dell. He didn't recognize that voice as Wayde's, or any other of the orphans at Abbeydrew. He opened his eyes to find an ugly pinched face with a scar across the right cheek smiling at him. He jumped out of his skin and cried, "Who the hell are you?" He was wondering if the home was being burgled.

"He do like to get snippy, though," said the man as he stood up and put his hands on his hips, "I say we toss him out on his arse now, too weak to be a soldier."

Dell jumped again then, remembering, with the sudden clarity of a slap to the face, where he was. "No, sir, I didn't mean any disrespect, just caught me off-guard."

"That's just it, Boy, we must always be on our guard. We are protectors of the king and his court," said the man who had met him at the door the night before. He was standing behind the gruffer looking man.

"I will not do it again, sir, I swear."

Sir Alyn, had a look on his stern face that said he wasn't so sure. "I am in the mood for some bloodshed this morn and these other buffoons are too well practiced to catch now so... We will see what you can do with a sword first, then we will send your arse away – bleeding and crying." With the last words he tossed a sword to Dell.

Surprising all in the room, Dell got his hand free of his blanket and caught the heavy steel weapon in midair, by its hilt, his fingers wrapping around it as if it was made for them. He had always been praised for his fast reflexes, which had saved his and other wards' lives more than once when they were on the steep roofs of the home making repairs and one slipped.

"He do have good reflexes though, don't he," said the man that had awakened him. "Can I have first crack at him?"

Alyn nodded and looked back at Dell, "Get up and to the yard."

Dell didn't even question him, only set the sword aside, grabbed the britches that lay on the bottom of the cot, pulled them on and took the sword back. He followed the rest of the men out of the barracks to the tourney field beside it.

The other soldiers ranged in age from not much older than him to gray and grizzled like the one that awakened him. This man quickly took up a battle stance, his own sword in his left hand. Dell didn't take up a similar position, he was looking at Alyn, expecting him to change the real swords for wooden ones, like he was used to fighting with. Because of this, he wasn't prepared when the man suddenly thrust forward and sliced his forearm with his very sharp and very real blade, leaving a thin line of blood behind. "The hell," asked Dell, pointing at his bleeding arm.

The other man was now coming at him again. By the look on his face he meant business, and none of the others looked ready to stop him. Dell threw the heavy sword up, catching the other's just as it would have taken him in the shoulder. His hilt guard was locked with the other man's, who was pushing for all he was worth. He used his other hand on the man's chest to push him away, then spun around and took up a similar stance to his attacker. He had now realized he did mean business and that none of the others intended to come to his aid.

The two parried and thrust back and forth across the dry yard, both got in several good hits, though only leaving superficial wounds. Dell, being the younger man, had more energy. The other was getting winded fast. He thrust one last time and went to his knees before him.

The gruff soldier held his sword up and said, "Enough for me."

Dell stumbled back to a wooden horse. He leaned on it as he caught his own breath.

Alyn helped the man he had just bested up then took up a similar stance to his, motioning the boy to come at him.

Dell was going to turn and leave, not wanting to do this. He remembered his promise to Wayde and knew he couldn't. He ripped what was left of his shirt off, wiped the sweat and blood from his forehead with it then threw it away and got into position again.

This went on for most of the morning, each man being bested and replaced with the next in line. None of them gave Dell a chance to catch his breath between. His anger and pride was the only thing keeping his swore and stiff muscles moving by the time the last, a boy about his same age, positioned himself before him. This boy stepped forward with a smile on his face; as if sure he was about to best the boy that had now put away twenty five seasoned swordsmen.

Dell wondered if he was another of the wards turned-out. He was dressed in fine woolen pants and his shirt, though plain white, appeared to be of fine linen. He didn't remember him from any of the sword battles between the homes. It didn't matter either way; he seemed to know how to use his sword. He thrust and parried as well with him, as well as he had the last twenty five men. He had now been fighting for close to three hours and he was beginning to get winded himself. He wondered how many more of the men he was going to have to best before they would consider him tested enough. At this point he had only taken on about half of them. He prayed this boy was to be the last. He wasn't a sore loser but he didn't like losing either.

He didn't like the holier-than-thou look on this soldier's face; this made him decide he wasn't going to lose this one either. He caught his guard on the other's and pulled hard, bringing them only inches from each other then he wrapped his left leg behind the other man's and knocked him to his back. He brought his sword down to take him in his exposed throat, stopping the sharp edge just before it sliced skin, then brought his right foot down on the man's sword arm, pinning it to the ground.

"Enough, Boy," said Alyn, stepping up beside him. His large hand took the boy's arm and directing the sword away.

Dell pulled his arm free of the sergeant at arms' hand and stumbled over to a barrel of water. He dunked his head into it quickly and threw it back. Water and blood was streaming down his sweaty chest and back when he turned back to the other soldiers, to see who was next. He watched the last man he had fought getting helped up by the others, unlike any of the others that had to get themselves up. This confirmed to him that this one was not another orphan and may not even be a usual soldier.

"The test is done. I think you will make a fine soldier, Boy," said Alyn coming up beside him and slapping him on the back. "Are you as good with a sword from the back of a horse?"

Dell had never tried so he only shrugged.

"I disagree. I do not think he will at all," said the last man he had fought. He was pulling his clothes back into place roughly. "I do not like him. He fights like one of the bandits."

Another man, who was tall and wide and looked a little like a god made mortal, stepped forward then. All the men save the one Dell had just fought and Dell himself went down on their right knees.

"Which is just why he will stay, Acthiel."

"What?" said the prince and Dell at the same time, though for different reasons.

The former not liking that his father was speaking to him like this before the serfs.

The latter couldn't believe he was looking at the prince and king – not from through a dingy window as they stood on their balcony on market day but less than twenty feet in front of him. One of them covered with the sweat and blood he had caused. He suddenly had an image of himself being hanged for assaulting the prince then.

The prince stamped his foot, gave Dell a glare to tell him he wasn't finished with him then turned and stomped away.

The king watched his son go then turned to Alyn. He waved the man to stand and said, "Train him as you see fit, Sir Alyn." He turned to Dell then and said, "What is your name, Boy?"

"De... Dell, my lord... your grace...majesty," sputtered Dell, as he dropped his head quickly. He realized suddenly he was looking the king directly in the eye. The two were of equal height and nearly equal build, he was very glad this man had not wanted to parry with him, he was certain he would have been bested then with little or no effort. He did not go gracefully to his right knee as the others did, he fell to them.

The king motioned for him to rise as well. "Just my lord, is fine, young Dell. You fight like this when you are before a real enemy and you will rise fast, Boy."

Dell felt like he had the wind knocked out of him by those words. He wanted to say thank you but he could not find the voice to do it. He nodded weakly and went down to his right knee again. He set the sword before him, the point of the blade in the dirt, dropped his head so the top of it was all the man could see and said, "I would proudly give my life in battle with the enemy to protect you, your majesty."

The king smiled. He held his hand out before the young soldier, so he could kiss his ring, then he turned and started back for the castle.

The others came over and introduced themselves to the boy the king had just honored.

****

King Vianor *was* very impressed with the new soldier but he knew his having bested and embarrassed his son before the other men would make it hard for him. He knew Acthiel would try his best to get the boy now, needing to save face. He should have punished the boy for his act, his son needed the men's respect too, but he could not fault him for it. He had not known he was fighting the prince of the realm. He would see what Alyn thought of him after his training, if he thought he would be a good addition to the rank he would have him assigned to one of the border guards, to keep him and his son from clashing.

He felt more than a little guilty when a stray thought crept into his mind. One of wishing that boy soldier had been his son instead of Acthiel. He had been intending to go to his bedchamber but instead he started toward the chapel, wanting to ask forgiveness for the last thought.

Kept to the Shadows

12

Life as a Blacksmith's Apprentice

Wayde did not need to be awakened by anyone; he was up long before the sun, as he often was when he was at the home. He was sitting on the top of a table in the yard, bare-chested, his hands in his lap and his mind clear. He had started every morning of the last five years this way and saw no reason to stop it now. He was just finishing his meditation and was opening his eyes when he heard a gasp from the direction of the house.

He and Hithal had arrived to the man's house late last night and he had gone directly to the room he said was to be his, above the barn. Hithal hadn't said anything about others living with them so he hadn't expected to see anyone other than the man there. He looked toward the house, wondering if this had offended the man but it wasn't a man standing in the doorway.

He wasn't ashamed of being without his tunic in front of a woman but he had only been that way before Cami, and the girl, Sara, for a brief few minutes, in the last five years, since he had been allowed to bathe himself. He wasn't *fancy-blood* as Hithal called the nobles but he knew that it wasn't proper to be in his manner of undress before a member of the opposite sex, that wasn't his mother, sister or wife, no matter what class he was. He grabbed his tunic and began to pull it over his head.

The person looking at him from the house was a young girl, probably about his same age, with black hair and big blue eyes. She was dressed in a short thin robe that clung to her curves. She was frozen in place, as if not sure what she should do, or maybe she thought if she stood still he might not see her.

"Pardon me, my lady," Wayde said quickly, "I was not aware there was anyone here but me and Master Hithal." He was fighting to get the sleeve of the tunic pulled out so he could get the thing over his head.

The girl before him blushed then, as her eyes traced his body. She liked how it moved with his ministrations. She frowned for a moment when he finally pulled the cloth over his skin then smiled at him.

Wayde had seen that look before, on some of the girls' faces at the home, ones that had made it more than clear to him that they would be happy to be with him. He suddenly felt very uncomfortable. He was about to ask who she was when Hithal's booming voice was calling out of the house.

"The boy's gone, Tabbie, he has up and run off... Oh, God, where is Jenna?" the last was said with a touch of panic.

The girl turned and shouted into the house, clearly and strongly, "I am here, Father, and the boy has not up and run off. He is out here."

Hithal was bounding out the back door moments later, a sword in his hands and a look of murder on his face. Seeing his daughter wasn't dressed and the boy looked as if he was only just getting that way stopped him dead for a moment. "What is going on here?"

Wayde wasn't sure what to say, still reeling.

"I did not know you had returned, Father. I wanted to get a little air, the boy was in the yard already."

Hithal looked at Wayde then, the accusation no less in the stare.

"I like to meditate in the morning, sir, to clear my head," said Wayde.

Hithal got a strange look on his face then it broke into a huge grin. He said through sniggers, "That's right, you want to be a monk!" He turned and ushered his daughter back into the house.

Wayde heard the girl saying 'A monk?' to her father with obvious disappointment and shook his head. "I promise to be true to you, Cami," he said to the clouds as he straightened his tunic and walked to the door himself.

Wayde found Hithal sitting at the table in the kitchen with a plate of steaming eggs and bacon before him, which he was making little haste at eating. Another woman, much wider in the middle and looking to be closer to Hithal's age, but no less beautiful than the girl, was standing in front of the oven. She was dressed in a simple dress in the prettiest shade of purple Wayde had ever seen. She had a white apron over her front to keep it clean. She was holding a metal spatula in one hand and the handle of a cast iron skillet in the other, two other eggs and three strips of bacon being fried in it.

She looked up when she heard the flooring shift and smiled. She took the pan from the flame and moved it to a plate on the stand beside her. "You hungry, Sweets?" she asked very pleasantly.

"Uh," started Wayde, he was caught by her beautiful eyes for a moment, the same eyes as the young girl had, except hers weren't looking at him as if he was a piece of meat as the young girl's had been. He dropped his eyes and looked to Hithal, unsure how to answer.

"Well, are you, Boy?" he asked.

"Uh, yes, sir, ma'am, I am," said Wayde. He ran his hands through his mussed up hair, trying to get it to lay better and make him look less like the monster the younger girl had thought he was on first seeing him.

"Sit down then," said the older woman, motioning him to the chair beside Hithal.

"This here is my wife, Tabitha, the girl you near accosted is our daughter, Jenna. She is gone to get bathed up and get herself to school so you don't need to worry about ogling her none more," said the man teasingly.

"I was not ogling her," said Wayde before he had realized it. He looked at the man quickly then and said, sounding quite humble, "I am sorry, sir, I meant no disrespect, I was not aware that there was any others at the house otherwise I never would have… certainly not without my tunic…"

"Hithal," barked the woman, just as teasingly, "Now you have the boy all upset. He will not be able to eat and I will not send him into that hot pit without a proper breakfast."

Hithal was laughing now, bits of half eaten egg and bacon falling from his mouth.

Wayde had a look on his face like he thought he had awakened in another dimension.

Tabitha eyed the boy up and down, easily seeing his fine physique through his thin tunic and said, making him blush as much as her daughter had. "Besides, why should a man with such a fine form wish to keep it covered? I never understood the need for such decorum; I like to look upon a fine male body as much as any man does a fine female one. I give you permission to walk around naked if you wish it," she said with a wink. She giggled when she saw him blush.

"I only wish I had a fine female body to look upon," teased Hithal, to which he got a loud harrumph.

She was intending it only as a tease but she slammed the plate down in front of Wayde a little harder than intended, knocking a piece of the bacon to the tabletop. "Now look what you have made me do," she said, starting to take it from the table.

Wayde took it first and stuffed it into his mouth.

Tabitha looked appalled at this.

Wayde noticed this and said quickly, "I am sorry, I have offended you again," he said.

"My wife is a *fancy-blood*, Wayde," said the man, a little less teasingly.

"I am not. My father was a lesser noble so I am only *middle* blood, and that's been tainted with yours, *Darling*. Wayde is your name, Boy?"

"Yes, ma'am. I truly meant no disrespect by that. I have had to eat things off the floor before if I wanted to have any and I know your tabletop is far cleaner than that ever was."

Tabitha looked appalled at this. She looked at Hithal and said, "Why would a boy need to be do this?"

"He is one of the orphans, from Ghorst. Remember I told you I was getting one of them this time?"

"He talks awful fancy for an orphan," said Jenna as she stepped into the room, having freshly bathed. The look in her eyes was still just as dirty though.

Wayde had thought she was pretty when she was unkempt but she was quite beautiful all cleaned up.

"You are supposed to be on your way to school, little lady," said her mother, motioning her out the door.

Jenna harrumphed as well as her mother had and turned and left. A door further in the house slammed moments later.

"Ooh, Hithal, that girl of ours is gonna end up in trouble, you mark my words. Did you see the way she was looking at Wayde? Why did you have to choose such a handsome one?"

Again Wayde blushed, now trying to sink under the table.

"We got no worries there, Tabitha, he wants to be a monk," said Hithal.

Wayde's head shot up to this, not sure if he wanted to refute it or not.

"A monk, say you? Now why would you wish to be this, Wayde? You cannot be more than sixteen, why would you want to limit yourself so young?"

"I do not want to be a monk!" said Wayde.

Tabitha looked at her husband for explanation.

"He says he don't want to bed no girls," said Hithal. He got a strange look in his eyes then and said, just under his breath, "You prefer boys then?"

"No, sir, I do not!" snapped Wayde.

Both Hithal and Tabitha were staring at him now.

"I am promised to another from the same home. *She* and I are promised to each other."

"Oh," said Tabitha then, turning back to the pan before the bacon she was frying burned.

"Jenna will be very disappointed to hear that."

Wayde jumped at that, wondering if they thought they were going to be able to have him for their daughter as well as a blacksmith.

"Would you like seconds, Wayde?" asked the woman then.

He had never had seconds of anything before in his life so he wasn't sure how to answer this; he looked to Hithal who was only smiling at him.

It was well into the morning, and three helpings later, before the dishes on the table were cleared away – an act it was hard for Wayde to sit through and not assist with. He looked over at Hithal, who had one hand in the beltline of his pants, the other rubbing his healthy stomach. He wanted badly to ask him a few questions but wasn't sure of his place.

Hithal seemed to pick up on this. "Speak your mind, Boy, I don't expect blind obedience and I sure as hell know you ain't a mute."

"I was wondering, sir, I have some friends... back in Ghorst... ones I was in the home with... I would very much like to write them... and maybe, visit them on occasion?"

"Well, Boy, the first you most certainly can do. It costs two pents to pay the messenger. You got any coins?"

"No, sir, I do not."

"Well then, at the end of the week you can send out five of them if you like."

"I was hoping... I want to send some sooner than that... I don't want them to worry."

"I pay at the end of the week, Boy, not before it's earned. I once loaned some coin to an apprentice and he went off on me. Never saw him again."

"I cannot go anywhere on two pents, sir," said Wayde, trying not to sound pushy.

"No, better to make you wait. Besides, you won't have anything to tell them until the end of the week in any case, yes?"

"Yes, sir," said Wayde, hoping he didn't sound too disappointed. "What about my other request?"

"We will see. If you work out well I might let you go with me to Ghorst in the fall."

In the fall? thought Wayde, that was not for another seven months.

"Now, we have to get to the mines in Elmsdune to get another load of iron ore. You know how to harness a horse?"

"I do, sir."

"Very good. See to that. I will meet you in front of the shop."

13

Pushing

Wayde was beside himself thinking all the things that could happen to his friends if he didn't get to see them for seven months. He vowed he would find a way to get there sooner if he had to *up and run off* to do it.

He walked through the front door of the house and walked to the side with the stable and carriage house. He had helped Hithal untack the horse and put him and the carriage away the night before so he knew where everything was. He opened the stable doors and jumped when the horse jumped and neighed nervously at him. He wasn't afraid of animals but wasn't as comfortable around them as Kyi was either. He pictured what the smaller boy would do in his position and smiled, he remembered watching him approach a horse that was new to the home a few years back, one that wouldn't let anyone else near it.

He put his hand down, palm facing up, and clicked his tongue as he took a step forward. "Hello, Boy, my name is Wayde. Hithal says you are called Reese? I am not going to hurt you, I only want to put your harness on you. What say, Reese?" he asked the horse softly, in a slightly higher pitch than his usual tone.

The horse started to prance in place and his eyes rolled a little as Wayde stepped closer then he sniffed his open hand and calmed some.

"Good boy," said Wayde as he brought the hand up and began to stroke the animal's nose and between the eyes. The horse nickered and nudged but didn't try to pull away. Wayde stepped away and opened the bottom half of the stall door. He reached to the wall and took the leather harness from it and stepped into the stall. "I am going to put this on you now, see?" he asked, holding the straps up so the horse could see them.

When he didn't back away Wayde slowly started to put the straps over his head. He held the bit in his hands and gently placed a finger in the horse's lower teeth, as he had seen Kyi do before, coaxing the horse's mouth open, it let him and didn't fight as he pushed the bone piece into its mouth. It licked at it with its tongue and bit down on it with its teeth several times, trying to get used to the taste, no doubt.

While it was occupied with this, he began to latch the straps around its chin and over its back, leaving a strap with a metal clasp hanging done on either side of the animal. He then took hold of the strap on its cheek and slowly pulled the animal to get it to walk forward, out of the stall. Once he was clear of it he pushed the door to with his foot and wrapped the loose reins around the outer door handle while he went to the other side of the barn to get the carriage out.

It took Wayde little more than fifteen minutes to get the horse hitched up and was in front of the stall as promised. Hithal wasn't there yet so he stood beside the carriage and waited for him.

He spent the time looking up and down the street. It had been dark when they arrived last night so he hadn't gotten to see any of the town he was now in.

He could see several other shops on both sides and across from him, telling him they were in the market district of the town, behind the stall was the house and the barn and beyond that was mountains. Most of the ride over had been through Bywood forest. He had never liked dark places, he was very happy to see the wide-open spaces around him.

The boy jumped as he heard a sound to his right, the sound of spurs. He turned to see a man, dressed all in black, on an equally black horse, coming up the road toward him. He guessed he was headed for the shop since there were only rundown homes to the left of him and this man was dressed too fine to be from any of them. He remembered Hithal telling him he was not to speak to the customers so he didn't immediately move toward him.

****

Prince Faelan had been in the mood for trouble since first rising that morning, he had already enjoyed messing with several of his father's staff and the pretty barmaid at the tavern had kept his interest for the few minutes it took to get her britches down, now he was intent on seeing what he could stir up in the market. His father would be very upset with him for doing this but he really could not care less.

His father was Henry Durbaith, High Lord of Arrachsnow, member of the Auldenway Council and good friends with the king – all points of contention with him. The lesser prince was next in line for the throne if something was to happen to his cousin, Prince Acthiel. A station his father could never aspire to even if he had the desire. His mother was King Vianor's sister meaning his blood was higher than his father's, who was only another lord's son.

Faelan saw someone he had never seen before this day coming around the corner of the blacksmith's stall. The boy's long blond hair was quite distinctive. He was pulling the smith's horse and carriage behind him so he guessed this was the man's new apprentice. He remembered the master smith asking his father for permission to request one of the turnouts. He smiled – someone who didn't know who he was yet.

The master smith was one of the few people in the town who really wasn't intimidated by him. The man knew his place well enough to keep him from being able to openly cause him too much trouble and was liked too much by his father.

There was no smoke coming from the chimney of the furnace, telling him it wasn't lit and there was no sign of the burly man who ran it. This made Faelan smile even bigger. His father was busy making preparations for the king and prince's up-coming visit to pay him any attention if he tried to push just a little. He would see how much mischief he could get away with before the smith came out and stopped him.

He stopped his horse beside the boy, who had long bits of hair hanging down over his face, and looked down at him. He was surprised when he raised his head to him and he saw his blue-gray eyes clearly. This was going to be almost too easy. "Who might you be?" asked Faelan.

"I am the new apprentice blacksmith, my name is Wayde."

The man dropped from his horse, took the two steps between them as one and the back of his hand connected with the side of Wayde's face moments later. "You dare to look upon me and speak to me, Serf?" the man barked. "And to not use my title when you speak to me?"

Stars lit the inside of Wayde's head, which felt like a melon that had just been dropped on a hard floor. That hit had come so unexpectedly that he was knocked to his knees, the gravel of the road ripped his pant legs and the skin beneath them. He stayed on his knees, praying the man wouldn't decide to punish him further. He knew full well what he could do to him if he wanted to. He *had* forgotten his place. He was a serf, he was not supposed to speak to anyone unless he had business with them and was never supposed to look at one of higher blood, which this man most certainly was, in the eye when he did so. "Please, my lord, I beg your pardon and your mercy," said Wayde as humbly as he could. He kept his head down and his eyes closed, to keep him from even accidentally looking.

Hithal had heard the last bit as he was coming from the house. He ran to the front of the stall, making his words come in huffs and puffs, "He is just out of a home in Ghorst, my lord, Prince Faelan. I just arrived last night with him. 'Tis my fault, not his, he's but a few hours into his 'prenticeship."

The man looked at Hithal, whose head was down so only a nasty scar that split the top of it clearly showed. He then looked at the boy, who was still on his knees, blood dripping from the place on his face the ring had hit, to the faces of other shopkeepers, who had come out hearing loud voices. He thought for a moment about making an example of the boy, not wanting to lose face, but he decided he would let it go, this time. "Very well," he said. "I accept your apology and will give you my pardon." He held his hand, palm facing down, in front of the boy's face. The same one he had just hit him with. Some of his blood still clung to the stone of the ring on the middle finger. He smiled when he saw the boy flinch, likely thinking he was going to get hit again.

Wayde wasn't sure what the man wanted at first then he realized and leaned forward. He kissed the ring on the hand that had maimed his face, tasting his own blood on his lips after.

The man smiled. He used the shoulder of the boy's tunic to wipe the rest of the blood from the piece of jewelry and said, "Teach the boy well, Hithal. You are nearing retirement and I do not wish to have to travel any further than here for my weapons."

"Yes, my lord, Prince Faelan."

"Is my sword ready?"

"It is, my lord," said Hithal quickly, none of the sarcastic humor in his words.

"Boy!" Faelan shouted, making both Wayde and Hithal jump, "Fetch my horse some water."

Hithal nodded to Wayde and motioned to the trough on the side of the barn.

Wayde slowly got up, took the reins from the man's hand, the same one that had hit him, without looking up, and clicked his tongue to get the horse to follow him.

Wayde found the trough Hithal had motioned to quickly but the horse didn't seem interested in it. He leaned over the edge and used it as a mirror to look at his face. He now had a two inch gash on his right cheek where the raised prong of the ring had sliced his skin. He dipped his hand in the water and wiped the drying blood away then used his sleeve to dry his cheek.

When he came back around to the front of the shop the man Hithal had called Prince Faelan was counting out coins. He watched him hand the blacksmith forty of them and take the shiny new sword from his hands.

Faelan looked up, hearing his horse neigh quietly, and motioned the boy to bring it over.

Being sure to keep his head down the whole time, Wayde did so.

The man smiled as he watched the boy flinch and jump again when his now gloved hand touched his face. He pulled it up and to the side so he could see the scratch he had left on his cheek. His other hand came forward then, moving the hair hanging over the boy's forehead away. He traced a scar the boy had there with his finger and said, "I take it you are a slow learner then?"

Wayde didn't answer, unsure just what he was asking.

"Well, tell me?"

Realizing the man thought that scar on his forehead was from another act of aggression toward a high-blood, he quickly, and as humbly as he could, said, "No, my lord, I have had that since I was born."

"Meaning?"

"I was told my mother suffered during labor and that I received the scar during my birthing, my lord."

"Killed your mother, did you?" the man said snidely.

"I don't know, my lord," said Wayde, trying hard to keep sounding humble.

"Yes, well, scars make you look more masculine, isn't that right, Hithal? Would not want too pretty a boy working for you. People might talk."

"Yes, my lord, I am sure he will not look so pretty as this in a few weeks," said Hithal, looking at the tops of his shoes.

"Do not be abusing the boy, Blacksmith. I do not want to hear any rumors of that kind either."

Hithal looked partway up, obviously not liking the implication in the statement. He mumbled, "Yes, my lord," and lowered his head again.

"This has been diverting but I must be on my way. I am expected at Auldenway Castle. Princess Anya of Elmsdune is coming for a visit and I wish very much to visit with her." The obvious implication was clear in that statement as well.

Wayde jumped a little at hearing the name of the castle in his hometown.

The man took the reins from Wayde and jumped onto his horse's back. He used the edge of the blade of the new sword to the animal's ribcage to get it to move. The horse let out a painful sounding nicker then started off.

Once the lord was down the road far enough Hithal hissed for Wayde to get inside.

Wayde jumped and did so, half expecting to get a beating from this man now.

The master smith grabbed a cloth from the side of the furnace and dunked it into the trough of water used for tempering the steel then grabbed Wayde's face and turned it so he could see the scar. He used the edge of the cloth to clean the last bit of dried blood away. "Looks like a clean cut, should not get infected none, but I should probably still cauterize it," said the master smith.

"Cauterize it? How?" asked Wayde, already knowing the answer even before the man started for one of the pokers in the small fire that was kept burning to start the furnace with. He remembered all the horrible scars on the man holding him and wondered if this was how he had gotten them. "No, sir, please, I will keep it clean so it doesn't get infected. I swear."

"Like the looks of your face, do you?" asked Hithal. "See to it you keep your eyes down, especially when Prince Faelan comes around again then, Boy. I will not defend you again."

"Yes, sir. I am sorry, sir."

"Some of the lords I deal with ain't so bad as him but we must remember our place, Boy, no matter how handsome you be."

"Yes, sir."

"Now, get your arse in the carriage, we are already late," the man snapped.

Wayde could see he was shaking as he dropped the rag and started for the door to the house, likely to tell his wife he was leaving.

Wayde had never been outside of Ghorst until he left the first day with Hithal, on the way to Arrachsnow. He had never thought the countryside could be so beautiful. Now he was seeing even more of it as they rode through the mountains to Elmsdune. They were going for a load of the metal they mostly used in their business – iron. They used the ore to make utensils, pots and pans, horseshoes and tools. They had a load of some of these, as well as some swords, daggers and shields, in the carriage to trade for it when they got there.

He was impressed with the workmanship of all the pieces, though he didn't have a lot of experience with swords and shields – he could imagine how Dell would have reacted to them. He had always said a well-made sword was like a work of art. "Do you think, one day, I could make anything so nice as these?" He asked Hithal this during a lull in their conversations, which had mostly been about the smith's own experiences in the home he'd grown up in, which was the one in Doveslade.

"If you have the passion for it, you can, indeed. You have to know the metal that you are working. Love it. Make love to it. Let it become what it wants to be," said the man fondly.

"How does one do this?" asked Wayde, truly wanting to know. He was the type that did a thing fully.

"When we return, if you like, I will let you have a try at it."

"Thank you, sir," said Wayde, honestly.

"Was your own life at the home so terrible?" asked Hithal.

"No, not terrible. Sister Jessa, the one you met at the coach station, was always real good to me, Dell, Kyi and Cami. She would deny it, I have no doubt, but I think we were like her own children. She always made sure we got the best of the chores and clothes and rarely punished us when we did bad."

"Dell, Kyi and Cami the ones you said you want to write to in Ghorst?"

"Yeah. We grew up together... I was... sort of their protector, I guess."

"Tough one, are you?"

"No, just don't like being *pushed*."

"Interesting choice of words," said Hithal, getting an odd look in his eyes.

Wayde had a feeling then the man knew one like Sabban too. "There was a boy there, one who is on his own, who tried to... recruit, I guess would be the word, me and my friends into a different life. One I was not interested in."

"Are your friends?"

"Dell wouldn't be. He is a lot like me in his thinking and he can take care of himself well enough. Kyi and Cami..."

"They easier to *push*?"

"Yeah, Kyi is... I hate to say it about a friend but he is a little simpleminded and Cami... She would like to think she could take care of herself."

"Is she the one you are promised to?"

"Yeah," said Wayde as he pulled a thin bit of wood from his jacket pocket. It was carved with the likeness of a female face. He passed it to Hithal, smiling at it as he did.

The older man took it and smiled back. If it was an accurate representation the girl was beautiful. "Quite the looker."

"She is that," said Wayde, looking at the scenery around him that was almost as.

"She got placed in Ghorst?"

"Yeah, at the castle, as a scullery maid."

"She who you wanted to visit?"

"All three of them, but yeah, her mostly."

"You will see her again, Boy."

"I know I will but... Time can do funny things," said Wayde, sounding far wiser than his sixteen years would suggest.

"There is a festival there in little more than a month's time, the Mid-summer Bazaar. I don't normally go to it but perhaps... if we can make enough to be salable, we could try for it," said the man, surprised at the act of kindness himself.

"I will learn quickly and make you a fortune," said Wayde, sounding very sure of himself.

"Now, you ever driven a horse?"

"No," said Wayde.

Kept to the Shadows

14

A Proposal for Cami

Cami was still getting used to her shorter hair and the life of a scullery maid a week later. She hated the former because the woman hadn't even tried to cut it straight. Sally tried to make it a little neater for her that night but the knife she was using was dull and little light was coming in through the window so it was hard to see what she was doing. She had actually only made it worse. She didn't like the tighter fitting clothing she had to wear. She was painfully aware of how much more developed she was than most of the other girls in the home had been, which was why she wore such loose clothes.

She didn't much like this new life. Her hands were almost constantly pruned now from always being in a bucket of mop water and her knees were sore and bruised from being down on them, scrubbing the floors. She was doing this in the Great Hall this day. She had only done three quarters of the room and it had taken her three days to get this far. Each night the lords and ladies would mess up the parts she had already washed so she had to start all over again.

She put the scrub brush back into the bucket and leaned back. She placed those pruned hands on the small of her back, trying to work out the kinks she had in it. Her eyes scanned the room as she did this. She used the back of her wet hand to push the hair that was tickling her cheek away. Over her head was several rows of huge square wood beams, laid out in right side up and upside down triangles. She guessed they were holding the roof of the castle's main hall up. She knew Dell and Wayde would know the name of those but she really didn't care what they were called.

She was amazed at the size of the beams. Each looked to have been carved from one piece of wood, which meant the tree they were carved from must have been massive. Those beams were mortised into the blocks that made up the walls of the large room. Huge windows broke the expanse of dark gray cement block walls but the room was situated so it only got sun first thing in the morning and at the end of the day, the only times it was really ever used. Dozens of candle stands were set along the sides of the room and a huge iron fixture hung from a chain to the center beam over her head. The chain to it was wrapped around a pulley wheel, which ran through a series of eyebolts along the beam and down the wall to a hitch so the fixture could be raised and lowered. The dozens of candles in it, and in the stands, were currently all lit so she could see what she was doing.

A colorful woven tapestry hung between each of the windows. Most of them were of battle scenes or mythical creatures but one always stopped her eyes when she looked around like this. This one was of a man leaning over an anvil, a hammer in one hand and set of tongs in the other, working a horseshoe. She smiled, thinking that was what Wayde was doing. She imagined him standing over the fire with no tunic on, his muscles rippling and sweat dripping down him.

She had waited every morning for the last week for a dispatch from Wayde but so far she had gotten nothing. The other girls got something nearly every day. She tried to tell herself this was because he hadn't been given permission to write yet but she was frightened it was because he no longer wanted to. Now that he was out in the real world he would have no desire for a simple girl like her, especially not if he saw how she looked today.

She wiped a tear from her cheek. She started to stand to take the bucket out to the yard to dump and refill with clean water. She jumped, nearly dropping that bucket, when the doors on the side of the room burst open. The sudden wind this kicked up blew the candles in the stands to either side of the door out and threatened to topple the stands over.

Cami looked over, half expecting to see Clara with the long wooden spoon she liked to brandish, and use on any part of her staff she could reach with it, in her hand; upset with her for something she had forgotten to do or had not done quite to the woman's preference. She was wracking her brain for what she could have done wrong this time and was trying to come up with the best way to apologize to avoid getting hit. The spoon left a nasty divot and bruise behind.

She relaxed a little when she saw it was a boy of about her age with long blondish brown hair. He was dressed in a coat and leggings the color of the sky. He apparently didn't notice that he was not alone because he never even looked at her; he only went toward the table at the far end. She watched him take up the carafe of wine on that table and proceed to drink directly from it, ignoring the three chalices waiting beside of it. This told her he was one of the nobles that hung at the castle. She turned and started to go in the other direction, hoping to get away before he noticed her. She stopped when she heard him shout to. Her hands were holding the bucket in front of her tightly, and she was trying her best not to shake with fright, not wanting to spill any of the dirty water on the clean floor. She heard his footfalls coming toward her then and prayed he was only going to ask her to get him more wine.

****

Acthiel had never been so angry in all his sixteen years, and that said a lot since most every day of his life was spent mad about something. He wasn't stupid; in fact he excelled at any subject put in front of him. He often ending up sending his teachers away because they could barely read the books on the subjects they were trying to teach him – often in tears – both men and women. He knew neither of his parents liked his treatment of the staff but he didn't care. Neither of them could, or would, do anything to him about it.

He secretly hated both his parents and had given up trying to please them long ago. His mother had never hidden that she was afraid of him. He knew he had nearly killed her during his birthing. He had overheard one of the midwives that had been present at his birthing telling the head kitchen wench about it once when she had been called to the castle to help birth one of his *errors in judgment*, as his father liked to call them. She was trying to explain why she thought he had such a low regard for women. It had taken all his effort not to show the woman just exactly why he had such a low regard for women – because they were weak. *Wouldn't his father have been so proud of him*? He thought then he spit on the floor and guffawed.

His father – now there was a bloody joke. He half expected to learn he was actually the stable master's son. Even that waste of human flesh had more backbone than his father did. He doubted his father even had the balls to do his mother well enough to have gotten her with child. He had heard over the years how hard the two had tried and knew they were both disappointed in what their efforts had gotten them. His mother didn't care about anyone but herself and his father only cared about his serf's. He could still see the look of pride his father had in his eyes when he looked upon the stupid serf brat that Sir Alyn had been putting through trials earlier that week.

That snotty little upstart would get his the first chance he got. He would have to do it discreetly. His father having made such a point of speaking directly to the boy told him the man would be watching him closely also, knowing his being embarrassed before the soldiers would irk him to no end. He hated that his father knew him this well.

The prince walked to the table and grabbed the carafe of wine on the corner of it, wanting to drown the upstart serf in it. He ignored the chalices beside it and upturned it, drinking most of its contents down in one gulp. He heard a sound behind him then and turned around, expecting it to be his father. He knew the man was expecting him to be at the stable right then, which was why he was where he was now – essentially hiding in plain sight. He saw instead a girl of average height. The ugly gray frock she was wearing told him she was a scullery maid. He knew the head kitchen wench made the girls all wear these in an attempt to make them less attractive to him but she didn't realize it didn't matter if they were covered in horse dung. There was only one part of them he cared about and that looked the same on any woman.

This one was new to him and looked good even in the shapeless garment. She looked like she had other parts he might care about seeing by the way she filled out the shapeless cloth. He shouted for her to stop where she was and smiled when he saw her jump and stand stiff. He set the carafe down and started toward her. His father wanted him to come to love his serfs and who was he to argue with the man?

****

"Who might you be?" The boy prince took the maid's chin in his hand and lifted it up.

Cami made sure to keep her eyes down as he did this, praying for it to be over quickly. "I am one of the scullery maids, my lord."

"You must be new, I know all the others," said the man, his eyes tracing her body. "You make this ugly frock look rather attractive. Too bad all of them don't fill it out as well as you."

Cami wasn't sure what to say to this.

"That was a compliment, Sweetie, you really should say thank you when someone gives you one, especially when it is a prince," said Acthiel.

Cami jumped, remembering what Maria had said about him and the stories she had heard of his exploits in the other homes.

"I understand you are from one of the orphanages. Which one?"

"Abbeydrew, my lord."

"Yes, that's why I don't remember you." He brought his face close to hers and whispered into her ear, "I can make your life here much more pleasant, Pretty. If you are nice to me I will be nice to you."

"Pardon me, sir, but I am promised already," said Cami quickly, hoping the man, who was supposed to be raised with proper manners, would follow the custom of not attempting to meddle with one who was already spoken for.

"Have you and your boy been before my father to ask for his permission yet?"

"No, my lord."

"Is he here at the castle?"

"No, my lord."

"Is he even in Ghorst?"

Cami said slowly, "No, my lord."

"Then, how can you be sure he is keeping his promise to you?"

Cami jumped again at that, she had just been wondering that very thing a moment before.

"You see, promises are not always kept, Miss... what is your name, Pretty?"

"Ca... Cameron, my lord."

"Cameron, that's a very pretty name, fits you well," he said as he moved the hair from her cheek. "Sometimes a man only wants a thing when it is right before their eyes and loses all interest as soon as another comes along."

Cami swallowed hard and fought tears.

"Look at me, I want to see your eyes."

"I cannot, my lord, it is forbidden," said Cami.

"Only if a lord has not given you permission."

Cami didn't want to but she did, locking hers on his very penetrating ones. She didn't want to think it but the boy before her was quite handsome. He reminded her of another, whose eyes were penetrating as well.

"Very pretty indeed, Cameron," he said, her name said softly, almost a whisper. "I am sure you could keep my interest for a bit, yes? I could get you reassigned... You could be one of my bath maidens if you wish it," he said, his lips brushing her cheek.

"Sorry, my lord, but I'm sworn to the kitchens for at least my first few months here," said Cami.

"I am saying I can get that changed, Girl." A touch of anger was tingeing his voice now, he wasn't used to being refused.

The doors he had come in through burst open again then, making the girl jump and the prince smile. Another man, older, much larger and more stately but looking very much like the prince stepped in.

"Acthiel!"

Cami heard a groan come from the prince's throat and watched him roll his eyes.

"What now, Father?"

"We have a riding lesson today, why aren't you in your riding gear?"

"I already know how to ride a horse, Father," said the boy arrogantly, stepping away from the girl further. He had not removing his hand from her arm yet so she couldn't go yet.

"Not in battle, you do not," snapped Vianor.

"Then I won't get into battle while I am on one," sniggered the boy. He looked back at the girl, expecting to see her smiling at his teasing. The look on her face actually more mirrored his father's.

"I am not playing games with you, Boy. Let the maiden get back to her work, get to your rooms and get yourself dressed!"

The prince did release Cami's arm then. He stood where he was for a moment, trying to find a way to get out of this farce. He found none. He guffawed and stomped to the doors he and his father had come through, slamming them shut behind him.

Cami stayed where she was, trying to get her heart back into her chest. She jumped as a hand touched her shoulder, thinking it was the prince coming again to try again.

"Are you alright, Child," asked the man behind her, his voice was much deeper than the prince's and sounded kind.

"I… I am, your highness," she said, realizing it was the king himself. She started to go down on her knees but his hand on her arm stopped her.

"Get yourself back to the kitchens, Girl."

"Yes, my lord," said Cami as she quickly did so.

Kept to the Shadows

15

Unexpected Visitors

Kyi's first week at the stable was the same thing each day: feeding the horses, watering the horses, brushing down the horses, oiling the tack, stowing the tack, mucking the stalls – he was beginning to hate horses. He was just sitting down to rest a moment when the stall doors burst open and a man that looked like a giant stepped into the opening, silhouetted by the sun beyond.

"You there, stable boy," said the booming voice.

Kyi spun around with a smile on his face and a name on his lips, both faded when he saw it wasn't who he thought it was.

"Ye... yes, sir?"

"Get my and the prince's horses tacked, we are going out."

'My and the prince's horse' replayed in his mind, that would mean... Kyi dropped to his knees in a pile of horse droppings then and said, "Yes, your majesty."

"Rise, Boy," said the king, then he turned and stepped outside.

Kyi did so, not even caring that he was now as dirty as the floor, and stumbled to the door of the bunkhouse and threw it open, "Galin?" he said.

Galin jumped up, climbing off the body of a girl, who was naked beneath him. "Damn you, Boy, I told you what to do already," he shouted, trying to get his britches back to his waist.

"I am sorry, sir," said Kyi looking at the ground. "The... the king... the king is asking for his and the prince's horses to be made ready."

"The who?"

"The king," said Kyi, his eyes shifting to the girl on the bed, he'd never seen a girl naked before and she had done nothing to cover herself up any so her breasts were just staring at him, they were so round and milky white, and looked like they had tiny pink bonnets on the ends of them. He was too stunned to move.

"Get dressed, Woman," Galin shouted at her as he grabbed Kyi's shoulder and pulled him from the room.

The two went to getting the horses made ready then Galin handed the reins of the prince's ride to the boy and motioned him to follow with the animal. They found the king still waiting, outside the stable. He was facing the tournament field beside the castle. The stable master could see a young man with no tunic on was riding a horse, bare-backed, around it, hitting targets set around the pen. He started to clear his throat to let the king know they were behind him when he saw the prince. Both of the stable hands could hear the boy swearing under his breath.

* * * * * * * * * * * * * * * * * *

Acthiel hadn't missed his father watching the new soldier boy, he knew it was him that was the reason his father had suddenly decided he needed more training. He already hated that boy for the humiliation of a week ago, now he was beyond even that. He had often gone down to the tournament field while the soldiers were training, to brush up on his own skills – the others all knew to let him win, the new one did not. A lesson he would enjoy teaching him. He could see the admiration in his father's eyes when he looked at him, as if wishing he were his son instead.

"Well?" he barked, making his father jump for once, as he climbed into his saddle.

Kept to the Shadows

16

A Proposal for Dell

Dell was hitting the target rings Alyn had set up around the field with the tip of the lance under his arm with ease. He rode the majestic animal under him equally as. He and the gray and white spotted stud were like one; he was barely holding the reins, using only his thighs to direct him around the field, and the horse was responding as if he knew what he wanted without needing to be told. He could feel the eyes of all the other soldiers on him as well as some of the female castle workers on the balcony across from him. He could hear them giggling foolishly and some of the comments they made as he came close enough for them to see him fully. He knew being shirtless was part of his allure, how he and the animal between his legs were moving – more than one of the women was saying they wished the horse were them. Him being a soldier in training was the only thing that made it all right to be in such a state of undress.

He wondered if Cami was among them. He had always had a bit of a crush in her but he knew she had eyes for another. He knew that other boy, his best friend, Wayde, felt the same for her.

He would never attempt anything with her as long as this was so; he cared too much about Wayde himself. Thinking of his best friend made him lose his concentration. This caused him to miss the next target. This, in turn, drew boos from the other soldiers and cries of whoa from the girls watching.

Alyn stepped in front of his path then, breaking the horse's stride.

Dell pulled the reins to get the animal to stop, which it did without hesitation. He slid from its back with ultimate grace. He took the towel the man had in his hands and wiped some of the sweat from his body. He waved to the ladies that had been watching and bowed nearly as gracefully as any true knight would have. He smiled at the cries of joy and giggles this got him. He turned and did the same to the soldiers watching him. From them he got rowdy cheers.

"Good show, Boy. I do believe you will make a fine soldier, and perhaps even, one day, a knight."

"It isn't nice to tease, Sir Alyn," said Dell plainly as he patted the horse's broad chest and stroked his snout then took the reins and began to lead the animal off the field.

Alyn left the field with him. "Nay, I do not tease, Boy. I saw the king watching you. He's very impressed with you, and he isn't with many. You keep at it and the Lord knows... you may one day be made a lord even."

"Can a serf do that?" asked Dell, stopping beside a barrel of water. He dunked the towel into it and used it again on his still sweat covered neck and chest then allowed the horse to drink from the top of it.

"Aye, one can, if he wins a lord's favor. It is not often, but it can happen."

Dell was speechless, he could have never dreamed of such. He wanted so badly to tell Wayde this news, the two of them had often spoken of what it must be like to be a lord and live in a fancy house with servants of their own. Many people had commented on his exceptional good looks and wondered if he might not have noble blood in his veins, he had always just shrugged it off but now he was thinking it again. "Sir? If an orphan's parents were noble blood, does that give the child any right to their affluence?"

"I dunno, Boy. I would think no. The edict as such, the parents would relinquish all rights to the child and that child, in turn, would lose them as soon as it was born, I should think."

"That hardly seems fair to the child," said Dell.

"The way of the world, Boy. Why, you think yours were?"

"I doubt it, sir," said Dell, having lost all interest in the question now.

"Well then, if you don't mind risking your blood, I have your first assignment."

"Yes, please," said Dell proudly.

"And, I don't mind telling you that you are the fastest ever to get one."

Dell beamed at that.

"Lady Anya, a princess from Elmsdune, is coming to the castle the end of the month, for a stay with the queen to complete her finishing. We are sending out a brigade to see her here safely. If you feel up to it, I have asked you be made a part of it."

"Thank you, sir," said Dell, smiling brilliantly.

"Get yourself cleaned up then, the stench of your sweat will likely draw every available wench from here to Elmsdune looking to lay with you," teased the man. He smiled at the color this brought to the boy's cheeks. For all his gruffness to him when he first arrived, he did truly like him. "We are being presented to the king this evening so that he can give us leave. You are about the same size as I was at your age; I have laid out one of my old suits of armor for you. It is not the newest design but it will keep your organs intact in case of a battle. You will also find one of the king's coverlets."

"Thank you, my lord, Sir Alyn," said Dell, bowing gracefully to him as well. He was still smiling as he started toward the stable with the horse in tow.

Dell smiled brightly as he looked at himself in the mirror on the door of the barracks, he was pleased with what he saw. The armor fit him like a glove and the stark white coverlet made his bronze skin seem even darker, which was giving him an air of godliness. His hair was clean and he was freshly shaved, wanting to be the epitome of a king's soldier.

He stepped from the barracks and felt equally as proud when he saw the look on the other soldiers' faces. Most were just as proud of him, though some had underlying looks of jealousy. They were all dressed as he was, except Alyn, who wouldn't be going with them; he was wearing his armor, which had a few dents in it, but no coverlet.

"We go down on our right knee, right fist over your heart, when we enter and remain that way until we are given leave to stand. You answer any question the king, queen and prince put to you, quickly, and keep your eyes to the floor unless directed otherwise."

"Yes, my lord," said all the soldiers quickly, most of them had been part of assignments before so they already knew to do this but Dell and three others had not been – this was said for their benefit as much as in a reminder to the others.

"Fall in." He led them across the field to the castle's inner foyer.

****

The king and queen were already on their thrones; their son hadn't arrived yet, which was obviously irritating the king. He was tapping his foot and looking at the doors frequently. Part of him was seriously thinking of sending the boy with the troop to get the princess, just to be away from him for a few days. Just as he was about to call the attendant to go and fetch his son the doors opened to him.

Acthiel was only half dressed. He was tying his leggings as he stepped through the doors, his tunic wasn't tucked in, as was proper, and his hair was a mess. This told his father what he had been doing instantly.

The prince smiled sickly, knowing that he could not stop him, nor would he dare to. "Sorry I am late, Father, my attendant hadn't gotten my britches as ironed as I like them so I had her try again."

Vianor wanted badly to have his son flogged right then but he held his tongue, as usual, not wanting to do it so publically, the guard was expected at any moment. He motioned the boy to his chair and said through clenched teeth, "You act up, Acthiel and I will send you to work in the mines."

Acthiel started to laugh then he stopped. There was a new look on his father's face, one that made him uncertain if he might have pushed his father far enough to actually follow through with his threat this time.

Vianor had no more gotten his words out when the doors at the head of the room opened. The sergeant at arms stepped in with the soldiers dressed in the king's colors in tow.

The king was obviously impressed with how good they all looked. The queen seemed pleased enough. Acthiel rolled his eyes, wondering when the underlings would stop trying so hard to win their favors. The men before him weren't built right to win any of his favors, though a few of them were pretty enough to be. The prince was shocked to see the one that had bested him in the sword fight among the men. He was only but a week into his trials – normally a soldier had to have been in service for more than six months to get a commission. He wasn't so surprised of this either though. He had already won his father's favor, which meant the other soldiers, especially Alyn, would go out of their way to include him in anything they could, hoping to glean some of the light shining off him.

****

The men stayed in close rank, two rows of five.

They came forward with Alyn, stopped in the center of the room and went down on their right knees at the same time, as if it had been choreographed.

Again, the king and queen looked please, again Acthiel only rolled his eyes.

"Your majesties, King Vianor, Queen Vela, Prince Acthiel, may I present my men to you for approval?" asked the knight.

"You may, Sir Alyn," said the king. He waved his hand to let them know they could rise.

They did so, taking up firm stances, their legs spread to the width of their shoulders, their heads held straight forward, their eyes aimed downward. All but one of them had their left hand resting on the hilt of their sword – Dell, being left-handed, had his sword on his right hip so it was his right hand on the hilt.

"I see the newest is among your chosen, Sir Alyn, pray tell, why this would be?" asked the king, smiling to himself. He already knew the answer but he wanted to rain some praise on the boy and build his confidence further.

"He has proven himself one of my best soldiers already, my lord, King. Word of bandits along the way have increased in the last days. I feel his passion and zeal could be the deciding factor to getting the princess here safely."

Acthiel let out a bit of a snort to this and said, "I bet he is good on his knees as well. He does have a pretty mouth, a smooth tongue and a plump backside," under his breath.

Luckily only the king heard him and he managed to ignore it. "Speak, Boy, is this the first assignment you wish to have? Surely you would rather something a little less hard to begin your life here? Perhaps a quiet border patrol?"

Dell picked up on the man's teasing quickly and said, "Nay, my lord, I have had a life of quiet, I wish for something with some backbone to it."

Alyn nodded to this and smiled proudly to the king, knowing he was getting a boost by his choice as well.

"Very well, Boy," said the king. He looked over the other men, most all of whom had been on escort parties before. He had only a few comments for them. After the soldiers had all had a turn being praised, the king motioned Alyn forward again and said, "I approve of them, Sir Knight. When do they depart?"

"At first light, my liege, so that they can make the pass before darkness falls."

"Very good, I will try to be out for the send-off," he said, his eyes lingering on Dell.

"Thank you, my liege," said Alyn, dropping to his knee, the men behind him did the same, in unison.

"Give the men the night off, father," said Acthiel suddenly.

Vianor looked sideways at his son at this odd remark.

"Haven't they earned it? It will be two weeks of hard travel to and from Elmsdune, surely they deserve a night to enjoy before?"

"Yes, son, I do believe you are correct. Sir Alyn, see to it," said the king.

"Aye, my lord," he said, smiling and nodding to the prince. He was wondering himself why the brat child would make such a kind gesture.

****

The knight escorted the men back out of the castle to the barracks again where he told them all they could go into town if they wished it, as long as they promised not to get too rowdy and weren't unable to ride in the morning.

All but Dell went to get changed into regular attire.

Alyn saw this and went to the boy's side. "What is it, Dell?"

"I have only one I would wish to see in town, my house-mother at Abbeydrew, and I don't feel like seeing her just now. My only real friends are either here at the castle or in Arrachsnow."

"You will be stopping in Arrachsnow for an evening; perhaps you will get a chance to see your friend there then?"

Dell instantly lit up, making Alyn smile.

"As for the ones at the castle, what part are they in? Perhaps I can assist?

"Kyi works at the stable."

"The little one?" asked Alyn. He was surprised one such as Dell would befriend such a boy.

"That would be him," he said smiling even larger. "He is quite a character, actually."

"Well, the horses will need to be made ready for the early morning departure. You may go and ask it of the stable master if you wish it."

Dell's smile continued to get brighter, "The other works in the kitchens."

"A girl?" asked Alyn, a knowing glint in his eyes.

"It is not like that, she is promised to my friend in Arrachsnow," said Dell, to that look.

"Who is to say they are still? He may have found another away from this one?"

"Wayde is as loyal as they come and he is too in love with Cami to ever see another like that," said Dell. He smiled to himself at how sweet it really was.

"Already so noble and not yet a knight, you are a true asset to this barracks, Young Dell."

"I am glad you find it enjoyable to tease me so," teased Dell. "I don't see a ring on your finger. Haven't you found the right one yet?"

"Too busy having fun with the wrong ones, my boy! There is no other girl you wish to see then? I can have a *wrong one* sent to you if you fancy it?"

"No, I haven't met anyone that could compare to Cami, and until I do… I want real love, not just a roll in the sheets," said Dell. He knew using Cami as a basis for his own love interest wasn't fair to the other women out there, how could any other hope to measure up?

"Well then, I will try to get the girl from the kitchen to bring you some refreshment if you are bound to stay here at the castle all alone."

"I am, sir."

"You say her name is Cami?"

"Cameron."

Alyn was shaking his head as he started out of the barracks.

"Sir?" Dell called after him.

Alyn turned back, his hand on the handle of the door.

"Why are you being so kind to me?"

"Because if you win the favor of the king, I will too. Sewage is not the only thing that flows downward."

Dell smiled at that as well, he was not against allowing this man into his spotlight.

17

Feeling Guilty

Dell didn't take his armor off or put away his coverlet as the others had before leaving, he wanted Kyi and Cami to see him dressed this way. He went to the door, excited that he was going to get to see them. He took one last look in the mirror hanging on that door then opened it and headed for the doors of the stable. He could see a light on inside so he knew the men that worked it would be inside it as well.

He was giddy as he knocked on the smaller door set into one of the swinging doors of the barn loudly and waited. It opened moments later to the small boy that was his friend. He saw Kyi's eyes start up him and quickly go back to the ground. He guessed he thought he was a nobleman or a knight by the armor and coverlet.

Kyi had thought this. He was still getting over seeing the king himself. He started to go on his right knee, "How may I serve you, my lord?"

"By stopping that," said Dell.

The boy's eyes shot up then. He stood up quickly, a huge smile broke his dirt-streaked face and he all but squealed, "Dell?"

"Hello, Kyi, see you are still up to no good," said Dell through a huge grin.

Kyi seemed to realize how he looked then, especially compared to the polished Dell. He tried to use the back of his hand and his shirtsleeve to wipe the mess from his face but the shirtsleeve was equally as dirty, because he had already used it for this before, so he only managed to smear it and get some in his mouth which made him start to gag, because it wasn't all dirt.

Dell realized this too as the pungent smell hit his nose. "I am here to ask the stable master to prepare ten horses for the morning. We are to act as escorts so we will need the king's colors and tacking for a two week trip."

"We?" Kyi asked.

"I am assigned to go with them. Sir Alyn says I am the fastest to be given his first assignment," said Dell. He had only wanted to show his friend how well he was doing but as he looked around the dirty stalls and saw how different their positions were he felt guilty.

"Where are you going?" asked Kyi eagerly.

"We are escorting a princess from Elmsdune back here. Sir Alyn says we will be staying a night in Arrachsnow so I hope to get to see Wayde."

"Oh, I envy you," said Kyi.

"Not liking the stables so much?"

"It is not like at the home. There was only three to look after there, here there are just... too many... and they need to be feed and watered and brushed down *every single day*," said the boy, dropping his shoulders.

"Have you had a chance to see Cami yet?"

"No, I haven't been given permission to leave the stable yard... I think I saw you getting run through your training once though, least I think it was you."

Dell nodded, likely it was. "I have been given permission to have the night off and I asked to get to see you and her. The sergeant at arms said he cannot promise but he is trying to get her free to come see me. If I do get to I will try to come here for a bit with her."

"I would like that... also... I cannot afford to send out a dispatch just now but I... I don't get my stipend until Sunday and it will take me two weeks to get enough... would you take one to Wayde for me?"

"Of course, Kyi, without even needing to ask."

"Thank you," said Kyi. He motioned Dell inside then and called out to Galin, telling him what the soldier was there for.

****

Cami was just getting back to the kitchens from cleaning the privy, trying to get the crud out from under her fingernails – not wanting to even think what was in that crud – when Clara shouted her name. She dropped the bucket and brush and ran into the room, frightened of the tone of her voice. "Yes, Clara?"

"Get yourself washed up, Child!" shouted the woman, pointing to the sink. "And try to do something with that mop on your head."

It took all Cami's efforts to keep herself from saying it was the woman's fault she looked like she had a mop on her head. She went to the sink and began to scrub her hands and under her nails with the pumas soap, when she was done she turned back to the head kitchen maid.

The woman now had a wooden tray with a plate of pork and steamed potatoes, a chalice and a carafe of wine in her hands, which she thrust at the girl.

Cami took it, looked at it funny then back at the woman before her.

"You are to deliver this meal to the soldiers' barracks."

"Why?"

"We do not ask that of our superiors, Girl."

"But..." said Cami, feeling uncomfortable. Her immediate thought was Dell but he was too new in the position to be getting such special treatment. Her next thought was the prince, whom she really didn't want to see. "Who is it?"

"I did not ask, and this is not a request you can refuse. This is one of the king's recent favorites."

Cami was all but in tears as she was escorted out the door she had come into the kitchen through the first day.

Clara pointed toward a long building along the west side of the compound and said very sternly, "Straight there. You stay as long as he requires you... as I said, he is one of the king's favorites," this last was said as if implying she shouldn't rush him and that she should be willing to wait on his *every* desire. "You return here immediately on your release."

"Ye... yes, Miss Clara..." said Cami. She was trying hard to fight back tears. She knew she was considered castle property now, just as she had been the orphanage's property before the turn-out, and she had to do whatever they asked of her whether she liked it or not, but she hoped this man didn't want her for anything other than to deliver his meal because she would refuse it and likely get herself flogged at the very least.

****

Cameron walked across the field, trying not to spill any of the items on the tray, and knocked softly on the door. She was hoping with all her being that it would be anyone but the prince.

Dell was anxious as he paced the barracks waiting for Alyn to return with an answer as to whether he was going to get to see Cami tonight. He was going over in his mind all the things he wanted to tell her when a knock on the door made him jump near out of his skin. He hesitated a moment, unsure why the man would be knocking, then walked to it and opened it.

It took Dell a moment to realize the girl standing outside was Cami.
It took Cami a moment to realize the soldier before her was Dell.

"Cami?" Dell asked tentatively. "What happened to your hair?"
"Are you one of the soldiers leaving in the morning?" asked the girl.
"Yes. I am riding to Elmsdune and back. I asked to get to see you before I go. What happened to your hair?"
Cami didn't want to lie to Dell but seeing he was so happy in his position made her feel even worse. She knew he would be

very angry if she told him the truth and she didn't want to get him into trouble, "I cut it. It was too long, it kept getting in my way."

"You did a fine mess of it."

"Yeah, I know. One of the other maids tried to help fix it but she didn't have the sharpest knife. I'm glad Wayde isn't here to see it."

"Wayde would still think you were beautiful, it is not your hair he is in love with."

"He loves?... He never said he loved me," said Cami quickly, though she had always felt he did, until recently.

"He may not have said the words but if you ever saw the way he looked at you, Cami."

"If he loves me then why hasn't he written yet?"

"I saw Kyi earlier, he said he hasn't been able to because he cannot afford to yet, it's the same for me, I am sure it is for him as well."

Cami couldn't argue that, she wouldn't be able to for at least two more weeks because she owed Sally two pents so that she could have a bath.

"I am going to be going through Arrachsnow on the way; I am going to try to get to see him. If you can find a way to get it to me I can take him a letter for you."

"I will try. Clara is very strict," said Cami, "If I don't get to can you tell him I miss him?"

"I will."

"I have to get back now, lights out for me is in about half an hour. I am glad to see you are doing so well, Dell."

"Are you doing well, Cami?"

The girl tried to put a happy looking smile on her face as she said, "I am. It is really tough sometimes but... It is not the same as at the home."

"Kyi said the same thing."

Cami didn't want him to ask anymore of her life now, afraid she might start crying and tell him, so she quickly said, "You be careful, Dell. Come back safe." She hugged him quickly then went to the door and disappeared through it.

Dell wanted to stop her but he didn't want to get her in trouble so he only nodded and stepped back. He was worried now about leaving Kyi and Cami, he had a feeling neither was being honest with him but there was nothing he could do about it now. He felt guilty for how happy he was in his placement. He looked at himself in the mirror again and got another rush of pleasure that he was getting to go on his first assignment and that he might get to see Wayde.

Putting thoughts of his guilt behind him he pulled the coverlet over his head, not wanting to get it soiled with the meal Cami had brought him, folded it up neatly then started to work the clasps to remove the armor.

Dell had just gotten the last clasp loose when he heard raised voices in the yard. One of them sounded like Cami. He went to the door quickly, afraid one of the other soldiers might think she was there without permission. He didn't want her to get into trouble because of him. He opened the door and froze. It was Cami's voice he had heard but it wasn't one of the other soldiers.

Kept to the Shadows

18

Stare Down

The prince had been watching the barracks since as soon as his father released him from the hall. He knew he had surprised the sergeant at arms and his father with his kind suggestion. He could see the latter honestly wanted to believe it was out of kindness but he had no doubt he suspected otherwise – who was he to disappoint?

He had expected to see the serf boy joining the other degenerate soldiers, heading for a local brothel. He was intending to make for it himself, and maybe accidentally run into the boy, with the tip of his sword, on his way. He didn't come out with them. He watched the old knight, Alyn, leave a few minutes after the others with a very satisfied looking smile on his face. This made him snigger. He wondered if this was why the boy was rising in favor so quickly. "Pretty mouth, indeed. I bet he is very skilled with his tongue," he said to himself. He had no desire toward men but he was tempted to let the boy have a go with him. Maybe he could have his father happen upon them, just for the chance to humiliate them both.

He jumped when the door of the barracks opened again, then Dell, still dressed in his full armor, stepped out and walked proudly and determinedly to the stables. He wanted to laugh; it only proved to him how simple the boy really was. "Put him in a suit of armor and he thinks he is a knight."

He moved to a better vantage point then and waited to see what the stupid boy was doing. It was only moments before he was starting back for the barracks, smiling nearly as bright as Alyn had been. "Sharing it with the stable boy as well, Ah?" sniggered the prince, "Equal opportunity man then."

He jumped when he heard the door to the kitchen pantry open then, he knew it was kept locked at night, he had tried to use it to sneak back into the castle on his nights of debauchery. He waited to see what debauchery this was and smiled when he saw the pretty new maid, Cameron, coming from it with a tray in her hands, heading toward the barracks. "Oh, I see, you like both sides and your pretties a little closer to home."

He moved back to his first position and waited.

It was surprisingly little time before the girl came back out. Either the brat orphan didn't have much stamina or having already spent it with Alyn and the stable boy had left him lax. The prince saw the girl was wiping tears from her face so he guessed it was the latter. "Don't worry, I will make up for his lack of ability," said Acthiel as he stepped out.

The girl had not been expecting anyone to be beside the barracks so she jumped, her hand going to her chest. She was even more frightened when she saw who it was.

"Evening, Pretty. It's Cameron, right?"

She dropped her eyes and said, "Yes, my lord?"

"Bestowing your special gifts on the soldier in there, are you? I assure you, they would be much better spent being granted to me."

"My lord?" asked the girl, sounding unsure what he meant.

"Come now, no need to act the innocent flower with me. A body like this has seen many days in a barracks, hasn't it?"

"My lord, I have never…"

"A virgin still? If you were planning to save it for your boy in Arrachsnow why are you so eagerly offering it to the soldier in there? Have you decided the other boy is unworthy of it now, or is it that he is too far away and you can wait no longer?"

Cami blushed at his implications and squealed when he suddenly pulled her to him.

"I can show you reasons why you should give it up now and why it should be to me. I can make you feel things you never thought possible," said Acthiel hotly as he kissed her neck.

She wanted to fight him but was afraid of what he would do if she did so she let him kiss her neck and run his hands over her back and butt, praying it would just be over with quickly. He had a sly look in his eyes when he stepped away from her, tugging at the apron around her middle. It was one she wouldn't mind seeing in the eyes of the one he reminded her of but not this one. "Please, my lord, do not do this," she said quietly, the tears she'd been shedding for herself and Wayde of moments ago now only for herself, hoping he wouldn't do this.

"I promise it will only hurt for a moment," he said, looking around for a place to use. "And the pleasure will make you soon forget that."

"Please, do not," she repeated a little louder.

They both jumped when the door of the barracks opened and Dell stepped from it.

"Pardon me, but I believe she asked you not to do this?"

Acthiel was surprised at this open act against him, not only because of the sound of threat in the question but that the soldier-serf was looking him the eye when he said it. "This is none of your business, Boy." The prince expected the boy to suddenly remember his place, lower his head and drop to his knees but hoped he decided to push it at the same time. He could take his building heat out on him as well as on the girl. He was surprised, and a little jarred, that the boy did neither.

"I am sworn to protect all in this castle, my lord, which includes this girl."

"Perhaps it is I that requires protecting from her, soldier. She has been begging me, with her eyes and these tight frocks, to do this, haven't you, Cameron?"

Cami looked up at Dell, hoping he wouldn't believe this of her.

"She has asked you not to do this as of now so it matters not what her eyes and frock said before, my lord," said Dell, his hand going to his sword.

Acthiel saw this and smiled wickedly, "You do realize, speaking to me in this manner can get your tongue torn from your mouth, looking at me, especially with such heat, can get your eyes plucked from you skull and threatening me is a hanging offense?"

Dell didn't back down, his sword now halfway free of its scabbard.

"I will see to it all three are done, in the order I spoke of," growled Acthiel.

"Dell, please," said Cami.

The prince had his sword fully free of its scabbard and was about to strike at Dell when a booming voice came from behind him.

One that made both him and Dell freeze.

19

A Bit of Sport

Vianor's eyes took in Dell, still in his armor, the girl from the kitchen, the same one his son had been taunting in the great hall only the day before, and his son and smirked. He could guess what had been happening. "Out for a bit of sport, Acthiel?" asked his father.

"Father, I was happening by the barracks, taking a walk to clear my head, to prepare me for our tour of a few days from now, when I heard sounds of a woman begging not to be harmed. I came upon a scene most distressing. This soldier was attempting to accost the maid here, who had only been bringing him some dinner," said the prince, his eyes locked on Dell's, daring him to deny it.

Vianor looked from the prince to the girl to the new soldier. He knew better instantly but he couldn't openly refute his son before serfs. "Did the soldier manage to harm you, Child?"

"N… no, my lord," said Cami, her faced aimed at the ground; she felt horrible for letting the king think it was Dell that had threatened her instead of the prince.

"Are you too upset to return to your duties?"

"N… no, my lord, King."

"Then do so."

"Yes, my lord, King," said Cami quickly; she all but ran across the yard.

The king then looked at his son and the soldier boy, whose eyes were still locked on each other. For all intents and purposes the boy, Dell, was violating the law by his actions; he knew Acthiel would've asked him to look at him, hoping to see the fear in his eyes.

There was none in Dell's eyes.

"He has spoken to me without my leave to do so, he is refusing to avert his eyes and has drawn his sword on me, Father. I demand him punished!"

"The boy is leaving on assignment in the morning, there is not enough time to choose another. He is new not yet aware of protocols. I will forgive him this time as a gesture of kindness. If he attempts such again he will be justly punished," said the king.

Acthiel looked shocked at this. He knew then his father knew he had been lying.

"Your mother is looking for you, I think she wishes you to tuck her in for the evening," said the king sternly, obviously dismissing the prince.

"Yes, Father," said Acthiel, finally breaking his stare with Dell. He slammed his sword back into its scabbard and turned with a huff, stomping back toward the castle.

The king remained, facing Dell. He had a look of sadness on his face. He couldn't tell the boy that he knew his son was lying.

"I did not do this, my lord. I swear," said Dell earnestly, then he added, "It was the prince trying to have his way with the girl." He knew by accusing the man's son, and his better, of this crime was an open act of treason, but then so too was looking him in the eye and drawing his sword to him. He watched the king shake his head slowly. He started to get to his knees so they man could take his head from his shoulders. "I beg you to make it quick, my lord, King Vianor."

Vianor's hand came forward, stopping the gesture. "You will keep your head, Boy. As I said to my son, you are not being released from my guard, young Dell."

It took a moment for Dell to find his voice. He knew what he said next would likely change the king's mind but he had to say it in any case. "I cannot go on this assignment, my lord, King. Cameron is very important to me. I made a promise to see her safe before I made the one to you. I cannot allow anything to happen to her."

The king wanted to praise the new soldier for how commendable his behavior was and say he wished the prince was more like him but that would be akin to admitting his son was a coward and an insufferable brat. "You *will* be leaving in the morning, Boy, and the prince will be leaving with me on my tour of the counties later this week," said Vianor, removing his gloves from his hands. "He will not have another chance with the girl."

Dell wasn't sure how to take that, not wanting to get her into trouble or thrown out either.

"Please, my lord, she has done nothing wrong."

"Your commitment to her is admirable, Boy. She will remain in the kitchen. Acthiel will likely find another that catches his fancy once he has returned."

"Thank you, my lord, King," said Dell, dropping to his right knee. "I swear I will earn the trust and respect you have shown me.

Again Vianor had a crushing feeling of pride in his breast. How was it the sisters in the orphanages could teach their wards such manners but he and his wife could not. "Rise, Boy. You have a long two weeks ahead of you, get what sleep you can," said the king then he turned and started for the doors of the castle.

20

A Proposal for Wayde

Wayde and Hithal's trip to Elmsdune went far faster than Wayde had wanted it to.

"We will start first thing in the morning, Lad. These tired bones only want to cuddle up to my wife for a few hours," said Hithal. He was happy to see the boy so enthusiastic.

"Alright," said Wayde, a little disappointed.

"Put the carriage away and brush down Reese if you still have so much energy, Boy."

Wayde nodded and moved over in the seat of the cart when the man climbed down.

"Tabitha should have dinner ready when you get inside so come to the kitchen when you are done."

"Yes, sir," said Wayde as he shook the reins to start the horse walking.

It was only a few feet to the barn. Wayde stopped the horse just before it and climbed down from the carriage. He tied Reese's reins off to the post then removed the harness from the carriage, pushed it into the storage side and closed the doors. He then took all but the bridle off the horse, leaving him tied up, and took the rest of the strapping into the barn. He hung it up then grabbed a bucket and brush from the bench beside the door, dunked it into the trough beside the barn and walked back to the waiting animal.

He was wondering if Kyi might be doing some-thing like this at the very same moment in Ghorst as he began to dry brush the dust from the horse's coat, then he wondered what Dell was doing, imagining him getting some more training with a sword, then, of course, his mind went to Cami, wondering if she was doing some dishes maybe, or beating out a tapestry. He so wished he knew. He was deep in these thoughts when he felt a hand on his shoulder, making him jump.

He turned to find Hithal's daughter, Jenna, leaning on the bottom half of the split barn door. The top of her blouse was open a few more buttons than was proper and a lot more skin than was proper was showing. "Hello, Miss," he said, keeping his eyes down, and well away from the exposed area. For all Hithal said he didn't expect it of him the man was free, which meant he was above Wayde, which meant so too were his wife and their daughter.

"You don't have to lower your eyes to me, Wayde, and you may call me Jenna," said the girl as she held a glass of something that was obviously cold, by the condensation sitting on it, up to her exposed skin. Some of that condensation dripped onto her exposed skin. Those drips traced the curves and disappeared under the cloth. She then held it out to him.

Wayde couldn't stop his eyes from following those drips, or his mind from wondering where they had finally stopped. He looked to the ground and said, "I already was taught what stepping over my bounds gets me once today, Miss Jenna. I think I would rather stick with custom." He did take the glass and take a sip quickly though, finding his throat suddenly dry.

It was lemon-flavored water.

He jumped again when her hand was suddenly on his face, touching the tender scab that had formed over the cut the lord had given him earlier in the day.

"Did my father do that to you?"

"No, Miss, it was one of the lords from town. I made the mistake of looking him in the eye."

"Lord Faelan," she said with such surety.

Wayde neither confirmed nor denied the thought.

"I think it is very unfair that the proclamation took so many from their families," said the girl as her finger traced the scar on his forehead.

Wayde knew he should pull his face out of her hand but was afraid of offending her. Her soft fingers felt good. "I do not think my life would have been any better out of the home." Jenna had removed her hand now so the boy moved to start brushing down the horse again, not wanting Hithal to come out and find him slacking off.

"How so?" she asked.

"My mother died during my birth and, since I was placed in a home, I would guess either she did not know who my father was or he did not care to know, since he obviously did not wish to keep me."

"I am sorry, Wayde," said the girl her finger now beginning to trace his shoulder blade and back.

He was wearing one of his thickest tunics but he could still feel that finger, which was making him feel other things. "Please, Miss Jenna, I do not want either of us to get into trouble."

"I won't. I know you are just getting to know my father but he is really pretty easy on his apprentices, especially if they really wish to learn the trade. I heard him telling my mother how many questions you had during your trip. He really likes you."

Wayde smiled at that, he guessed he really liked the gruff old man as well.

"You have a beautiful smile... and eyes, when you show them," said the girl, bluntly.

Wayde blushed a little and lowered his eyes again; he hadn't realized he was looking at her. "You are beautiful as well, Miss Jenna."

Jenna stepped up before him again then and placed her hand under his chin, pulling his face up gently. "I told you, you do not have to lower your eyes to me, Wayde."

He raised and locked his on hers then. He would be lying if he said he didn't like what he saw looking back at him. He realized her face was coming closer to his then and felt her soft lips touching his, without realizing it he was then kissing her as well. When he felt her hand running down his side and over his buttocks and moving toward his crotch he jumped back and said, "I am sorry, Miss."

"You do not seriously want to be a monk, do you?"

"No."

"Don't you find me attractive?"

"Very much."

"I am not a virgin, Wayde. For all my father is very respected in his trade and my mother is *middle* blood, as he calls it, they aren't high enough to expect me to marry well so there was no need to remain pure. I can have as much fun as I like, and you look like you'd be a lot of it."

He knew he couldn't afford her kind of fun, on more than one front, "I... I'm promised to another."

"Have you gotten the king's permission to marry this other girl yet?"

"No," said Wayde.

"Then, in principle, you really are not," said Jenna as she stepped closer.

Wayde was now against the edge of the building so he had nowhere else to go. This didn't stop the girl who was stepping closer to him now, pressing her firm body against his.

"I'm of marrying age this fall; if you were to marry me it would make you a free man, Wayde," said the girl as she took his empty left hand and placed it on her right breast, moving it over the very thin fabric herself. "You wouldn't have to work even the three years my father is asking you to."

Wayde could feel her body reacting to his hand and started to get lost in how his was reacting in turn then he pulled the hand away and placed it on her waist. He was about to push her away as her lips met his again. He knew he should stop her but he was afraid of what she would do if he turned her down. That and a part of him suddenly didn't want to. Her hands were starting to pull his tunic from his belt as the door to the house opened and Tabitha's voice was calling out.

"Wayde? Is Jenna out there with you?"

Jenna pulled her mouth from Wayde's then and said, "Yes, Mother, I'm helping him with the horse," she called out.

"Well get it done with, dinner is on the table and I will not reheat it."

"Be right in, Mother," said Jenna. She kissed Wayde again then and whispered, "My room is far enough away from my parents that they will not hear us and I promise to stay quiet if you can sneak out tonight."

Part of Wayde wanted to say he would try but he kept thinking about Cami. He nodded, more just to get her to step away from him than as an agreement to her proposal.

She kissed the end of his nose then dropped the brush in the bucket and stepped back, she ran her hand along the horse's side, over its rump and along the other, her eyes locked on his the entire time, then ran toward the light coming through the door.

Wayde leaned his head back, trying to get the wave of feelings coursing through his body to ease then he dropped the brush he was holding into the bucket.

He untied the horse and led him into the barn, put him in the stall, put the bucket of oats in easy reach then stepped out and closed the upper door. He took his time walking to the house, not ready to see the girl again just then.

He was exhausted, for more reasons than one, when he went to his small room over the barn a few hours later. He didn't even think about Jenna's proposal and was asleep in seconds. He was soon dreaming of the beautiful countryside he had seen earlier and of chasing a wildly giggling Cami around one of the fields they had passed through – catching her, falling into her arms in the tall grass and making love to her for hours.

****

Wayde's next days as a blacksmith's apprentice were spent learning the tools of the trade. He never got to use any of them, only name them off and what their uses were. He was given a lesson on metallurgy next – how different types of ore, cooper and steel are used for different things and how different metals are mixed to make still harder metals. It was his seventh day in Arrachsnow before he finally got to see something being made.

The local woodsmith was in need of a new set of chisels, since these didn't take a lot of finesse to make, forging them would be his apprentices first lesson.

It was hot sitting near the furnace but Wayde had to be close to it to watch the bit of iron ore Hithal had in the fire.

"It has to be bright orange-yellow, Boy. Don't let it get to white or it's useless."

Wayde didn't take his eyes off it until he saw it change from red to bright orange, then he shouted for the smith who came running over and pulled it free.

Hithal smiled and nodded, "That is your first true lesson in forging, Son. If you can get the heat just right you are on your way."

Wayde was feeling very proud of himself as he moved to watch the man begin to shape the pointed chisel then.

He also spent most of the week spurning the advances of Jenna; who seemed to appear at the most inconvenient of times, like she was just looking for such opportunities.

She claimed it was purely by accident but he had no doubt she had known he was still in the tub when she had barged in on him one morning since she was at the table when he asked her father permission to take the bath. She had refused to leave or avert her eyes when he asked her to so he could get out of it. And there was no way to deny that she had fully intended him to find her lying on his bed in the room above the barn, naked. She claimed she had simply gotten hot and tired while hanging out the laundry and knew the room was always very cool. She claimed she had no idea he would be returning to it at that time of day since he typically worked well into early dusk most every night. He might have believed this if she hadn't began to touch herself and ask him if he cared to join her. He finally had to tell her he would tell her father if she kept at it to get her to stop, whom he had no doubt, would then send her off to a convent to become a nun.

Now she was either not speaking to him at all or was calling him *monk boy* every time she walked by.

The final night of his first week found him sitting at the small table in his room, a quill in his hand, a bottle of ink and three pieces of parchment before him. All he'd written on each was his friends' names though, unsure what to tell them or how much of it to tell.

21

The Send Off

Morning found Dell up, fully geared and waiting outside of the barracks with the other soldiers. It was a chilly morning so each had a mug of steaming grog in their hands. He was blowing across the top of his as he watched Kyi and the stable master, Galin, getting the horses out of the barn and lined up for them. He could tell by how stiffly his friend was walking that he hadn't been given the same pleasurable treat to warm himself up with.

He would be riding the same spotted gray and white stud he had used for training. Alyn said since the two worked well together and no one else had claimed him he was essentially his to use if he wanted. He had named him Sledge, since he was like a hammer when it came to how he nailed any command he was given.

Dell wished he could go and speak to Kyi, the boy had stopped and waved at him three times, but he knew it wasn't his place to. Other than for direct business or on personal time he shouldn't even acknowledge him now.

He hoped Kyi would understand.

He didn't have long to think about it as Alyn, dressed in his full gear as well, stepped from the castle with the king beside him.

The guards moved into formation. Many of them were whispering about the honor the king was giving them by seeing them off. More than a few looking at Dell, to say they had a feeling it was because of the king's obvious interest in him. Dell tried hard not to let that thought settle in his breast, though he desperately hoped it was so. He feared the actions of the night before had squelched some of the king's interest.

The two men walked across the field and stopped before them. In unison the ten men all dropped to their knees and remained there until the king told them to rise.

"This task is very important. Princess Anya is my niece; she is precious to me, whereby her safety is paramount. The roads you will be traversing have been known to harbor bandits but reports of their activities of recent have declined, it is hoped it will be an ordinary mission."

The king motioned to Alyn then, who stepped forward and handed each of them a leather scrip, heavy with coins.

"This is a partial commission for this task, when you return you will be given the balance of it," Alyn said to the men.

Dell's mouth dropped open; he had never held so much money in his entire life.

Alyn motioned for the men to drop to their knees again as the king turned to leave them. Once he was away he told them to go to their horses, calling Dell back.

"Yes, sir?"

Alyn pulled a sword from the scabbard at his side and handed it to the boy. "The sword you have by your side is only made for practicing. I doubt it could slice butter straight. This one has seen me through many a battle and has served me well. It is not yours to keep but it will get you until you return. What you have in your scrip there and the balance of your commission should be enough to afford yourself one."

"Thank you, sir," said Dell, finding his throat suddenly very tight.

Dell ran over to the other soldiers, a proud smile on his face as they greeted him cordially. He found Kyi holding the reins of his horse, beaming at him as proudly. He said, "Thank you," to his friend, who was smiling at him too. He found a folded up piece of parchment in his hands with the reins. He smiled down at Kyi and nodded.

"Be safe," said Kyi as he patted the horse, "This is a good horse, high-spirited, but he will do you well."

All of the castle staff were lined up along the wall to see the soldiers go, they all cheered as they rode by, some of them shouting the names of the ones they knew, throwing roses at them.

Dell looked for Cami and saw her just as he reached the gates; he called out her name and waved. He saw her hand move like it was tossing something, likely a flower as well. He smiled at the gesture and blew her a kiss as he and the other soldiers went through the gate.

****

Cami stepped down and picked up the piece of parchment she had been trying to toss at Dell, to take to Wayde. Her heart felt like it was going to explode as she stepped back into line on the wall.

"Do you know him?" asked Kathy and Sally in unison, one on either side of her.

"Yes, that is Dell," said Cami proudly, "We grew up together at Abbeydrew. He is one of my best friends."

"He is so handsome," said Sally.

"Is he the one that gave you the glass heart?" asked Kathy, obviously jealous.

"No, that was Wayde. He is in Arrachsnow," said Cami, her hand going to the object, which she now kept in her pocket, not wanting Clara to find it and take it away from her.

"Is he as handsome as Dell?" asked Sally, holding her hand over her heart and swooning.

"More so, I think, just in a different way," said Cami.

"Dell was out training in the yard the other day with no tunic on and he was covered with sweat," said Kathy, rolling her eyes dramatically. "What I would not give to be one of his bath maidens."

"Or his horse," said Sally, her hands going to her heart and her eyes rolling back.

Cami left them to their talks of which of Dell's features they liked best and went back in the kitchen.

22

Arrachsnow

"We will be riding in a wide circle through several towns on our way to Elmsdune. Always remember, you are representing the king. You are expected to be on your best behavior when in ranks," said the man riding beside Dell, named Nox.

The man before him, Evan, turned in his saddle then and said, "Once we reach town and are out of our armor we are free to do as we please though," jingling the purse at his side.

The look on Dell's face must have said it all because the two of them and the other before him, Leb, all burst into laughter.

"Doveslade, my home town, is the first town we come to. It has several places that offer a young soldier plenty of ways to release tensions," said Nox.

Dell knew what they meant, he laughed as well, though it was forced. He wasn't a virgin but he wasn't intending to be with anyone he didn't know and care about. "How long will it take us to reach Arrachsnow?"

"Someone there you are saving yourself for?"

"No, just a friend I want to see," he said, his hand going to the sword Alyn gave him. Not wanting them to tease him, as he knew they would, he added, "He is the blacksmith's apprentice, I hope to commission his master to make me a sword."

"Aye, the smith there is one of the best sword-smiths in the county," said Leb.

Dell smiled on hearing this, hoping that meant Wayde was enjoying what he was doing then.

The two day ride to Doveslade came and went quickly. They rode into the town in a double line and went directly to the local inn where the commander, Weatherby, procured them rooms and stalls for their horses. The other soldiers all quickly headed for the local brothel, Dell told them he wasn't feeling well and stayed at the hotel, purchasing himself a bath instead.

The glade of trees that separated Doveslade and Arrachsnow was dark and a little eerie but they made it through it in little more than five hours, which would put them reaching town early the next evening. They would be stopping there for the night so he should be able to slip away to see Wayde; he hoped his friend would be able to see him.

Dell was feeling quite excited as the first signs of the town came into view. According to Nox they would be riding through the center of the market to reach the inn so he began to look for the smith immediately. Columns of smoke and the sound of a hammer hitting against metal drew his eyes to the right side. He saw an open stall with a large stone fireplace and a stalky man with no shirt pounding a long piece of ore on an anvil but he didn't see

Wayde. Still he smiled, guessing this was the place he would be. It was rare for a town this size to have more than one smith.

He was giddy when they reached the inn and just as anxious as the others to be given leave to see the town, though he didn't head for the local tavern as the others.

****

Wayde was just coming from the side of the barn, a bucket of water in each hand, to refill the trough used to cool and temper the worked pieces. He had only two chores left to do before dinner, this and to clean out the dust shoot of the furnace; if it was allowed to build up the oven could explode.

He looked up to see where he was going, not wanting to trip, and saw a man in full armor and the king's colors approaching the stall with intent. He quickly turned, not wanting a repeat of his previous encounter with a lord. He stopped when he heard his named called out by a voice he would have recognized in an instant no matter where he was. He wasn't expecting to hear that voice where he was though so he wasn't sure if he dared to let himself believe his ears. He turned back and looked at the soldier's face and about dropped the buckets.

Hithal, also hearing his apprentice's name called out, stepped to the front of the stall then. He wasn't sure who this soldier was, or how he knew the boy's name, but he wanted to prevent a repeat of the boy's encounter with Lord Faelan before it began, if at all possible. He saw the young soldier approaching and stepped out to stop him. "May I help you, my lord?" asked Hithal quickly, keeping his eyes lowered.

Dell was too overcome to speak at first. "I am not a lord, sir, I am same as him," said the soldier, pointing at the stunned Wayde.

Hithal looked up then, unsure what to say.

"Dell?" asked Wayde, unsure himself what to say.

"Excuse me, sir. I am a little out of sorts. I was at Abbeydrew with Wayde, might I have a few moments to visit with him?"

Hithal looked like he wasn't sure whether to say yes or no.

Wayde quickly went into the stall and emptied the buckets he was holding then stepped back to the street and said, "I will clean out the dust shoots by light of a candle if I must, Hithal, please, just ten minutes?"

"Very well, Boy, I suppose you have earned that," said Hithal, trying to sound hard.

"Thank you, sir," said the boy as he motioned Dell to follow him back around to the barn.

Once they were behind the wall of it the two hugged, though it was far from satisfying for either since the armor made Dell unsqueezable.

"How are you," asked Dell.

"I am well," said Wayde quickly.

"He sounds gruff, is he a good master?" asked Dell. He watched Wayde looking toward the stall, as if to make sure he wasn't going to get into trouble. His hair shifted as he did this so the new scratch on the side of his cheek was now showing clearly.

"He's really rather kind." Wayde saw Dell's eyes lingering on the new mark on his face he added with a snigger, indicating the scratch, "I ran into the barn door, was quite stupid actually."

Dell tried to laugh as well but he knew when Wayde was lying, just as he had Cami. He knew his friend's pride wouldn't allow him to admit what actually happened so he didn't push.

"Are you well?" asked Wayde.

"I am."

"Take a look at you? Are you a knight?"

"No, but I am on my first assignment as one of the king's guard. We are riding to Elmsdune to escort a princess back to Ghorst."

"Wow, done yourself good, you have. Sister Jessa would be so proud," said Wayde.

"And, you?" asked Dell, feeling worse than he had with Kyi and Cami.

"I haven't gotten to do much yet," said Wayde, looking at the ground. "Mostly cleaning up when Hithal is done forging. What about... How are Kyi and Cami? I have been... I haven't gotten to send any dispatches."

"I haven't either, though when I learned I was coming here, I hoped I would get to do it in person. I did bring you something though," said Dell, he reached into the scrip at his side and pulled out a folded up parchment.

Wayde couldn't help but hear the sound of the coins hitting against each other in the scrip as Dell took the parchment out. He could tell there were quite a lot of them. He was glad for his friend but a little envious too.

"Is it from Cami?"

"No, she wasn't able to get me one for you. It's from Kyi."

"Oh," said Wayde, trying not to sound too disappointed. He was happy to hear from him as well.

"She said to tell you she misses you very much though," said Dell, hoping to help.

Wayde nodded, guessing Dell was only saying it to comfort him. He stuffed the note into his pocket and said, "I will read it later."

The two fell silent then, not sure what to say. So much had happened in only a week that neither of them knew just where to begin, or how much or it, good and bad, to tell.

"I am here also to ask that you forge me a sword," said Dell proudly.

"You will have to talk to Hithal on that. He has said I am not to speak to the customers."

"Oh, I guess..." started Dell, he had never felt uncomfortable around Wayde before, the sudden change in their social class made him unsure how to act.

Wayde was about to ask Dell to tell him more of his assignment when Hithal's bald head appeared from around the corner, telling him he wanted him back. He motioned Dell to follow him and said, "My friend wants to commission a sword, Hithal."

"Well, well, a fine young soldier should certainly have one of them. It will take us a few weeks. Any ideas of size and weight?"

Dell pulled the one Alyn had loaned him from his scabbard and said, "About like this, maybe a touch more heft toward the hilt but equal to it in length."

Hithal took it and looked it over, "Fine quality, it's been carbonized... I should think I could have one like it completed in a few weeks."

"I'm not to be back to the castle for two weeks, I'm not sure of my schedule from there."

"My apprentice and I are planning to make the Midsummer Bazaar in Ghorst end of next month; perhaps we can try to make an exchange then?"

Dell watched Wayde's eyes light up at this, getting back the sparkle they used to have, and smiled as he said, "That would be perfect."

Hithal did another thing that made Wayde's eyes even brighter. "Would you like to watch you friend attempt to forge an item?"

"I would, sir."

"May I?" said Wayde excitedly.

"You have watched me do it enough times now, Boy, go pick out a bit of ore and make what you will with it, be it kitchen utensil, tool, sculpture, weapon. Let your inner eye decide."

Wayde was smiling brightly as he went to the crate holding what they had picked up the trip to the mine. There was a piece he had his eye on, one that had spoken to him the moment he saw it. Hithal had told him to discard it because it wasn't big enough to be used to make anything practical but he had stuffed it into his pocket anyway. He took it from the crate now and carried it over, showing it to the smith and Dell.

The two men looked at the misshapen mass, unsure what he could see that they weren't.

"Odd shaped, that one is," said Hithal.

"Would you mind terribly, sir, if I was to get out of this armor while I watch? It is mighty hot by this fire."

"You must be roasting in that suit though," said Hithal, smiling, "By all means, Son."

Dell motioned to Wayde that he would be right back then went around to the side of the barn. He pulled the coverlet off and unstrapped the breastplate, he placed these both into the saddle bag on his horse and went back to the front of the stall, now only wearing a thin tunic.

While he was doing this Wayde had the piece of iron ore held in the flame of the fire on the end of a set of tongs. He smiled at the two men watching as he pulled it out, at just the right time by the look on Hithal's face, and went to the anvil. The men moved to get a better view as he picked up the hammer the smith had given him his first day and began to use the ball end of it to work the piece into a bowl shape.

"He's making a bowl," said Hithal, sounding as proud as a father would.

Wayde smiled sneakily, then, again using the ball end, began to warp the ends, pushing them in.

"A fluted bowl," said Hithal, even more impressed.

Wayde shook his head. He took the tongs, pinched the center together and twisted it then used the end to grasp the fluted edges and turn them down, curling them around.

Hithal was scratching his head as he watched, completely confused now. He was about ready to tell the boy if he wasn't going to take this seriously he wanted him gone.

Dell, on the other hand, was completely mesmerized, watching his friend work the metal like a professional.

Wayde dunked the piece in the trough and set it behind him on the bench before the other two could see it. He took the other piece of ore he had grabbed from the fire then, it was now the right temperature to work. This he used the hammer on, drawing it out to a very long length. He took one of the half-moon chisels, used for shaping wrought iron work, and used it to mold the elongated metal into a long thin tube, he then stuck the tongs into the flame of the furnace, until it was red hot and touched the end of it to each of the pieces and set them together so the two melted together to form one piece. He thrust the whole thing into the trough for a few seconds then held it up to Hithal.

The man, who had been a full blacksmith since the age of twenty, was now looking at a very realistic looking rose. "How did you do that, Boy?" asked the smith, flabbergasted. He took the rose from him and began to look it over, obviously impressed with it. He then passed it to Dell.

"You said I should let the piece of ore decide what it wanted to be. I saw a rose. Do you think we could sell it at the fair?"

"If you can make more like it, I surely do."

Dell was beaming at Wayde as he handed him the flower back.

Wayde took it and held it up back up to Hithal.

"No. That is your first piece, Wayde, it is yours to keep."

Wayde then moved it back to Dell. "Take it to Cami for me," he said, smiling brightly.

"I think you should keep it and give it to her yourself when you come to the bazaar."

Wayde brought it back close to his chest and said, "I would like to do that."

Dell looked up the road then and said, "I have to get back to the inn now."

Wayde nodded and forced down the lump of anxiety, not wanting him to go so quick.

Dell felt it too. He bowed to the smith then and said, "Thank you for letting me watch him, Master Smith. I will be waiting with anticipation for the sword you will be making me."

"If this boy is as good at other things, it may be him making it for you."

Wayde beamed at that, he had dreamed he had made his friend a sword.

Hithal took the flower and started for the house with it, to show Tabitha and Jenna.

Dell stepped forward and pulled Wayde into a hug, this one was more satisfying for both since he no longer had the bulky armor on. Both were wiping their eyes when they stepped back.

23

Elmsdune

Dell was still smiling about how happy Wayde seemed to be as the soldiers formed ranks and left Arrachsnow the next morning. He would have liked to see him again before they left but they were heading in the opposite direction. It helped to know he would be seeing him again in a few weeks, in Ghorst, for the fair though. He couldn't imagine this assignment getting any better, then the soldiers came over the final rise to Elmsdune and he saw a magnificent castle before him.

He had always thought all castles were cold and harsh, all blocks and angles, like the one in Ghorst, and the ones depicted in the few books the home had, but this one was all curves and arches and looked quite inviting. It was set on the top of a natural plateau so it overlooked the town, which was wrapped gracefully around its base. He imagined a princess from such a castle must be beautiful as well. He got his answer as they rode through the double portcullises and found the lord of the manor, his wife and a girl about his age standing on a balcony overlooking the courtyard.

All the soldiers were looking toward the three of them, their heads held high as they did, in honor of them; Dell's eyes were locked on the girl. She was the most beautiful thing he had ever seen. All thoughts of never finding an equal to Cami were gone, at that moment this girl become his choice for comparing to.

This girl had long flowing amber hair, her face had a healthy glow. She was dressed in a flowing gown in the softest shade of pink, which set her skin off nicely. He thought his heart had stopped beating as soon as he saw her, then, as her eyes met his, a smile came to her full pink lips and color came to her cheeks, he was sure it had. He would've died the happiest man alive if he had just then.

The man on the balcony beside the princess, her father, called out then, "Fine soldiers of King Vianor's guard, you are welcome in my town and castle. My sergeant at arms will escort you to the barracks where you can rest then we wish to see you in the great hall for a dinner."

Weatherby answered for them all, "Thank you, Lord Colmstead, it would be our pleasure."

Lord Colmstead waved them on then turned to his wife and daughter, motioning them to enter the room beyond then.

****

Princess Anya didn't immediately follow, still watching the handsome soldier riding by. She hadn't wanted to go on this trip; she knew she needed Queen Vela to complete her finishing so she could then be introduced to society but she really didn't want to see either of her cousins; knowing both Acthiel and Faelan would be there.

The last time she was near Faelan, end of last summer, when he and his father came to their castle for Beltane, he had made advances at her. Acthiel had made it more than clear when she was last at Auldenway Castle that he wouldn't mind if she wished to fulfill the requirements of their soon being wed before it came to be. She, being of noble blood, had been able to tell them both to leave her be but she knew others who had been afraid to, including her friend, Ashlynn. She didn't want to think of what might have happened if she hadn't walked into the room at the very moment she had, stopping Acthiel's advances.

Her mother had asked her once, when discussions of her future came up, if being Prince Acthiel's wife, and the future queen, would be all that bad, luckily she had never had to answer. She didn't like her cousin. He was handsome, yes, but far too arrogant for her. She had never seen any of her would-be-suitors, or any boy, that had made her turn her head. They were all so soft, plain and uninteresting – until now.

She hadn't especially wanted to be on the balcony to see the soldiers that would be taking her to the castle in Ghorst either, expecting them all to be grizzled old men who would know of nothing but horses and war. She had begged her father to let her stay in her room until she had to leave but he insisted that she present herself. She was glad now that he had when her eyes locked on the last one in the row on her side. She saw he was also looking at her and smiled.

He was sitting up straight in his saddle, looking proud to be on his horse and in the ranks. His armor looked like it fit him like a glove, if this was so he was very well built. His face was like that of a dream. His wavy brown hair was bouncing playfully as he cantered with the horse, as opposed to forcing the animal to carry him. The bright smile that came to his face after she smiled almost stopped her heart. The fire behind his eyes was threatening to consume her, and she was willing to let it. All the soldiers looked quite stately in their armor and the king's colors, but this one was just awesome. He was taller than most of them, a good head over the man beside him and the two before him. She wondered if he was a lord's son that she had not yet met; she hoped so, she would very much like to dance with him at her introduction.

She felt a heat rise in her belly when she saw he was watching her still as the men started to move further into the courtyard, to meet up with Sir Dale, her father's first knight. He even turned in his saddle to keep his eyes locked on hers until they were around the corner.

She heard her father giving their chatelaine instructions for the meal and thought for once she might actually enjoy a public function. She felt giddy as she tried to think of ways to get near this soldier to find out who he was.

"Away from the balcony, Anya."

Anya jumped a little. She had been leaning over the railing wanting another glimpse of the handsome soldier. She stepped back and walked to the center of the large room. "May I be excused to go and get myself ready, Mother?" she asked politely.

****

Dell had never been to a formal dinner before so he had no idea what he should be doing. He had always felt very self-assured but suddenly he felt like he was the ugliest thing in the room. He tried to follow the lead of the other soldiers but it was obvious none of them were all that comfortable either.

He was standing with Nox and Leb near the back of the great hall, well away from the bulk of the soldiers. They were all hoping to get through the dinner without making fools of themselves or their king. The other two men had joined the king's ranks only a few months ago themselves, neither had been in society very often either so they were just as unsure how to conduct themselves. They were telling him of their previous assignments, hoping to give him an idea of what the life of a soldier was, he was only half listening; too busy looking around for the girl from the balcony.

The doors to the great hall opened, everyone stopped what they were doing and watched the princess walk in grandly, followed by two other women – one twice her age, the other close to the same as her.

The rest of the room just disappeared; the girl in front was the only thing Dell could see. Her hair, which was in a tight bun on the balcony, was now loose and flowing in gentle curls along her shoulders with a few strands of baby's breath weaved through it. She was wearing a forest green gown with a tight bodice, showing a touch of cleavage, just enough to flatter and tease, that set her hair, that was more blonde than red, and the flowers off beautifully. His eyes traced her tight body; a heat lit in his belly as thoughts of touching it flooded his mind. He would be willing to die to have just a moment with the beautiful creation. He was so enthralled by her that it took Leb three tries to get his attention.

"You want another ale, Man?"

It took him three tries to get his voice, "Yeah."

****

Anya was feeling quite nervous as she entered the hall that she had eaten, played in and attended many functions in over her fifteen year life. It felt like this was her first time here. Her eyes panned the room quickly, looking for the gorgeous soldier. She was sure her heart had burst when her eyes stopped on him. He was standing in the corner with two of the men he had been close to in the ranks. Standing on his own feet she saw he was indeed a full head over one and closer to a head and a half over the other, making him close to the tallest person in the room. He was no longer wearing the bulky armor, only a tunic with the coverlet over it, showing his body was as large without it. His chest and arm muscles were bulging out from under the material, which clung to him perfectly.

She had never been with a man, as was proper for a princess, and had never once wished to be before she was married but she wanted to be with this one. She was imagining him walking over to her, taking her in his arms, lifting her up and taking her off to one of the suites to have his way with her. She would not have put up any fight at all if he had.

Anya had thought he was handsome looking down on him from the balcony, in profile only, she watched his head turn toward her then and thought he was even finer looking. His face was perfectly proportioned, with strong cheekbones, full pouty lips and bright, gorgeous, eyes. She couldn't tell what color they were. She wanted desperately to go to him to find out but she knew she couldn't. He smiled then, at something one of the two with him had said she thought, and, if it was possible, he got even more handsome. She thought she would die of happiness then. She wished it was her that smile was meant for.

She wanted to go to him and ask his name, but, as her retinue, Tish, who was right behind her, reminded her he was beneath her. The older woman had overheard the princess telling Ashlynn that she thought one of the soldiers was attractive. Luckily, for them both probably, the woman had no idea which soldier it was otherwise she could have had him removed from the rank.

"It's best to ignore them, Child, not give them any hope or ideas. They are here only to protect us on your trip. Your virtue must remain until you are wed and it will not be to one like any of them so it isn't fair to lead them on," said Tish as she saw her eyes lingering on the three youngest soldiers in the corner.

"I know, Tish," said Anya, trying to sound like she meant it. It took all of Anya's effort to look away from of him but she didn't want to be improper. She saw her father waving to her then so she went to his side.

****

It was actually the princess Dell's smile was meant for but there was no way for him to tell her or let her know without drawing attention to himself and run the risk of getting hanged for his improper behavior. He thought he was going to turn into a pile of warm mush when her eyes stopped on him, watching her eye him over. He wanted to believe he saw true desire in that look but he knew it was more likely thinking he didn't belong there. He didn't care; he enjoyed her eyes being on him anyway. He thought he was going to stop breathing when she looked at the floor then the women behind her, saying something to them. He wanted to get her attention again, if only to have her beautiful eyes on him again, even if it was in utter disgust, but knew how inappropriate a wish this was. He couldn't stop himself from having it though.

He saw the princess looking around the room again. He moved to a more open position, so she couldn't miss him. This time she looked right past him as if not even seeing him. He felt like someone had doused him with a bucket of ice water. He wondered if he'd been mistaken in the connection he thought he had felt between them. Of course he had been, it was foolish of him to think it, she was a princess and he was only a step above a serf, to one in her position he would be invisible.

24

Friendly Fire

The next morning the soldiers were in rank again, waiting for the carriage that would be carrying the princess, her retinue and friend to be made ready. The sun was just reaching its apex in the sky when the doors to the castle opened and the princess, her two companions and her father were walking down the stairs.

Anya looked down the ranks of soldiers, looking for the handsome one. She didn't see him. She hoped he was only on the other side of the carriage. She was about to walk around to find out when her father spoke, making her jump and reminding her who she was and where she was.

"I will miss you my dear but this will be good for you as well. Your mother and I will be seeing you at Michaelmas for your debut."

"Thank you, Father."

"Listen to your retinue. I know you think she is cross and cruel but she really does have your, and our, best interests at heart."

"Yes, Father," said the girl.

He leaned forward and kissed her forehead then stepped back.

Anya took one last look as the castle she had called home for fifteen years then climbed into the carriage.

****

The first day was uneventful; as evening fell they stopped in a thicket in the forest and set up camp. The princess would sleep in the carriage, her friend and retinue would share a tent set up close to it, and the soldiers, two to a tent, were set up around the perimeter. Though they had seen nothing of trouble, they set up a perimeter guard. Four men walked along the sides, back and forth every few seconds, a fifth would stay by the fire at the center of camp, to keep it roaring, while the other five soldiers slept, then they would switch places. Dell was the one sitting by the fire for the first watch.

Dell had now gotten over his happiness at seeing Wayde and had forced himself to forget what he thought he had seen in the princess' eyes. He knew that pursuing that desire would do him no good but that left what he would find when he returned to the castle, which was making a knot form in his belly.

The king had said he would keep Cami safe but he wondered how he could. He had no idea what the life of a king was like but surely the man would not be able to keep his eyes on his son every minute of every day, nor would he care about the fate of a lowly scullery maid only days out of an orphanage. His stomach was also twisted up that he had lied to Wayde when he said Cami was fine. He had never once lied to his best friend. He didn't like how he felt having done it now. He tried to tell himself it was for his own good, because he knew he would let nothing stop him getting to Cami if he thought she was being harmed in any way and didn't want to frighten him needlessly.

What would he do if he returned to find that the prince had harmed her? How would he be able to explain to Wayde that he had left her knowing she that was in danger? How could he explain not telling him in time to perhaps have stopped it? Or, for lying to him in the first place? His nerves were so taut that he jumped when he heard the leaves beside him rustle.

He looked up and saw someone was approaching the fire. He couldn't tell if it was one of the soldiers or one of the women they were escorting. He started to stand up, in case it was one of the latter, the princess' friend and her retinue had both been out to the fire before the sky darkened, looking for warmth. He drew in a thick breath, dropped his head and fell to his right knee when he saw it was, in fact, the princess herself.

Anya couldn't believe how bold she was being or how excited she was at the thought of being it. She watched the tent that held her retinue and best friend for close to fifteen minutes to make sure they were both asleep before she finally, slowly, stepped from the carriage and snuck around the back of it.

It was dark behind the carriage. It took a moment for her to remind herself to breathe as she looked into the even deeper darkness of the forest around them. She was suddenly thinking of all the things that could be hiding inside it, just waiting for the perfect opportunity to strike. She forced herself to take a breath and move to the end of the riding compartment of the horse drawn vehicle. She saw the fire, lighting her way like a beacon. She had overheard the commander of the king's guard telling the handsome soldier he was to take this watch so she knew he would be by that fire, by himself. She had hoped the man would say his name but he had not. She knew she shouldn't be doing this but she couldn't stop herself, she had to know the man's name.

The princess was trying to be quiet so she would not wake her companions or draw the attention of the other soldiers. She did not want the man she was moving toward to get into any trouble, because it would be him that got into trouble for this not her. She had been so quiet she saw she surprised him even. She had known he would be very formal with her in her heart but she had hoped, for a brief moment, that he might treat her like an average person. As she watched him realize who was before him she knew that was a silly hope – she was always going to be a princess.

"Please, Sir Knight, you do not need to be so formal when I am not at the castle and with my father," said the girl sweetly, barely over a whisper.

Dell remained on his knee, his head down, as he said, "I am not yet a knight, my lady."

"Oh," said the girl.

Dell's heart sank; she sounded so disappointed.

Anya was disappointed. If he was a knight she could speak to him without risking him getting flogged. Still she had hope – he could still be the son of a lord that simply had not taken the vows of knighthood yet.

"Is…is there something you need, my lady?" Dell wanted badly to look at her beautiful face up close but he knew he had no right to.

"No, just wanted to warm up a bit and stretch my legs. Please, sir, seeing you still in that position is making them hurt worse." Anya wished he would look at her, she wanted badly to see what color his eyes were.

Dell rose just enough to take the folding carpet stool he had been sitting on and move it so she could sit on it then he took one of the logs that hadn't yet been chopped for firewood and sat on it beside her.

"You are new to the king's army, yes?"

"I am. I was just turned…" Dell stopped and swallowed hard. He had never been ashamed of being an orphan before, it certainly wasn't by choice, but he knew telling her he had just been turned-out of a home would cement the fact that he was so far beneath her that *she* could be punished for sitting near him and speaking with him. "…I just joined a few weeks ago," he finished, hoping she wouldn't immediately turn and go back to her shelter.

Anya stiffened, realizing what he had been about to say. She had been sure, by his look of grace, that he was at least of some noble blood. Thinking, like her, he had been sent to the castle to be finished so he could be introduced as well. Now being a soldier would have raised his place in society a little but not enough for her to be speaking so openly to him. She knew she should go then, as her retinue had said, it would do no good to lead him on, but she just couldn't. "You already know my name, may I ask what yours is?" she asked.

"Dell, my lady." He had always liked his name but it sounded terribly dull on his lips just then. He knew most nobles had grand names like the prince did.

Anya smiled; she liked the name and thought it fit him well. She watched the flames of the fire dancing off his face muscles and their reflection in his eyes as he looked up at it and poked at it a little. She still couldn't tell what color they were but she liked how they sparkled as the light played in them. She felt a warmth coming to her middle again then and smiled. She was about to speak to him when she saw him lower his head, as if just realizing he had raised it too high and saw him tense up. Hoping to put him at ease, Anya said, "You don't need to lower your eyes to me."

He did still.

Anya heard one of her companions coughing. She knew if whichever it was woke up they would feel compelled to check on her so she stood and said, "I will retire now. Good eve, Dell."

Dell felt a warmth flood his middle as his name left the beautiful woman's lips. He liked the way his name sounded when she said it. He quickly stood up and went down on his right knee, bowing to her again. "The same to you, this night and always."

Anya smiled at this. There were few she had heard so well-spoken that were high-bloods. As was custom, the princess put her hand out to the soldier so he could kiss the top of it. This was an act she had never liked. It made her feel like she was demeaning the person having to perform it and some of the people having to perform it made her feel demeaned by doing it – namely her cousins. She didn't mind it this time. She was doing it this time because she very much wanted him to kiss it.

Dell felt his heart beating so hard as he took the delicate hand. He pressed his warm lips to her soft skin. It wasn't the physical contact he really wanted to have with her but at least it was contact. The scent of roses, flooded his senses and made him a little dizzy, in a good way. He forced himself to remove his lips, not wanting her to think him a letch.

Anya forced herself to take her hand back and to turn from the soldier. She started back to the carriage. She touched the spot his lips had been to her own, wishing it was him instead of her hand.

Dell watched her walk back to the carriage and wondered for a moment if he shouldn't offer to escort her, it looked very dark. He wasn't supposed to leave the fire without telling anyone though, and to do that he would have to admit he had been speaking to her. He relaxed as he saw a small flicker of light inside the carriage, telling him she was inside. He wished he was inside it with her. Shaking himself back to reality, he put another log on the fire and poked at it to get it roaring again. Just as he was settling back onto the carpet stool Nox came up behind him.

"Your turn in the tent, my friend," said the man.

"I'm more than ready," said Dell. He handed the other man the stick he had been using as a poker then went to his tent, which was across from the carriage, on the opposite side of the camp.

Dell had thought he would fall asleep as soon as he got into his bedroll, having spent the last hour fighting to stay awake. Now his mind was working too fast to even give it a thought. His mind was trying to tell him the princess had only been out to stretch her legs. His heart was wondering if she would have come to the fire if it had been Nox sitting there instead of him.

He knew this wasn't helping him to get over his growing infatuation of her. It also didn't help that he could see the carriage from where his tent was. He could see the candle was still burning inside it, telling him she was still awake. Could he dare hope that she was thinking of him too? The compartment went dark then. He pulled the flap closed, curled up under his blanket and began to count backwards from one hundred, a trick Sister Jessa had taught him to stop his mind from running.

25

Clumsy Footing

The princess' escort took their time leaving camp the next morning. They would be stopping in Pemberley about midday. The princess wanted to be a little more presentable than she felt she was when they did. Anya had sent her retinue to Weatherby as the sun was clearing the treetops to ask that he send a soldier out to find a decent bit of the river for the ladies to clean up.

"Nox, Dell," shouted the man quickly.

The two men kneed their horses quickly and came up beside their commander.

"The princess has requested a decent place for her and her companions to bathe. Scout the river ahead and report back."

"Yes, sir," both men said.

They returned about twenty minutes later, saying there was a cove up ahead.

"Take the princess and her companions to it and remain there until they are done and we have come."

The two dropped from their horses and waited for the ladies to get what they needed then, in a line, they started in the direction of the cove on foot. Nox took up point, the retinue next, the princess and her friend, side by side, next, and Dell in the rear.

Dell tried hard to keep his eyes on the landscape around them, or the ground before him, but they kept going to the princess' back. She was wearing only a thin dress, most likely an under dress. It hung loose on her body and he liked how the morning sunlight shined through it. Her voice was melodic as she and her friend softly spoke of the scenery around them and what they thought they might do when they reached Pemberley, which had a nice dress shop. He felt his heart leap in his chest as she giggled at something her friend whispered to her, making him smile. H jumped when he saw her notice he was. He looked away quickly, not wanting her to know he was listening to them; he could be hung for doing that.

****

Anya kept glancing over her shoulder. She felt a little nervous but also strangely safe about having the handsome soldier behind her. Learning that he was one of the turnouts should have squelched any more thoughts of him but it only made her want to know more of him. *Dell,* what a stately sounding name, she thought.

She had caught his eyes leaving her body several times and knew it was because of the under dress she was wearing. It was quite thin and with the sun in front of her, reflecting through it, he could likely see far more than he should. She knew it wasn't nice to tease but she liked thinking he found her attractive. She knew her retinue would be angry with her for doing this but luckily the woman hadn't picked up on it yet. Chastising her sternly was about the only thing Tish could really do to her but if she was to send a dispatch to her parents, or ahead to the king, she could make her life and the soldier's far less enjoyable. At this moment she considered the risk worth taking. She hoped the smile she had caught on Dell's face and how flushed he got at having been caught looking at her meant he did as well.

She started giggling when Ashlynn pointed out an oblong leaf and made a joke about it looking like a certain male body part. She glanced behind her then, her eyes panning the soldier's body, wondering if it did. She caught him smiling again and again saw the slightest color coming to his cheeks as he looked away, realizing he had been caught. She smiled to herself. She quickly looked back at her friend then and went back to the conversation with her.

They reached the small setback the soldiers had found in about fifteen minutes. Floods of the distant past had etched niches out of the huge boulders that made up the river's banks making a small cove where the water remained relatively stable. A slight current came through it to keep the pool from getting stagnant but not enough to make it dangerous to be in. A ledge, just under the water's surface, had been cut out of the rock by the current – it was perfect for a person to use to ease themselves in easily.

Nox stopped them when they reached the hillside above this cove. For all he did have some noble blood it wasn't as high as the princess' so he kept his eyes on the ground as he said, "We will remain up here to give you some privacy, ladies."

"Thank you, sir," said Anya, her eyes drifting over to Dell quickly as her friend and the retinue started to work their way down the steepish bank. As soon as they were down she started down it. She slipped halfway down, squealing a little.

Without even thinking, Dell quickly went down to her and offered her his strong hand.

Their eyes connected as she took it. Both of their hearts leapt from the feel of the other's hand in theirs.

"Are you hurt, my lady?" asked Dell quickly.

"No, sir, just need a bath even more now," she said, brushing the dirt from the side of her dress where she had slid in the soft damp moss, leaving a line of green stain and bits of foliage behind. Her arm was covered with bits of earth as well.

Without thinking about it Dell gently brushed it off then rubbed at the stain underneath to make sure she hadn't raised any skin or bruised herself in the process. He felt her trembling and goose pimples rising on her skin as his hand moved over her. He realized what he was doing then. "I am sorry, my lady, did I hurt you?"

"Not in the least," said Anya.

Dell looked down to where the other women were and back up the hill to be sure Nox hadn't seen him, not wanting it to be reported to Weatherby, and in turn, Alyn, then to the king. "I did not mean to overstep my place."

"Don't be sorry, Dell," said the princess, her heart leapt as she said his name, not having meant to. She saw he was getting stiff then and added, "I will not let you get into trouble for only offering me assistance, sir."

Dell's heart leapt hearing her say his name. He was pleased she had remembered it. It was dangerous to let himself think why she might have remembered it.

"You are as gentle as you are strong. Would you and your strong arms remain here to assist me gently back up when we are done, sir? It would do me little good to slip down again on the way up and need another bath. As clumsy as I am we could be here all day."

Dell wasn't much in the world but he knew when he was being flirted with. It warmed his insides but made him nervous at the same time. He knew he was risking his neck being stretched by even speaking with the girl but he so wanted to. "I will, my lady," he said.

Dell tried not to listen to the ladies splashing in the water as they got themselves cleaned up, or think of the images it was creating in his mind – knowing the fabric of the thin dress would be clinging to the princess and would be rendered all but transparent. He felt his face flush when he saw Ashlynn and Tish appear from the shrubs before him.

They both had a blanket wrapped around their shoulders, hiding all but their faces and the skirt of their dresses below their knees.

He lowered his eyes, anchored his feet in the soft and shifting ground and held his hand out to the younger one first.

She took it, smiling at him as she passed him, then continued up the bank with little or no problem.

The retinue was equally able to make it up the hill.

He turned to the princess, who was also wrapped in a blanket, though it wasn't pulled up nearly so high as the other ladies, the left side of her shift had fallen off her shoulder. The skin was glowing at him like a beacon. He forced himself not to look at it as he offered his hand to her.

Anya was waiting patiently below. She was enjoying watching the man's muscles work as he hoisted her heavy-set retinue up. She smiled and caught her breath when his beautiful eyes came up enough to see their color for the first time, as he watched her friends to be sure they made it up safely. They were the prettiest shade of blue she had ever seen. She jumped when she realized they were now looking directly at her and saw his large, strong hand, waiting for her. "Thank you," she said as she took it, holding on tight to keep from slipping backward.

Her footing wasn't as sure as her friend's so she slipped a little as she reached him. She let go of one side of the blanket to try to keep her balance and realized just how thin the shift was then – she might as well be naked before him. He proved himself a true gentleman when he only reached over, took the blanket and helped wrap it back over her shoulders then placed his hand on the small of her back, stopping her from falling further. She leaned on his steady frame to catch her breath without thinking about it then realized she could feel his heart beating through his tunic.

She was mesmerized by its steady rhythm for a moment. She could feel it speeding up and drew in a quick breath. She looked into his beautiful face, which was only inches from hers now and watched his lips trembling slightly; she wasn't sure if it was from the effort of holding her up or desire for her, at being so close. She knew which she wanted it to be. She didn't want him to let her go, he felt warm and safe and he smelled so good. She had been around other soldiers, when she was being escorted to other relations' castles. Most of them smelled of wet horses and sweat. He smelled like sweet apple wood, the wood they had used in the fire the night before, and a heady musk she guessed was distinctly him. She wanted to sink her nose into his chest and just breathe him in.

"Careful, my lady," Dell said, smiling at her.

Dell had noticed the blanket falling open, and how transparent the shift was, it was hard to ignore, as was the pink skin it was showing through it. He quickly averted his eyes, as was proper, and helped wrap the blanket back around her shoulders then steadied her.

He allowed her to lean on him as she got her footing back, and enjoyed the closeness for all he knew he should not be. He could smell the rose scented soap she had used in her bathing and liked it very much; it was all he could do to stop himself from sinking his face into her hair. He could feel all of her curves and her back muscles through the thin material of the blanket and her shift. He also could feel she was trembling. He tried to tell himself it was only because she was cold, her hair being wet and a breeze blowing up the bank at them. It was safer to think this.

Anya's heart was beating double time as she let him push her up the bank a little further. She used a small sapling beside her to get herself up the last bit. She felt flushed and gladly took the handkerchief her friend offered her to wipe her brow when she reached the top. The other soldiers and the carriage had caught up to them. Seeing the look on her retinue's face, as if wondering if she had hung back intentionally, told Anya she shouldn't linger any more so she went with her and Ashlynn to the carriage.

Nox went immediately to his horse so Dell walked with the ladies to the carriage to assist them into it then the group began to ride toward Pemberley.

26

Pemberley

Weatherby procured rooms for the ladies and his men and stable space for their horses when they reached town then told all but three of the soldiers they could go into town if they wanted to, those three being Nox, Dell and Clem. The third man was one who was riding toward the head of the ranks. The three of them were to remain at the inn to be sure the ladies had no needs.

Nox and Clem immediately went to the dining hall, for some food and ale; Dell wasn't hungry. Instead he was wandering the grounds.

****

Dell was trying to get his head back on straight, it was now bouncing between thinking of the princess, worry at whether Cami was safe and still feeling sick for having lied to Wayde. Some of his anxiety dissolved as he took a look around the garden before him. It was a warm spring day with only a slight breeze from the east. It gently blew through the flowers around him making their beautiful scents fill the air, making him smile. He started down the slate stone path before him. He had no idea where the walkway led but knew it wasn't far; he could see the next building over, another inn, from where he stood. He stepped up to the branch of a rose bush hanging over the path and smiled. It was hard to think any ill thoughts with all the beauty around him. He turned one of the blossoms to him and smiled more at how much it looked like the one his friend had forged from the dead ore. He was just leaning in to smell it when he heard the gravel further up the path shift. He looked up to see something of even greater beauty before him.

****

Anya told her friend and retinue she needed some fresh air as soon as they reached the room they were sharing. She thought sure her Tish's head was going to explode when she told her it was too be alone. It had taken her several coarse words, and a few threats, to convince the latter to remain in the room. She was sick of her constant nagging about how she should and shouldn't act around the king and prince, as if she had never been around them before. She had become belligerent about it since they would be arriving there the next day. She could imagine what Tish would say if she knew she was dreaming about being with an indentured soldier, only one step over a serf.

She knew the woman suspected she was attracted to one of them but, luckily, not which one; she wouldn't dare say anything to the commanding officer at risk of naming the wrong one. She knew as well that what she had done was unfair to Dell. She was risking his life by continuing to try to get near him but she couldn't stop herself. She felt a connection to him, even when he wasn't near her, as if she could tell he was thinking of her at the exact same moment. Thinking that he might be thinking the same was both excited and frightened her.

She had been sitting in the gazebo in the center of the patch of greenery and had actually gone into it to avoid the chance of meeting up with him, not wanting to put him at any more risk. She was equally surprised and not so when she stepped around a tree the pathway turned beside and found herself staring at the man. He was bent forward and smiling, as he smelled of a large pink rose on a shrub beside the path. She didn't want to disturb him but she wasn't upset when she saw him look over at her, or when his smile got even larger, for a brief moment.

****

"Good day, soldier," said the princess, dipping into the slightest curtsy.

"Same to you, my lady," he said as he bowed and lowered his head.

"Beautiful gardens."

"Indeed, they are."

She watched him reach into the shrub and snap the stem with the flower he had just been enjoying on it then he brought it out to her clutched in his fingers.

"It all pales in your beauty though, my lady," he said, his eyes looking at the pebbles by her feet.

"Thank you, sir," she said breathlessly as she took that flower. "I love roses." She held it to her own nose then looked around them. "Magnolias are my favorite though. This garden doesn't have any of those."

"I like them as well, my lady." Dell was pleased she had shared the bit of personal information with him.

She knew she should walk by him and continue to the inn but she couldn't, "Would you walk me back to the gazebo just up the path?"

Dell looked around quickly. He knew he should say no but he wanted to be near her, even if only for a moment. "It would be my pleasure, my lady."

Dell stayed just behind her as she turned and went back to the structure, holding the flower to her nose the whole way. When they reached it she took his hand and allowed him to assist her to the bench on the right. He then stepped back and remained on the lower step, his face turned away from her and his eyes down.

"I would like to ask you a question but I'm unsure just how to," said the princess after a few moments.

Dell looked at her delicate slippers and said, "I am at your service, my lady."

"It's of a personal nature." She knew she was treading on thin ice.

He knew he was dangerously close to getting into real trouble now. He knew he should end whatever this was now but instead he found himself saying, "You may ask me anything you wish, my lady."

"I saw you watching me as you escorted me to the cove, and helping me up the bank... Am I mistaken that you find me attractive?"

Dell wasn't sure how to answer that, unsure if she was serious or was only trying to make him incriminate himself for a nefarious purpose. He had heard stories of how high-bloods liked to toy with serfs, knowing it was the serf that would suffer for it. He didn't want to believe that the princess would do this but the prince, who was her cousin, certainly seemed to.

"I promise I mean nothing ill by asking, I am only looking to satisfy my curiosity," said the girl.

"Yes... I find you very attractive, my lady," said Dell then.

"I think you are quite handsome," said the girl, surprised at how forward she was being.

"I am adequate, I suppose," said Dell modestly. He had always thought Wayde was better; he wished he was half as rugged looking as his friend.

Anya wanted to tell him he was the most splendid thing she had ever seen in her whole life but knew that would be stepping too far over proper decorum for high-blood to soldier. "You started to say, the other day, in the woods before Pemberley... were you... were you one of the orphans in the recent turnout?" she asked, steeling her heart for the answer.

Dell felt all the color leave his face in an instant and the look that came to hers made him feel even worse, obviously confirming her thoughts.

Anya's face drained of its color and she thought her heart had stopped beating; if he had been a lesser noble's son she could have at least been able to play with the idea of them having a chance.

"I... I should go, my lady. If you have need... if you require an escort back I can send out one of the other soldiers in a few minutes."

Anya knew she was really pushing the limits now but she didn't want him to go. She wanted to know if he even felt a little bit of what she did, even knowing there was nothing she could do about it if he did, just wanting to pretend she could for a moment. "I feel drawn to you. I... I wish..." said the girl, fighting the difference in their stations and her desire to be with him. She wasn't sure how to say what she wanted to say, or what it was she wanted to say.

The rose he had given her fell from the bench beside her, caught by the breeze, both of them reached for it at the same time, their hands touching as they both reached it.

"I wish it as well," said Dell. His eyes met and locked on hers, intentionally for the first time.

That brief moment of intimacy was all it took; neither of them could stop, or deny, what was happening.

Dell saw her face moving toward his, as if wanting him to kiss her. He knew she was as attracted to him as he was to her. He thought sure his heart was going to burst with pleasure at the thought. He stopped moving when he saw tears coming to her eyes. He released the flower, stood up quickly and dropped his eyes to the floor of the wood structure. He guessed he had let his desires cloud what was actually happening. He thought sure he would die even before anyone could put him to death for what he'd just done. He could almost feel the chaffing rope of the noose going around his neck.

"I am sorry, my lady," he said, going down on is right knee before her, "I did not mean to presume or to overstep my boundaries. I... I will have my commanding officer come around to take report of my misconduct."

It took all Anya's effort not to reach out and touch the hair that was cascading down the soldier's head; it looked so soft and shiny. "Please, sir, it is I that has done the overstepping. My retinue has been telling me I should not... I do not seem able to stop myself though... I want... I don't have many friends, I would very much like it if you would be one," she said quickly.

"I... I will be anything you wish me to be, my lady, I am your humble servant."

"Not like that," she said quickly, "as an equal."

"That I can never be," said Dell, how much he wished it were different clear in his voice.

"If I give you leave to be?" said Anya.

Dell wasn't sure how her ordering him to be an equal would be treating him as one; that would only make the differences between them painfully obvious.

Anya realized this at the same time. "I'm sorry... I didn't mean... May I call you Dell?"

"If it pleases you, my lady," said Dell, beginning to feel uncomfortable, sure someone was going to come around the corner and see him doing this awful thing.

"It would please me if you would call me Anya."

"I cannot," said Dell. He wanted very much to call her by her name but that was more intimate than he would allow himself to get with her. He started to shake his head, about to tell her this when she spoke again.

"Please, Dell. I have so many people that call me princess and my lady, all frightened of getting flogged for being improper, even my best friend refuses to call me by my name unless I beg her to… I want to be… I wish to feel like just a normal girl for a while. Like I was one of the wards at the home you grew up in."

He knew she hadn't intended this to hurt him but it had, reminding him again that they were from entirely different worlds. At the same time he very much wished she was because then he could be with her without worry. "I would never wish you anything except what and who you are, my la…" his voice hitched. He knew he had already half-doomed himself and he wasn't one to do anything half way so he swallowed hard and said, "You are absolutely perfect… Anya."

Hearing him say her name made butterflies take flight in her stomach and her heart beat erratically. She knew there was nothing anyone could do to keep her from wanting to be with this man now. "Say that again," she begged breathlessly.

His eyes met hers again, "You are absolutely perfect, Anya," his own heart beating erratically.

"I would very much like it if you would kiss me, Dell," she said then, taking his hand that was on the railing beside her into hers.

Dell wanted very much to kiss her then, her full lips looked like they would be heaven to touch and taste. He forgot who he was and who she was as he leaned forward, intending to do what she asked.

Their lips were just brushing each other's when a dove suddenly burst from the shrubs behind the gazebo, sending white feathers and green leaves flying and making them both jump and her squeal.

When the leaves the bird had disturbed finally stopped rustling they heard voices drifted to them on the wind, approaching them, one of them the shrill pitch of her retinue's.

"Please Go, Dell, I don't want you found here. If Tish finds us together she will know you are the soldier I... she will bring it to the king's attention."

Dell was looking back up the path, knowing she was right. "I don't... I... thank you for treating me like more than a serf, Anya, even for just a moment," he said then he turned and ran up the path in the direction away from those approaching voices.

The way he said this made her heart hurt, like he knew they would never see each other again, or at least not like this again. She wished he had been able to kiss her then, at least once, just so she would have that memory of him if this was to be their only time together. She was fighting back tears as she tried to straighten her dress and sat back down, so it would look like she had been there, alone, the entire time. She jumped up when she saw Dell running back toward her. She thought then others must be coming from that direction as well, meaning they would get caught and he would get punished.

She was about to tell him to stand true, that she would tell them she asked him to escort her here so he was not at fault and had done nothing wrong when she watched him take the steps to her then he was pulling her into his arms.

Dell knew what he was doing was wrong but at that moment he didn't care and would die willingly. He took her breath away when his lips met hers.

Anya had kissed boys before, mostly other lord's sons, mostly experimentally, but this one sent shivers and tingles over her entire body. She thought she might lose herself in it. She felt one of his large hands go into her hair, cupping her head and the other touch the small of her back, pulling her close to him, so their bodies were now pressed tightly together, and heard herself moan softly and felt herself going weak in the knees. She wanted to tell him to take her then but knew she couldn't. She didn't want it to ever end but it did.

Dell backed away, knowing if he didn't then he never would. "I would risk all that I am, my very life, for this one moment in time with you, Anya."

"I... I..." Anya couldn't think of anything to say back, feeling very dizzy just then.

The voices were even closer now.

"Go, Dell, please," said Anya then; dreading the thought of him letting her go but not wanting him caught.

Dell took her hand in his and kissed the top of it then released it and ran up the path.

Anya put that hand to her lips, kissing the place his lips had just been then she turned so she was facing away from the path her retinue was coming down, facing the path Dell had just gone up, wishing he would come back. She wiped tears from her face and held her hands against her stomach, trying to get it to stop quivering. She took several deep breaths and let them out slowly then turned, sat back down. She brought the rose Dell picked for her up to her nose, hoping to hide that she was so flushed, as Tish appeared before her. The soldier, Weatherby, was by her side.

"My lady," said the soldier. He dropped to his right knee for a moment then rose and looked around the structure, "Are you alone here?"

"I am, sir," said the girl.

Tish had a look on her face like she wasn't so sure.

"The innkeeper said one of my soldiers had also come into the gardens, your retinue was concerned with you being alone."

"Surely none of you soldiers would consider harming me, sir," said the girl, giving Tish a stern look.

"Surely not, my lady, they were handpicked by the king himself, but I had to consider the distress of your retinue. She was concerned about your safety."

"As would all your soldiers certainly be, yes, Sir Knight?" said Anya, not backing down any. "I am quite appalled that she would even think to suggest one of your men, handpicked by the king himself, as you say, would consider harming me in any way."

Tish realized then that, for all she was entreated with the princess' safety, accusing, or even suggesting, one of the king's soldiers had done a wrong against her was an affront to the king himself. "My lady, Master Weatherby, I am sorry for my over-zealousness. I am very tired from the trip and my nerves are overwrought," she said quickly.

Weatherby bowed to her and the princess and said, "I have little doubt this trip has been long and trying on the nerves of both of you, my ladies. Please, if there is anything you desire to assist in easing them, do not hesitate to ask it."

"There is nothing other than you getting us safely to Auldenway Castle, Sir Knight," said the princess. "I have had enough of the gardens and fresh air for one day, Tish. I will go now to our room. Please ask the innkeeper prepare some dinner for me and have it brought up."

"Of course, my lady," said the woman humbly, she curtsied deeply, backed herself away then moved quickly up the pathway.

Weatherby was just about to ask the princess if he could escort her back to the inn when he heard the gravel up the path shift. He stepped in front of the princess, placing himself in the line of danger, tightened the grip on his sword and said, "Who is there, step out now."

Dell did so, boldly; ready to take whatever punishment the man might give.

The path Dell followed led only to the inn next door, which shared the use of the gardens. He didn't want to get caught going in the front door of their inn so he had planned to stay hidden and then go in once his commanding soldier, the princess and her retinue were safely inside. A spider slowly descending from a branch of the tree beside him had made him jump, causing him to lose his footing and make the gravel shift noisily.

"Dell, is that you, Boy?"

"It is, sir, I..."

"Having trouble keeping your footing on the loose gravel, Soldier?" teased Anya. "I have been listening to you for the past twenty minutes. I thought at first there was a bear stalking me. To think, a clumsy soldier?"

The sneaky smile that came to the princess' lips made Dell want to smile back. He lowered his eyes and said, just as teasingly, "I'm sorry if I disturbed your time of peace and reflection, my lady. I'm all of grace on horseback but my feet apparently are too large for my body on land."

Weatherby was looking hard at Dell now, catching an undertone he wasn't sure of. "Why aren't you inside with the other soldiers?"

"The air inside was stifling, Master Weatherby, I've always preferred the outdoors. I had not realized how long this pathway was. I heard voices and thought perhaps someone was in trouble, so I came to check."

"Very commendable of you, Boy, I will tell the king of your thoughtfulness."

"Thank you, Master Weatherby, being one of his soldiers is merit enough for me."

Weatherby smiled proudly to this, he could see why Alyn and the king were so taken with this boy. He turned to the princess then and said, "Surely the lady would prefer an escort back to the inn by a handsome young soldier than an old crotchety one."

Dell looked up quickly then, wondering if the man was playing with him.

"It would please me to have either of you escort me, Sir Knight," said the girl gracefully.

"Yes, well, I will hand you off to this young lad in any case. I need to see about alerting the stable hands to have our rides ready for first light. We need to be through the pass before midday to make it to the castle before dusk," said the man. He bowed to the lady then quickly made for the inn, not even looking to see if they were following.

Dell waited a moment to be sure the man didn't return before he turned to Anya and said, "May I escort you back, my lady," holding his arm out to her.

She took it gladly, wanting the intimate contact with him, no matter how fleeting. Feeling how tense he was and hearing him call her *my lady* instead of her name made her heart clench, it suggested the intimate moment they shared had passed. "What is the matter, Dell?"

Dell stopped and looked down at the princess. He put his hand on her cheek, brushing a stray hair from it as he caressed it. For all it hurt him to say what he was about to say, he knew, for both their sakes, he had to. "Please, my lady, call me soldier or serf, if anyone hears you call me by name... and I must call you my lady or princess only, otherwise... I could not live if you were punished... I would give my life for you in an instant if you ask it but I don't want to die."

Anya didn't want to admit he was right but he was, she began to tremble for a different reason then.

"Please don't cry," said Dell, "it is the way it must be. I've been told, if I continue to do good as a soldier, one day I may strive to becoming a knight. I very much wish for this, but, even then, I cannot hope to aspire to one such as you."

"It isn't fair," said Anya.

"I would do anything to make it otherwise... We must be realistic; it will do neither of us any good to wish, hope or try to make it otherwise."

"I don't want to go to Auldenway, I despise my cousin, Acthiel. He thinks, because he's the prince, he can have anything he wants. And our cousin, Faelan, is worse still. I understand he is to be at the castle as well. Me being a princess is all that keeps them off me."

Dell tensed up again then, for another reason. "I swear to you, on my life, neither of the princes will ever lay a hand on you."

Anya was frightened by this heated acclamation though it made her feel good to think he cared that much for her safety. She could see he had more reason than only her to say this in his eyes, he had experience himself with her cousins' rudeness, she guessed. She was scared then that if he hated them that much he might do something he shouldn't, looking for a confrontation or to make himself feel like more than just a soldier and a serf.

Dell felt her tense and relaxed a little, not wanting to frighten her. "I am sorry, my lady, I sometimes let my passions control my emotions."

Testing that, she said, "Take me away somewhere, to a place no one knows who we are, a place where we can be together."

"I wish such a place existed... I am sworn to the service of the king, Anya, and I cannot dishonor that pledge," said the soldier. It was the hardest thing he had ever had to say, looking into her eyes was making his heart break. He *would have* taken her away then if she had asked it one more time, never wanting to be away from her.

Anya could tell, from the first moment she saw him, how proud he was to be a soldier, so she had expected the remark. It only made her love him more, knowing he would not dishonor himself no matter what the reward. "You are so honorable," she said as she stepped into the inn.

Dell wished he wasn't so at that moment. He leaned on the wall, wanting to cry, laugh and be sick all at the same time.

27

A Proposal for Kyi

Kyi was just returning from the privy yard with the wheelbarrow, after emptying it from the morning mucking, when the stable master called his name. He audibly sighed, wondering what the man wanted now. He was already tired to the bone. He ran the few feet to the side of the barn, set the barrow against the wall and ran around to the front. He called back, "Yes, Galin?" trying to look eager.

"We have a horse that has thrown its shoe. Take it to the smith in town to get it reset," said the man as he held out a piece of parchment to him and a small scrip with coins in it.

Kyi took the items and opened the paper; it was a writ giving him permission to be out during the day, on castle business.

"You are to go there and back here, straight away, no detours," said the stable master. "This horse is needed for the prince to ride on the tour."

"Yes, sir," said Kyi.

The man disappeared back inside then brought out the horse the boy was to take to the smith.

Kyi was surprised to see it wasn't his usual ride.

Galin picked up on this and quickly added, "The prince's regular ride has gone lame from the training the king has been putting the boy through. Most of his trip will likely be in the carriage, he shouldn't have to do any fast riding so this one will get him well enough."

"Yes, sir." The boy took the reins and started it toward the gates.

Kyi was nervous and excited about being out; especially by himself. There weren't many serfs out this time of day so it took him little time to make it to the corner of the street across from the smith's stall. It was awkward since the horse wasn't allowed on the sidewalk. He stood on the corner, waiting to be given permission to cross for close to ten minutes and then it was the smith himself that gave it, likely seeing how the horse was standing.

The man held his hand out for the paper the boy should have with him without saying a word. He wanted to be sure the boy was out by permission before he did. He didn't want to get himself into trouble either.

Kyi passed it to him quickly and waited for him to read it and respond.

"Alright, boy, bring the horse over here," said the man, motioning toward a padded bench by the anvil.

Kyi was not sure what to do with himself as he waited. He had watched a horse being shoed before so he wasn't paying any attention as the man used a pry bar to work the nails holding the partial shoe still to the horse's hoof and began to clean up the hoof to prepare it for the new one. He didn't want to look around the stall either because it made him think about Wayde and wonder how he was. With nothing else to do he looked up and down the street before him. He was surprised when he saw someone he knew.

Sabban wasn't moving along the side of the street with the serfs; he was walking quite proudly out in the open. He watched him stop at a door in the center of a building and walk inside without knocking. The sign on the door said it was the bailiff's office. Wayde had said it was the local bailiff that had been at their home assigning them all to their positions. He wondered what the man had to do with Sabban. He didn't have long to think on it because the smith was done and was walking the horse back over to him then.

"Tell your master to make sure he stays off this a couple days, no running or heavy riders," said the smith.

"Yes, sir," said Kyi quickly. He handed the man the scrip Galin had given him to pay for the service. He waited for him to count it then asked, "Might I bother you for permission to cross the street, sir?"

The man grunted and walked with him to the corner, waving him on.

Kyi was about halfway across the street when he heard his named called. Knowing whom it was already he finished crossing then turned and waited.

"Hello, ah… it's Kyi, yes?"

Kyi nodded.

"How are your three friends? What's it been, two weeks now?

"Just about, yeah," said Kyi, wondering why this was important.

"Wayde said he thought you would all be fine, said you didn't need my services, guess he was right."

Again, Kyi only nodded, though he really didn't know if this was true.

"So, are you fine?" he asked. Sabban could tell the boy wasn't, in fact he looked ready to start crying.

"Yeah, I guess."

"You got placed at the stable, I'm guessing," said Sabban, looking at the horse.

Kyi nodded.

"Do you like it?"

"It's a lot more work than I thought it was going to be. Did I see you leaving the bailiff's office just now?"

"I do work for him on occasion," said Sabban, stiffening up.

"Can you get him to reassign Wayde to something here in Ghorst?"

"I am not sure that there is anything for him here," said Sabban gruffly, "I might be able to get him to move you though."

"The stables aren't that bad. I promised Wayde I'd at least give them a fair try," said Kyi.

"Well, you know, even if Wayde doesn't think this, you are now an adult, you can decide you want to do something different. I personally thought he was always a bit overbearing of you all, and never liked how dumb he seemed to think *you* were."

Kyi jumped at the implication that Wayde thought this of him. "I *can* make decisions for myself."

"I know you can," said Sabban. "How much are you getting paid at the stables?"

"One pent per week."

"Hell, Boy, it'll take you forever to earn your freedom that way. I can show you how to make ten times that. Or more."

"How?"

"Well, we can start with something simple. Have you heard any interesting news at the castle?"

"Like what?"

"Comings, goings, the like?"

"Dell is gone out on a commission to Elmsdune and the king is getting ready to go," said Kyi, not sure why Sabban would want to know this.

"Where's our beloved king off to?"

"His annual tour, I think. He's bringing the prince with him. That's who this horse is for."

"See, easy," said Sabban. He reached into his pocket, brought out five pents and handed them to Kyi.

Kyi wasn't sure what he had done to deserve the coins but he took them.

"You know, you could come to work for me and earn that much every day," said Sabban.

"How?"

"No different than what you did before leaving the home, collect the town folk's leavings."

"I don't know," said Kyi, remembering Wayde telling him to stay away from the thug.

"Think about it, we'll no doubt see each other again soon," said Sabban, starting away.

Kyi watched the man walk away then began to walk quickly back to the castle.

Kept to the Shadows

28

Reevaluations

The morning sky was gray and overcast, matching the king, queen and prince's moods, though for different reasons.

The king knew the queen was unhappy with him for forcing the prince into this trip, no matter what she said, and he was upset with his son for acting like a spoiled brat that needed to be spanked and sent to his room without supper. He was also feeling guilty because he wished the soldier, Dell, was with them. He would have liked to see him in the field, in action. He had actually considered postponing the trip until the boy returned so that he could be.

The queen was angry with the king for making her son go and for making her have to tell him he had to go. She was angry with her son for acting like a spoiled brat. Mostly she was angry at herself because deep down inside she was glad the two of them were leaving. She was tired of listening to them constantly fighting.

The prince was angry with both of his parents. He hated going out in the world, he hated to see the people because they looked at him like he was a horrible monster. He knew they hated his father and many projected that hatred on him. This made him hate the people. He could care less whether the proclamation was reversed or not, it really didn't affect him in any way.

He was also upset because he'd been run hard in training the last two weeks, training he didn't feel he needed, because of that stupid up-start soldier his father had taken such a liking to. He was about ready to tell him to adopt the idiot and get it over with.

Because of him he hadn't been able to have his way with Cameron, the pretty scullery maid, yet. Every time he got near her his father was there. And, he wouldn't be here to see his cousin, Anya, arrive, which meant she'd find someone else to pass her time with, again leaving him out in the cold. He suddenly just wanted to jump on his horse and run away.

The party leaving the castle was to be a total of fifteen strong; the king and prince, the steward, Rehldach, a cook, the carriage driver and ten soldiers, four on horseback and six on foot. They would be away from the castle for nearly a week. It was a round trip, beginning in Lichland, through Arrachsnow, Doveslade, Bywood Forest and back to Ghorst.

They would inspect the crop fields and livestock of farms between each town, the storage facilities, hospitals, orphanages and hospices of each and take a census of the current population. They needed to inventory the amount of food stores available to be sure the supply wasn't short if the population began to grow quickly.

This trip was more important than any of the previous years had been. About a month ago the children born during the first years of the drought had been turned out of the homes, meaning there had been an influx of serfs. Any time the facilities turned out wards it meant an increase in crime; this time there was almost twice the number of any previous year. The king wanted to be sure the number of soldiers in each area was adequate to handle the increase.

All these thoughts weighed heavy on Vianor's mind so, needless to say, seeing the gate of Lichland was more than welcome.

They didn't stay long. The small town was mostly only a farming community. The king made his obligatory appearance, with the pouting prince in tow. Then they went back to the carriage while the steward went to count the livestock and check the food stores. The king spent most of the five hours in the small town talking to his captain of the guards about the upcoming Feat of Arms at the Mid-summer Bazaar, in only a few weeks. The prince spent most of it asleep in the carriage.

Lord Durbaith was waiting for them when they arrived in Arrachsnow, two days later. His town was not nearly as big as Ghorst but it was a thriving community with a full market and several well-known tradesmen. The main street has lined with the locals, all come out to greet the king and his entourage. They rode into town on horses rather than in the carriage, so the people could see them. Yet another thing the prince fought with the king over. They were greeted with everything from screams of elation to boos and hisses. Both the king expected.

Lord Durbaith met them at the head of the street, in front of the city gardens. He hushed the crowd and addressed the pair,

"Welcome to Arrachsnow, my lords, King Vianor, Prince Acthiel. All is open for your inspection. Please do not hesitate to ask anyone for assistance. No one will refuse you."

"Thank you, Lord Durbaith. My captain of the guard and I will go to view your guard then to the warehouse district to meet with your steward, to view the stocks. Will you take the prince and my steward on a tour of the orphanage, hospital, hospice center and the merchants? I expect I will meet up with you by the time you have reached the trade stalls."

"Aye, my lord," said Durbaith, bowing deeply. He couldn't help but notice the look of surprise and distaste on the young prince's face. He knew the struggle the king was having with the boy and that he didn't want to break him, only make him see the world for what it was – harsh. He hoped in doing this that when he became king he would think of the consequences of his actions. He waited for the boy to dismount. After the usual and customary salutations, the lord, prince, steward and half the guard started toward the hospital.

Arrachsnow was only about half the size of Ghorst but was just as prosperous. Its seaport offered trade with many other counties but mostly dealt with Idlefort. The ocean beyond the port was rich with fish, one of the only foods that didn't decline during the droughts. This had helped the town become a wealthy province, and, in turn, its lord rich as well. Lord Henry Durbaith was a just lord, and one of the few that believed the proclamation had served its purpose and should be at least lessened. His province hadn't suffered as much as Ghorst or Doveslade but it had to destroy many children to survive.

The lord placed his hand on the prince's arm, respectfully, to direct him through the street to the hospital.

Acthiel wanted to pull away but knew he couldn't without angering his father. He wished he had his own horse with him; then he could slip away and take off. He wondered if his father had told the stupid stable boy to say his was lame for this very reason. He wondered if the stupid half-dead horse he had would even make if back to Ghorst.

There was a farm between Arrachsnow and Ghorst he liked to visit from time to time. The farmer had several daughters that liked entertaining princes. It had been weeks since he had been there; likely they thought he had forgotten them. Maybe he would go there. Or he might take off on one of the trails that led into the mountains. He could meet up with the troop bringing his cousin to Ghorst. He could order the fat retinue he knew her father would have sent along to ride his half-dead horse and enjoy the ride in the carriage with his cousin. The formal announcement of their betrothal was now only days away so she shouldn't feel the need to refuse him any longer. Either way, in a matter of a few months they would be married. He would be able to have her any time he wanted and she would no longer have a say. This thought made him smile. He liked it when they struggled; it made muscles they didn't usually use tighten up. Maybe he could find a way for the stupid soldier boy, Dell, to swallow his sword on the way as well…

He couldn't even enjoy getting to see his cousin, Faelan, while he was in this miserable town, because he had already left for the castle. He had gone to Ghorst to greet the princess himself, no doubt. They had a running wager to see which of them could bed her first. At this point he had the better chance, given the future plans, but if Faelan had time alone with her, with him not around, the odds might tip. He would still have to marry her but he would never let her live down that she would be nothing but a disgusting whore to him then.

The prince barely paid any attention to any of the inspection of the hospice and hospital. He asked a few well sounding questions, so the lord would report back to his father that he had been, but only enough to appease. He had learned ways to placate his father; he only had to nod, say uh huh and look attentive whenever anyone looked his way. It was hard though; he didn't want to open his mouth, he didn't want to even breathe – he didn't want to catch anything the sick and foul people had. The conditions were sterile enough and everything looked neat and tidy, except for the people who were coughing and moaning as if they thought they might get something from him, other than disgust and pity.

He knew his father was hoping him seeing what life in such a place was like might make him feel some compassion; he had refused to visit the ones in Ghorst when his mother made her visits and she had never pushed him to go. His mother wasn't with them so he couldn't refuse it now.

He managed to make it through the hospital, and hospice without even a pang of guilt. If anything he was sickened more that the people were allowed to live in their condition because they were taking from the stores. He thought it smarter and far more humane to destroy anyone that was too sick or old to work.

The orphanage had an impact on him, one of making him feel he needed a bath. One of the children had the gall to run up to him and throw his arms around him, begging him to take him back to the castle with him. He was very glad Arrachsnow had only one, which had never gotten as full as any of the three in Ghorst or either of the two in Doveslade. He would've pulled his sword and begun to kill all the bratty wards if he had to enter another.

Needless to say, the prince was very glad when they left the service district and started for the market. On a typical day at the market would have been crowded. Today only the shop keeps were around. Durbaith had given each half a day's typical earnings so the king and prince could do their inspection with little or no hindrance. Another reason the people loved him so.

The street had shops and stalls on both sides. The usual attractions: butcher, baker, cooper, grocer and cloth merchant, spices and liquors. At the end of the street were the taverns and inns. The king, prince and party would be staying with Lord Durbaith at his manor so they had no need to go there.

They stopped first at the butcher. The king's steward, Rehldach, was with them to inspect the quality of the meat, and to show the prince what he should be looking for if he had to lead an inspection himself. Some of it wasn't as lean or as fresh as the king's man, or the king, would have liked to see but was still high enough quality to be sold, as long as it was consumed within the next twenty-four hours.

The smells in the butchery – raw meat, blood and guts – made Acthiel gag. He managed to keep from vomiting by placing a large amount of snuff into each nostril. He almost lost it again when the butcher handed him the cleaver expecting him to slice off some portions of the half steer on the cutting board; an act he got through only by pretending it was one of the pathetic wards in the orphanage they had just left.

They found much the same at the baker. The grain was dry and didn't harbor any insects and the yeast was a little lax but still alive enough. The sample of bread the baker offered the prince tasted like paste and the flour used made him sneeze but he didn't dare refuse, knowing that Durbaith and Rehldach would tell his father if he did.

The clothier's inspection was of the quality of the cotton, linens and wool. Some of the dyes were a little watered down and there was a few moths but nothing unusual and, again, was adequate. The woman offered the prince his choice of the scarves she had available. Their colors were muted and barely discernable. He had no desire to have one but he took what was supposed to be a blue one, figuring he could use it to pay the next whore he was with.

Some of the spices at the grocers' had to be confiscated because they had been allowed to stay out too long and had gotten stale but only a light fine would be levied. The shop sold mostly only edibles that were already preserved so a quick inspection of the wares he sold was all that was needed.

The candle maker's wicks had more lead in them than the king's steward liked. They were told to discard the lot of strings and procure more before the beginning of the next business day or face being closed down. Though the men were not pleased, as it would cost them a trip to the next town over, they could not refuse. Not so surprisingly, they did not ask the prince if he wanted to try his hand at dipping; nor did they offer him any samples.

They went through several other shops where Acthiel did have to try the trade or sample the wares. He managed to smile through most of it. He thought his day was finally done when they left the last shop on the street but then, just when he thought this day couldn't get any worse, they came to the blacksmith's stall.

The smithy had barrels of water, piles of copper, iron ore and steel, wrought iron pulleys and chains and various tools for shaping and forging hanging around a huge stone furnace that was spewing heat and black smoke, leaving a fine black coal dust heavy in the air and coating all the surfaces. The popping of the fire, the hissing of steam escaping the bellows and the sound of hammer against metal rod made the prince's head ache.

Acthiel didn't like the look of the master smith. He was a burly looking man, almost twice his size with muscles on top of muscles. He was bald and scarred badly. The younger man didn't look any older than himself. He wasn't quite as muscled but was equally as large. He guessed he was either the smith's son or his apprentice. He had wavy blonde hair that was hanging down in his face, as if ashamed of how he looked.

The younger one stayed in the stall when the smith came forward to greet them.

"Good day, Lord Durbaith... is it the time of the annual inspection already?"

"It is, Master Smith. We have the proud distinction of having Prince Acthiel with us on this tour as well," said the lord as he indicated the boy.

Prince Acthiel hated being shown off to those that were beneath him and could do him no good but he wanted it reported to his father that he had been nothing but kindness and cordiality so he stepped forward and placed his hand out to be kissed. The smith did so. The way he was smiling as he stepped back made the prince nervous.

"Please, sir, go about your business, we are only here to observe," said Lord Durbaith.

Acthiel watched the two men moving around the stall like they could read each other's mind, not speaking just anticipating the other's needs – handing each other tools and taking turns at the anvil.

He watched the younger one take a bright yellow bit of metal from the furnace, walk it to the anvil and begin to work it, surprised that he had a fluted bowl with cutouts along its rim in a matter of moments. The prince was trying not to be or look impressed but it was hard not to; he could see the elder smith, Lord Durbaith and the steward were equally as. He was instantly jealous of this boy. He was about to make a snide comment, not liking that this nobody was getting so much praise from the men around him, when his father stepped up behind him.

"Good day, Sir Smith," said the king.

Hithal was speechless. He was fine in front of Lord Durbaith and even the prince and his entourage but not the king himself? He started to go down on his right knee but stopped when the king told him to rise.

"I must say, sir, I am watching this lad moving about like he has been here for years, yet he appears so young. Is he your son?" asked the king. He smiled when he saw the boy smile. He was impressed that it did nothing to mess up his stride.

"Nay, my lord, King, though I could ask for none better if he were. He is only but three and a half weeks here," said Hithal, beaming.

This surprised the king. "Has he forged before?"

"No, my lord, but you would think it," said Hithal. "May I be so bold as to show you a few of the items he has made. Quite the eye for art, he has."

"By all means, sir," said the king. He expected to see rudimentary metal items a teenage boy would create so he was more than astonished when he saw a cartful of items any full smith would be proud to present. Well-formed bowls, perfect utensils, tools and, surprisingly, several realistic iron roses in various stages of bloom. "Did he honestly make all of these?" asked the king as he picked on of the latter up.

"He did, sir," said Hithal.

Acthiel was getting very bored now. He began to kick at a rock half imbedded in the dirt road at his feet, wondering, if he got it loose, if he could kick it hard enough to kill a man? There was more than one before him he wouldn't mind testing this thought out on, beginning with the handsome, young, smith's apprentice.

"We are planning to take a chance at the bazaar next week in Ghorst," said the smith.

"You bring items such as these along and set up a demonstration and I am certain you would do yourself very well," said the king's steward. He was now eyeing the wares himself.

"Where did you come by this wonder at the ore?"

Wayde had a smile on his face as he set the new articulated bowl before them, along with the other items.

"He is from your own Ghorst, my lord," said Hithal then. "One of the turn-outs."

Acthiel stopped digging at the rock with the heel of his foot and lit up at that. He took a closer look at the boy then. This must be the one the pretty scullery maid was so hot to wait for. He sniggered.

"Would you like to try your hand at it, Acthiel?" asked the king.

"What?" Acthiel coughed. The look on his father's face, the same one he had when he looked at the soldier boy, saying he was truly impressed, told him he didn't dare say no. The prince stepped forward and stopped beside the serf boy. He was upset to see he was a head taller than him as well, and, if he was honest with himself, far handsomer. This didn't make him any happier. He had hoped to see he had a pitted face or a cleft lip but all he saw was a fresh looking scar on his right cheek and an older looking scar on his forehead. Neither of which took away from his looks. It was extremely hot next to the furnace and the smell of the hot metal was making his nose burn. He saw the boy wasn't sweating at all and didn't seem bothered by the odors. He refused to cover his face or remove his cloak, overcoat or jerkin, unwilling to let him show him up in that way either.

"Show him how it's done, Wayde," said the smith as he handed the prince a hammer.

"Yes, Hithal. Do I have permission to speak freely, my lord?" Wayde asked the prince respectfully, keeping his head lowered and his eyes on the ground.

Acthiel shrugged, not particularly caring.

"You have it," said the king.

"Thank you, my lord, King," said Wayde, bowing his head to the king. "I will show you how to make the roses, my lords," said Wayde, "First off, I work it into a bowl shape."

Acthiel watched the boy hit the edge of the heated iron slab before him a couple of times, flattening it into a roundish shape then he stepped back and held the end of the tongs out to him. The prince stepped up, took a halfhearted swing and completely missed the piece, he hit the anvil quite hard instead, making the muscles of his arm, back and jaw, which was clenched tightly, all ring out in pain. Hearing the disappointed breathes from the master smith, his father and Lord Durbaith angered the prince greatly. He was ready to throw the hammer away from him when the boy spoke.

"That wasn't bad; I wasn't so accurate my first swings either. Just bring it in to your body a little more, and hold the hammer looser," said Wayde, sounding more like a master smith.

If there hadn't been so many around him right then, Acthiel would have taught this serf what it was to belittle a prince. He took another swing and barely connected with the piece this time. He cried out, fell back and dropped the hammer as the vibrations raked his body. He saw the look on his father's face then and hardened his jaw. He didn't think this was work for a prince but he wasn't going to let this serf show him up. After a few more tries he was hitting the metal, doing as the serf was telling him to do. When he was done he had a pathetic looking rose but a rose all the same.

"Very good for your first time at the anvil," said Hithal, trying to sound like he meant it.

The prince shrugged and held the metal flower out to the smith.

"You may keep it," said Hithal, "It's my policy to let my apprentice's keep their first."

The prince started to say he didn't want it as he watched the smith point to one stuck in the crux of the rafters over his head, implying it was the boy's first piece. It was as perfect as the others in the cart.

Hithal could see the prince was feeling quite abused and, by the look on the king's face, he wasn't especially happy that his son had essentially been shown up by a serf either. Hoping to make it better, he quickly said, "Perhaps you would prefer one of the other flowers instead? Your majesty, Prince?" pointing at the others in the cart Wayde had made.

Acthiel looked over the ones in the cart then back to Wayde's first piece. He guessed the boy was saving it to give to the pretty scullery maid. He smiled quickly, and put what he hoped was a truly impressed and gracious look on his face, as he said, "I would very much like that one there."

Wayde jumped at the request. He started to say he couldn't have it but knew he could get worse than hit if he did. He knew he had no say in this, if a high-blood asked something of a serf they were required to do it without complaint. He held his tongue.

Hithal saw how upset Wayde was. He wanted to say no, he knew he was saving it for the girl in Ghorst. He didn't dare insult the prince or king further either. "Get it, Boy," he said. He would make it up to him later.

Wayde took the piece from the notch in the rafter and held it up to the prince.

Acthiel was smiling wickedly as he took it from the boy. He could see how much it was hurting him to do it, which made it even more pleasurable. He looked at the flower and felt anger well up inside him again. The thing was a hundred times better than his first try. How could this serf, this uneducated piece of horse dung, make something so beautiful on the first try. He hated this boy even more then. He turned so only Wayde could hear him and said, testing his earlier theory, "There is a pretty new scullery maid at the castle I have recently found much pleasure with. Cameron is her name." The prince looked over his shoulder to make sure he wasn't being noticed doing this then at the boy's face. Seeing it turn pale white told him he was right that this was the girl's friend. He twisted the verbal dagger further. "Quite the bucking little filly, she is, and quite eager too. *Every night*. I am doing my best to tame her, but you know her kind..."

Wayde flinched. Cameron had promised to wait for him but then he had promised to wait for her and he had broken that promise at the home, and almost again with Hithal's daughter only a few weeks before.

"She's quite taken with me. She was quite upset when I told her I had to leave. It was a little embarrassing actually but then... not so familiar with proper manners, I suppose. She said she wasn't sure how she could go even a day without me... I think maybe I will take this to her, to show her how much that means to me."

Wayde suddenly felt like his whole life was over.

"You wouldn't mind if I was to tell her it was me that made it though, I am sure. Should be an honor for you, to think I would be willing to say your work was good enough for me to claim, is it not?"

"If… if it pleases you, my lord."

"You know a serf's mind better than I, would it please her?" asked Acthiel smiling wickedly. Seeing he had cut the boy to the bone, the prince turned to the master smith, frowned and said, "Actually, this one isn't so nice either, now that I look at it. I don't think I want this one after all."

King Vianor had noticed his son speaking to the boy and wondered what he was saying. The look that came to the boy's face, which lost about three shades of color, and was twisted up like he might be sick told him it wasn't anything nice. His son then announced loudly that the rose in his hand wasn't so nice and he didn't want it either. This was an insult to both the boy and the smith. He couldn't punish his son before them but he could try to smooth things with the boy, whose pride had likely just been trampled by Acthiel. "Master Smith, might I purchase one of the beautiful roses. I believe my queen would very much enjoy one."

"Nay, my lord, King, you may have one at no charge," said Hithal as he took the nicest from the cart and held it out to the man.

"I insist, Master Smith. You have lost any chance for other sales due to our visit; I feel it is only right."

Hithal was going to say Lord Durbaith had taken care of that but could see the man was going to be steadfast and would be insulting him to continue. He was proud that the king would want to pay for an item he could take without needing to ask for it. He knew, in doing this, the man was praising Wayde's workmanship – to say it was worth paying for. He looked at the boy then, expecting to see him beaming with pride but he was looking at his feet. Not wanting to embarrass him in front of the lords, he turned back and said, "I should think that ten pents would cover it, my lord."

The king motioned the steward over and held his hand out to be given his forest green scrip. He counted out the coins and handed them to the smith.

Hithal took them and held them reverently.

"There is to be a contest at the bazaar this year, for fine craftsmanship, I put forward that you enter a few of your wares here in it. I, for one, would be surprised if you didn't at least get an honorable mention."

Hithal was speechless; he had never been given so high a compliment. He looked again at Wayde, expecting to see him equally as pleased, since it was directed more at him. He was being far quieter than he would have expected. He looked at the prince then, who looked like a cat that had swallowed a canary, and finally to the boots of the king again. He tried to sound as happy as he had started out at as when he said, "I very well may do that, my lord, King. Thank you for the gracious suggestion."

"We've taken up enough of your time, sir. Thank you both for showing us your trade," said the king.

Hithal and Wayde both bowed as the men turned and left them.

Hithal turned to the boy, upset with how slouched he was. Some would consider him not so very astute but he hadn't missed Acthiel talking quietly to the boy, he knew the idiot prince had said something that hurt Wayde's feelings. Once the men were far enough away he stepped up to him and gently put his hand on his shoulder. He jumped when Wayde jumped. "I didn't want to offer the prince that rose, Wayde… but we must remember our place."

"Consider me thoroughly reminded," said Wayde under his breath, with more than a hint of sarcasm.

"I am sorry the prince was so harsh. Told you he was arrogant, didn't I, Boy? He knows nothing of fine workmanship. Lord Durbaith and King Vianor both said your pieces were quite fine. The king would certainly never offer to purchase a piece from you if he didn't think it well worth the price," said Hithal, holding the coins out to him.

Wayde took them, letting them fall from one hand to the palm of his other hand. There was a day having ten gold coins would've made him feel like he was rich. He couldn't bring himself to feel very good about them because he felt the king was only looking to buy his silence for his son being a bastard.

He really could not care less what the prince or king thought of his work; a few kind words from them would do nothing for his future. He'd never before needed another person's praise; he was comfortable enough with himself.

"I think we should get the stall cleaned up and knock off early," said the master smith. He was about to suggest that the boy go and spend some of the coins he was holding on himself. He knew he hadn't spent any of what he had given him to date, not even to send dispatches to his friends. This had surprised him since he had all but begged him for an advance his first day there.

Wayde shrugged then stuck the coins in his pocket and went to get the bucket and shovel beside the furnace. The rose the prince had made and his own first piece, which the prince had discarded, were both setting on the railing beside it. He picked the two pieces up and looked at them for a moment.

The prince's rose really wasn't bad for a beginner. He had been surprised himself that his own first one had come out so well. Comparing the two was like apples and oranges though. At that moment his didn't look any better to him than the prince's though.

Hithal watched Wayde put the prince's ugly rose and his own prized rose into the rubbish bin beside the furnace, the one for missed pieces, to be reheated and worked into something new, as if to say they were both junk, and frowned. "Now boy... no matter what the idiot prince said yours is a fine piece."

Wayde thought it was as well but he still didn't move to take it from the bin. He didn't want to tell the man he didn't want it anymore because the sentiment it had been made from was a falsehood. He had Cami in mind when he made it, thinking how much she would love it, especially because he had made it for her. She had won the favors of a prince, how could he compete with that? She would likely have laughed at his silly gesture now, likely having been given precious jewelry and furs by the prince.

Hithal walked over, took the boy's flower out of the bin and held it out to him, "Come now, Boy."

"I am not feeling so well, sir, would you mind if I just wanted to go to my room now?"

"Dinner will be ready in a little more than an hour. Tabitha made her famous lamb stew. She's looking forward to seeing just how many bowls you will eat," said Hithal. It had become a contest of sorts between his wife and the boy; she could tell how good a meal was by the number of helpings he had of it.

"I'm not hungry, sir," said Wayde, leaning on the far post and playing with the string of his trousers.

Hithal thought he did actually look like he was going to be sick. "Are you angry with me for telling you to give the prince the flower?"

"No. I know we have to do anything they ask," said Wayde, he really wasn't.

It had been a long day and the boy had worked quite hard through it, without complaint, making more than a dozen pieces and the anxiety of having to put on an unexpected show for the king and prince was likely to have taken quite a toll on his nerves. "Alright then, yes, you may go." The smith watched him stump out of the stall then looked down at the wrought iron rose in his hand and frowned, it really was a fine piece of workmanship, especially for his first piece.

****

"Everything seems well in order, Lord Durbaith," said the king as they walked back to the carriage to prepare for their departure.

"Thank you, my lord," said Durbaith, smiling.

"I do believe this trip has cemented my thoughts on the status of the edict," said the king.

Durbaith had hoped to hear that. "I'll see you at the next council meeting, my lord, King. Safe journey to you, the prince and your men."

The king put his hand out for the lord to kiss the ring of then climbed into the waiting couch. He watched the prince do the same then motioned to the driver to begin to take them out of the city.

The king felt a sense of relief. He had seen several of the turn-outs in the cities and all of them seemed to be fitting into society well. The soldier, Dell, of his own guard, and the boy in Arrachsnow, Wayde, were proof that they had been raised well enough to be so. He slowly twirled the cast rose he had purchased in his fingers and smiled then set it down on the folding table before him.

He had heard nothing of any real issues to worry about in their visits. It seemed Lord Durbaith was right, the proclamation had served its purpose and he could suggest that they at least back off on the requirements with a steady heart. Perhaps they could start by allowing two children per couple, that shouldn't put too much of a strain on the supplies. The younger wards of the homes might even be able to return to their parents, if they lived and their parents wished it.

He felt confident all was now well in his lands.

29

Trouble Afoot

The king's entourage entered the forest just as the sun was reaching its apex their six day out, it would be close to setting before they would leave its dark roads but they would be home this time tomorrow which made them all quite happy.

King Vianor felt the trip had been well worth it and had hopes his son had taken away a few good lessons from it as well.

He was proud of his son for being willing to work beside the blacksmith's apprentice in Arrachsnow, with little to no complaints. It was one of the few times he had ever had such a feeling for his son and he wanted to savor it.

He gave the captain of the guard the signal they were ready and sat back.

The soldiers formed ranks along each side of the carriage as protection since bandits were well known to frequent such places; all seemed quiet and safe. They began to move slowly along the wooded road. The trip started uneventfully… About a league into the trees the air became thick with tension and the horses began to fight the driver, causing the carriage to have to be stopped while the man tried to calm them down. The other animals also seemed to be tense; making their riders just as, sensing something was amiss as well.

The captain of the guard walked his horse to the king's side of the carriage and called out to him, "Something doesn't feel right, your majesty. I ask for your permission to get the horses moving again."

Vianor was playing a game of cards with Rehldach so he hardly even noticed that they had stopped. "Is there a problem?" he asked, not even taking his eyes from his cards, putting a red seven on top of a black seven on the pile of cards facing up between them and taking another from the draw deck, a stack of cards facing down.

The captain was about to answer but instead he gave a painful sounding grunt that got the king's attention.

Vianor looked out his window and saw an arrow protruding from the soldier's right thigh.

"Protect the ki…" the man started to shout just as another arrow pierced his throat, killing him instantly.

A volley of arrows took out three more soldiers as nearly a dozen bandits, dressed in bits and pieces of rags and armor, came out of the trees and surrounded them.

The king told Acthiel to stay hidden as he pulled his sword, jumped from the carriage, ran toward the bandit closest to him and fell into battle with him. The steward followed right behind, doing the same. The prince had no intention of disobeying his father's orders this time; he got on to the floor of the carriage and cowered in the corner, two pillows on top of him.

The remaining soldiers, the steward and the king couldn't overcome the numbers. All but one of the men they had with them lay wounded or dead but only two of the bandits were dead and only half of the twenty or so were even wounded.

Rehldach was about to shout for Vianor to escape with the prince when he saw him take a slice to the thigh, knocking him to his knees. The steward turned from his fight trying to get to him in time but took one himself shortly after.

Acthiel finally got up the courage to see what was happening. He peered over the edge of the window frame and froze in horror as he watched the steward and his father fall. He shouted frantically, and a bit pathetically, for the driver to get the horses moving. The man whipped the animals and they bolted forward. The carriage lunged forward a few more feet then stopped abruptly, throwing the prince into the front wall inside it. The horses only made it a few feet before their legs were cut out from under them then the driver was pulled from the seat and killed, leaving the prince alone and defenseless.

Acthiel shrank back into the corner of the carriage he had always felt safe in. He realized, with sudden and frightening clarity, he was about to die. He knew if he didn't do something so too would his father. He was about to reach for the sword kept hidden under the seat, for just such an occasion as this. His eyes fell on the perfect rose the serf boy had made; it apparently had slipped off the table in the attempt to flee. He remembered the look on his father's face as he watched the serf boy making the iron items and the look he had when he watched the boy soldier being put through his training then. He had never once looked at his son that way – with pride. Something inside him snapped then.

The prince threw the door of the carriage open, jumped from his hiding place and ran to the closest riderless horse. Some of the soldiers were still fighting around him and his father lay bleeding and dying but he gave them no thought as he swung himself onto the animal's back and kicked it hard in the hindquarters.

Acthiel began to laugh wildly as he increased the distance between him and the battle. He saw the edge of the forest and hooted, thinking he was now safe. He jumped as he felt a stabbing pain in the left side of his back, just below his shoulder blade. A wave of pain radiated out from this point of impact. The next thing he felt was himself falling from the horse. He never felt himself hit the ground.

****

Wayde opened his eyes as the ray of sunlight that had been slowly moving up his face finally reached them. He was surprised he had been able to sleep after how hurt and upset he had been the night before. He tried to tell himself it had all been a stupid dream but the damage he had done to the room – furniture upturned, the sheets from the bed in a pile on the floor, the mattress half off its frame, all the paper from the writing desk on the floor, a large black ink stain on the far wall, the bottle that once held that ink in pieces on the floor beneath it and his rumbling stomach, upset with him because he had gone to bed without any dinner, were all telling him it had all been too real.

The sun was just coming over the treetops across from the barn his room was in. This meant he only had about an hour before the smith and his wife would be up. Normally he would be down in the yard sitting on top of the table doing his meditation by now but seeking peace was the farthest thing from his mind at this moment.

He jumped out of the bed and began to pace around his small room. He was fighting the urge to steal Hithal's horse and go to Ghorst to find out for himself if Cami was truly now with the prince. He didn't want to believe she could do this to him but she had promised to write him and he hadn't heard anything from her since he left. Dell said it was because she hadn't been able to afford to yet but neither had Kyi yet he managed to get him a dispatch through Dell. He hadn't sent her anything either, which he was now upset about as well. Maybe if he had she wouldn't have let Acthiel near her.

There was truly nothing he could do or say against her being with the prince, except that he hoped she knew she would be nothing but a plaything to him. He was about to kick the wall when the door burst open. He turned with an apology for the damage he had done to the room on his lips. Hithal had told him he expected the room to be kept neat and tidy. It wasn't the master smith. It took a few seconds to believe who it was.

"Hello, friend," said Sabban. He was being supported by Beau. The older boy's left pant leg was soaked in blood, a belt tied tightly around it, he had cuts all over his arms and the side of his face was one massive bruise. Beau was a little less bumped and bruised but barely.

"What the hell are you doing here?" asked Wayde.

"I happened to be in the area and thought I would stop in for a visit and to bring you news of Ghorst."

Wayde knew better than them being there just on happenstance. He set his feet, crossed his arms, which had gotten larger since he had last seen the thugs, over his chest, which had also increased in size, and gave them a look to say this.

"We need to hide out for a few hours," said Sabban. "I will pay you for your hospitality, of course," said the boy, nudging his friend in the ribs.

Beau quickly held out a forest green velvet purse. It looked like it had come from a noble's belt.

"Come across someone who fought back, did ya?" asked Wayde.

"Only for a moment," said Sabban, smiling sickly.

Wayde could see the scrip was full but he wasn't interested in coins, Hithal paid him well enough. He hadn't spent any of his stipends yet and he had been given ten pents by the king the day before so he had nearly that much in a box under his cot. "No, I'm sorry. I cannot offer you this room to heal up. My master is very strict, he said if he finds me with anyone up here he will throw me into the furnace, and I believe him."

Sabban gave him a look to say he doubted this, looking around at the mess around him.

"*He* did this," said Wayde, "He caught me up here with his daughter yesterday."

"What about Miss Cameron?"

"I'm here and she's in Ghorst, isn't she," said Wayde, quite snidely.

The tone of the boy's voice surprised Sabban a little bit, it sounded quite convincing. He remembered the look in his eyes when he and his friends were last before him when he looked at the girl too though. What could have happened to change that?

"You're lying," he said.

"No, seriously," said Wayde, putting on his best impudent look. He had never been good at lying but he didn't want these two here even for a moment longer. He turned his face so the scar the local lord had given him three weeks ago, that was only now healing, showed and said, "He did this my first day here, said he wanted me to know my place right away and said he'd do it again every week until I did." Then he pulled up his sleeve to show a burn he'd actually given himself the day before when a drip of melted ore fell from the tongs, "He did this just yesterday because I wasn't as fast as he thought I should be."

Sabban still thought he was lying.

Wayde was about to add more when a male voice from outside shouted out.

"*Get your bony arse down here*, or I'll brand you into next month, Boy," growled the man, sounding quite mean and angry.

"Please, Sabban, I don't wanna be marked up any more," said Wayde, with a quiver to his voice that sounding true. He knew Hithal's shout was only in jest but he could see it had convinced Sabban.

"Alright, I will go, but I won't forget that you refused us help," said the older boy.

"We leaving?" Beau asked.

"Yes, Beau, we are leaving."

"Be quick and quiet about it," said Wayde, "The man is three times as big as me and his arms are twice the size of mine."

Sabban and Beau stumbled back out, down the stairs, to the side of the barn, around the back of it then disappeared back into the darkness within the woods.

Wayde was just closing the door of his room when Hithal appeared at the bottom of the steps, just missing the two thugs as their backs went into the trees behind the house.

"Come now, Boy, I will not have you going without dinner and breakfast. We got a lot of work to do if we are going to Ghorst in two weeks. I will not have you fainting on me and falling into the fire," sniggered the older man. "Tabitha would have *my* arse then."

"Yes, Hithal," said Wayde.

"We need to get your friend's sword completed as well," said the master smith as he put his arm around the boy and squeezed him affectionately, "I will let you finish it up, if you like."

30

Serf's Day

Life at the castle for Cami the last week had been much better, the last four days better still. The prince had left five days ago so she no longer had to look over her shoulder, constantly wondering when the prince might sneak up behind her. She had gone to Clara two days before the prince left, the day after he had tried to force himself on her outside the soldiers' barracks, begging her for a sweater, complaining about being cold. She wasn't sure if the kitchen maid knew what she was up to or not, she didn't say either way if she did. She did get her one, for all it was two sizes too big, was moth eaten and smelled sour. She had also begun to wear her hair in a tight bun, as Clara did, which didn't detract from her beauty much but helped keep it from tickling places she wasn't used to feeling it and kept it from getting ratty and soiled as she sweated. Her long thick hair had always been one of her best features. For all it was less beautiful now that most of it had been cut off, it was still nicer than most of the other maids.

She had been frightened to go into the castle the day after Dell left, unsure if him being away now, and unable to protect her, might make the prince more attentive. She had seen him start in her direction a few times but it always seemed like his father was there to stop him. She knew it was silly to think the king might be watching out for her but she very much wanted to thank him. Clara had even stopped barking at her so much and actually praised her a few times.

It was on the fourth day after the prince left that the woman went to her and told her she could have the next day, which was market day, off. Most all of the servants had been given the afternoon off and were being allowed to go into town to spend their earnings. Cami's stipend was only two pents per week, she had to give Sally her first two, to repay the two she borrowed to pay for the bath her first day and Clara had taken her second two back because she broke one of the fine porcelain dishes when she was helping Maria wash them, so she only had two pents. Those she was going to use to send Wayde a dispatch.

She had seen Kyi the day before; he too had the afternoon off, so they had made plans to go into town together. She hoped Dell might be back at the castle in time so they could try to see him as well but so far there had been no news. She was thinking about all of this as she finished up the floor of the dining hall.

Cami woke in the morning of Serf's Day before the rooster and was half dressed before the other girls were even opening their eyes. She was surprised how good she felt since she had stayed up late the night before, using the light of the moon, to write the last bit of her dispatch to Wayde.

She wrote that Dell wasn't back at the castle from getting the princess from Elmsdune yet but they expected him any day and of how beautiful all the maids said the princess was; teasing that she hoped their friend didn't fall in love with her. She ended it with how much she loved him, remembering that Dell had said Wayde loved her even though he had never said it in words. She couldn't wait to get it to him. She was sitting on her cot, trying to be patient, as the other girls, who were talking about what they were planning to do for the day, moved out of the room.

Cameron had a hard time keeping her mind on task but she managed to complete all Clara had asked her to do quickly and well. Thus, the woman had no reason to say no to her when she went to the kitchens to get her permission to go out.

She saw Kyi pacing in front of the stable doors as she came around the corner of the kitchen. Her heart leapt with joy. She missed the days of spending time with him, Dell and Wayde. She looked toward the barracks and saw a lot of activity but didn't see Dell. She wasn't sure if she would get him, or herself, if trouble, if she went over and asked for him so she didn't. She walked over to the stables calling out to Kyi as she got closer. She knew the look on his face as soon as he turned to her.

"What's the matter?"

"Dell hasn't returned yet," said the boy.

She knew he had hoped the three of them could go out together. "I'm sure he'll get with us as soon as he is able to, Kyi. He is trying very hard to make a place for himself."

"It seems he has. I heard the sergeant at arms talking about him just after he left for the assignment. The king really likes him."

Cami was surprised how jealous the boy sounded.

Kyi realized himself how that had sounded; he quickly added, "I didn't mean it that way... I am happy for him, I just am feeling..."

"I miss him, and Wayde, too, Kyi," said the girl.

Not wanting to spoil their day together by making them both upset, Kyi tried to smile as he said, "So, where are we going?"

"I have only enough to send Wayde a dispatch," said Cami. "Dell didn't get mine to take to him, so I really only want to go to the dispatch office, anywhere else is up to you."

The two quickly ran to the gate and followed the other castle workers that had been given the day as well. They stayed to the right side of the street, keeping in the shadows, and stopped with the others when they came to the corner before the market. This was the first time Cami had been in town during the day. Sister Jessa had given all her wards lessons on what they should do when they were out during the day but she never told her how awkward it would be to see the looks people gave her. It was hard to look at everything going on around her, as she wanted to, and keep her eyes lowered, as she was supposed to.

They stood on the corner with a group of other serfs, most they didn't know, just waiting – they couldn't cross the street until they'd been given permission. It was a long wait. By the time one of the merchants noticed them half of their day was gone and most all of them were ready to turn back.

Once they were across they were allowed to walk along and browse. By this time of day most of the nobles had already been out and were back to their homes so they wouldn't have to worry about being seen.

Kyi was immediately drawn to the bakery. He had always had a sweet tooth and a fresh tray of fragrant honey cakes were calling his name. Cami didn't stop though. She wanted to go to the dispatch office first. She was afraid she might lose the note or the office would close before she got it there.

"We will go back, Kyi," she said when she saw he was pouting.

By the time they got back to the bakery the pastries he had been eyeing had sold out. The next batch wouldn't be ready for another hour, which was after the time they had to be back in the castle.

"I'm sorry, Kyi."

"It's alright," said the boy, sounding like he only barely meant it.

"Maybe we can find something up the next stalls?"

Kyi was about to say he wasn't hungry anymore when they heard someone behind him call his name.

Cami looked behind her and was a little surprised, and nervous, to see Sabban.

"Hello, you two," said the thief boy as he stepped up and put an arm over each of their shoulders. "Where is Dell?"

Kyi started to say, "He is…"

"… coming along shortly," finished Cami, giving Kyi a hard look. She remembered how tense Wayde was around the older boy. She knew he wouldn't have been that way without a good reason. Because of this she didn't trust the boy either. She could see cuts on his arms and his right cheek was all bruised up, his hair was hanging down over it to trying to hide it, and he was walking with a limp. She wondered whom he had gotten into a fight with.

"I saw you eyeing the empty tray there, Kyi, and I see they appear all out. I can get you one."

Kyi's eyes lit up to this.

Cami stiffened up.

"I have some I just purchased if you would like one," said Sabban as he motioned the boy to follow him.

The thug had noticed the two as they walked by but he didn't want to catch their attention while they were around so many others. He heard the girl say they would come back so the boy could buy one of the sweets he had been eyeing and knew then how he could get them to stop and speak to him. When they were far enough down the street he stepped out and purchased the last of them.

Cami was about to say they were expected else-where when Kyi nodded and followed him. She didn't want to go but she didn't want her friend to go alone so she followed as well.

Sabban led them into the alleyway beside the bakery. Beau, was leaning against the side door of the building, beside a tray of honey sweet cakes. "Go ahead, Kyi, eat as many as you like."

Kyi held two pents up to Sabban, which was what it would've cost to purchase one from the vendor.

The older boy waved his hand away, "Don't be silly, I'd never charge a friend."

"Thanks, Sabban," said Kyi as he took one of the biggest cakes and bit into it.

Sabban put his arm around the boy's shoulder and asked, "Have you given my offer any thought?" just loud enough for him to hear.

"Not really. I have been awfully busy... what with having to get horses ready to go for getting the princess from Elmsdune, then pulling more for the king, prince and ten others," said Kyi, without thinking about it, stuffing a second cake into his mouth.

"Yes, the king's tour," said the man getting a strange look on his face and a sneaky smirk splitting his lips. "Any other news?"

"Another prince, Lord Faelan, I think my stable master said his name was, has arrived as well. I think he came to greet the princess. I heard him asking my master if she had arrived yet."

Sabban got a pleased look on his face. He smiled, pressed five pents into the boy's hand and waved for him to take as many cakes as he liked, then he turned to the girl. "Hey, Cami," he said, motioning her to come into the alley further, "I have something for you as well."

Cameron was standing close to the edge of the opening of the alley. She didn't want to get blocked in by the two older and larger boys. "I'm not hungry," said the girl.

"It's about Wayde," said the thug. "I saw him the other day, in Arrachsnow. I was there on business. He was working the smithy. He actually likes it quite a lot, he does. He made you something."

"Really? What?" asked Cami, stepping a little closer.

"It's back here," said Sabban as he went deeper in.

Cami couldn't imagine how Sabban could know that was where Wayde was or what he had been assigned to for a job unless he had actually seen him. Her heart leapt in her chest at the thought of him having sent her something he made; it was better than a letter that would be full of empty words. All her nervousness forgotten, she followed him deeper into the alley.

Sabban was leaning near the end of the alley with something in his hands. She couldn't make out what it was. "How was he?" she asked. She was hoping he wasn't upset with her for not writing to him.

Sabban grabbed her arm, pulled her to him and turned quickly so she was pinned to the wall by his body. He pulled the collar of her frock open, exposing the thin shift underneath, and began to kiss her neck.

Cami started to struggle but he was bigger than her so she couldn't move and one of his elbows was pressing on her chest so she could barely get any air to breathe let alone scream for help. She felt his hands starting to pull the skirt of her frock up and began to panic. She could see Beau had moved himself so he was blocking Kyi's view, meaning what little help her friend might have given her was not there either.

"Quit fighting, Woman. Wayde said he wanted me to show you a few things. Just some things he wants you to do for him when you next see him," said Sabban. He began to bring his mouth to hers. His left hand squeezed her breast as his right one went up her skirt, forced her legs apart and began to pull at her underpants.

"Please, don't," Cami barely managed.

Kyi finished his third cake. They were better than he had expected them. He was so full of sugar now that he felt very jittery. "Hey, Cami, maybe you should take one for yourself, for later," he said, looking around for her. "Cami?"

Beau moved so he was blocking most of the alley beyond, "Go ahead, take one for her," said the tall boy.

"Cami?" asked Kyi, trying to see past the thug. He was sure he had seen her walk past him a minute ago.

"Don't worry about her, Boy, Sabban's giving her what she wants."

Kyi was about to say more when he heard Cami's quiet plea. Being shorter and smaller than beau, he was able to get under the man's arm and behind him before he could move to stop him.

"Please," cried Cami, in barely a whisper. She was trying to squeeze her legs together to stop the man's hand from getting her further exposed.

"That's right, Baby, work them thigh muscles. Men like it when you wrap 'em around 'em and hold on tight," said the thug. He released her breast and took hold of a handful of her hair. He pulled it hard, which made her legs loosen without her wanting to. He smiled as he started to bring his hand home then he jumped as he felt something jab him in his left kidney.

He fell back, released the girl and grunted. He swung around to find Kyi with one hand balled up, the other holding a broken bottle. The thief's blood was shining on and dripping from the jagged edges. He reached around and touched the area that hurt then brought his hand out to find more staining his fingers.

"Stay back," growled the small boy, "Cami, you alright?"

Cami was in tears, trying to get her underpants pulled back up. She nodded and stumbled back up the alley, past Beau.

The stunned thug didn't make a move to stop her.

"Aaayow," cried Sabban, "Now, Kyi, that any way to treat a friend?" he asked, showing him his bloodied hand.

"You want more?" asked the boy, as he wiped bits of the honey glazing from the cake he had just eaten from his chin.

Beau started toward him then, finally figuring out what was happening. He was figuring to take him by surprise but Kyi ducked under his hand and slashed his arm on the way by. Now the boy was on the open end of the row and the other two were pinned in.

"Come on, Kyi," cried Cami.

Keeping the broken bottle, now with both of the boys' blood on it, before him, and Cami behind him, Kyi backed up. Once he was in the open street he threw the bottle away from him. He doubted the thugs would try anything in the open. He turned and followed behind Cami, who was heading back toward the castle fast.

Once they were far enough away to know they weren't being followed, Kyi asked, "Are you alright, Cami? Did he..."

"No," said the girl, breaking into tears again.

"I'm sorry. I didn't want one of them cakes that much," said Kyi. "We should report this.

I bet Dell would come down here and take care of that scumbag for you."

"No! Promise me that you will not tell Dell, or Wayde, about this, Kyi. Ever," said Cami with a look of fright, equal to the one she had after what Sabban had been trying to do.

"But..."

"Promise me," said the girl desperately.

"Alright, Cami, please don't cry."

Cami felt so dirty and ashamed that she wished she hadn't just spent her only two pents on the letter to Wayde. She wanted a bath and the next one she would get for free wasn't for another two days.

"Did you want anything, Cami? I will buy it," said Kyi, showing her the pents he had in his hand still. They were the five coins Sabban had just given him.

She knew he felt horrible for what had happened and it wasn't his fault but she wanted that bath. "Can I have two of them?"

"Of course, Cami," said Kyi. He wanted to ask her what she was going to spend them on but the look of pain on her face made him hold off. He could feel her trembling beside him.

They hugged when they got through the castle gate then went to their separate parts.

Kept to the Shadows

31

Arriving at the Castle

Two days later the king's soldiers and the horse drawn carriage holding the princess and her companions rode through the gate to the courtyard of Auldenway Castle. The sun was just starting to disappear from the sky as they stopped before the main stairs. Not many were there to greet them, unlike their send-off, because the castle staff was busy making everything ready for the king and prince, who were five days out on their tour of the counties and were expected back in two.

Dell saw a few of the servants waiting, including Kyi, to take the horses to the stable, but no Cami. The queen was there, to greet her niece, and a man that looked like a high-blood, by how he was dressed, but that was it for nobility.

The soldiers remained in their positions around the carriage as it stopped before the steps into the castle. They would remain in place until its passengers had entered the castle and they had been released.

****

The queen was a little tense as the soldiers and carriage pulled up, mostly because of who was standing beside her. Faelan was her husband's sister's son so he was also a prince. He was next in line for the throne if anything unfortunate was to happen to her husband and son. A fact he loved to remind everyone of as often as he could. Although he always added that he personally hoped he never sat in the chair for the sad event that would bring him to it. He was only supposed to be at the castle for the bazaar at the end of the week, to act as a judge of the contests, but, from how he was now smiling, she guessed it was more to see her pretty niece.

She tried to put a genuine smile on her face as the carriage and the soldiers on horseback stopped before her. She was truly proud of the men, though not filled with as much pride as her husband would have been. She waited as the attendant went down the steps, folded out the carriage step and opened the door. He helped out a young woman Vela didn't recognize first. She was about her niece's age, so she guessed she was a companion. The princess' retinue came next. Her niece was last. The girl looked a little weary but no worse for wares.

The queen couldn't help but notice the girl's eyes going immediately to a soldier at the end of the rank on her side. She thought it was the same soldier her husband had taken such a fancy to. His face and eyes were straight ahead, like the others. She could see how stiff he was sitting, unlike the men around him, and that his larynx kept moving up and down repeatedly, telling her he was swallowing hard. This implied he had noticed the glance and was trying to act otherwise. She wondered if something inappropriate had happened between the two of them.

She thought the boy soldier was quite becoming as well, especially in his full armor and coverlet. He reminded her very much of Vianor when he was first introduced to her. She could understand her niece being attracted to him but he was only a step over a serf so it would do her little good to encourage it. She didn't especially like her son mingling with the low-bloods but it wasn't seen as amoral for a male to cavort. She wondered if she needed to have a word with the girl, to remind her of her rank and station and the need to remain pure until after she was wed, which would be to a nobleman's son at the very least, not a soldier serf.

She put the thoughts away and put a smile on her face as her niece stopped before her.

****

Faelan knew his aunt didn't care much for him and would really rather he not be at the castle when her son wasn't but he didn't especially care. He was higher blood than her, in point of fact. If not for her marrying his uncle she would likely be nothing more than a country lord's wife. He was formal whenever he was before her though, as the queen she could have him punished for ignoring custom if she wished it. He knew she didn't have the strength to do it.

He was at the castle partly to be a judge in the Mid-summer Bazaar, it was a task he didn't want but his father and the king had insisted on, but mostly to see his niece. He knew that Acthiel was going on the tour with the king, a fact his cousin had complained sourly about the last time they saw each other, so he wouldn't be there to get in the way of him seeing her. He knew the prince wanted to be her first but he intended it to be him, which he knew would ruin her for his cousin –in more ways than one.

She had been planned for the crown prince from birth because she was high-blood, again, higher even than the queen herself. Whether she was a virgin on the day of her wedding mattered little, except to the man she would be marrying. Faelan enjoyed the thought of his cousin having to spend his wedding night with a deflowered woman very much.

He heard the cheer of the castle workers announcing the king's soldiers and the carriage had entered the gates and stiffened his back. He wanted to look regal when the princess pulled up. She hadn't seen him in close to a year. He had changed a lot in that span of time. He had filled out, so he now had some muscle tone, and hair coming out on his chest. Many women had told him that he had grown quite attractive. He was anxious to see how this one would react to him.

Faelan was an attractive man, more so even than Acthiel, who was considered to be quite handsome, but, as with the prince, his personality ruined his good looks. A fact both he and Acthiel were arrogantly unaware of.

He put what he considered his best smile on his face as the carriage came to a stop across from him. He watched the attendant go to it to open the door for the lady and smiled even bigger when the first young lady stepped out. He couldn't remember her name but he knew she was the princess' best acquaintance. Like Acthiel, he would be more than happy to be with her as well. His smile faded a touch as his cousin's retinue stepped out. He'd had more than a few heated run-ins with her, threatening him with bodily harm if he came near the girl with any sort of nefarious thoughts.

The smile increased again as his cousin stepped out. She had changed quite a lot in the last year as well, she was far less pudgy with baby fat and she had much larger breasts. She looked like she would be quite a lot of fun now.

He started to bring his hand out in greeting, expecting her to look at him immediately. He watched her head turn and her eyes go immediately to a soldier at the end of the rank – to one that looked like he could be the son of a lesser noble himself. He saw the young soldier's eyes go to her quickly then away just as and could tell, by how tense he was suddenly, that he knew she was looking at him too. This angered Faelan. He wondered if he had been beaten to the prize.

Whether or not the man was a lesser nobles' son, it was a hanging offense just to have spoken to the princess, as anything other than asking her what her needs were. If the soldier had touched her he would be flayed before he was hanged and if he had lain with her, even if it had been consensual, it would be a drawn and quartering offense. He would very much enjoy getting to see this man punished if this was the case.

He looked the man, this rival, over. He supposed he could see what it was about him the princess was attracted to. He was almost too pretty to be a man. He had dark wavy hair that even the wind seemed to like to play with. His features were well structured and shaped and his dark eyes were penetrating even from the distance between them. He wondered if the armor he wore was true to size, if so he would be formidable in a fight. He knew if he had been chosen for this assignment he was good with a sword as well.

He remembered Acthiel once telling him that he often trained with the guard to keep his skills sharp. He thought maybe he would request the sergeant at arms set up a session for him in the morning and ask that all the best be among his opponents. He could then find out how good this soldier really was. He knew the king's soldiers liked to use real weapons in their training, an accident could easily happen. He smiled, getting to best this man with a sword before running him through with it might just be as pleasurable as being first with the princess might have be.

****

Anya was nervous as the carriage came to a stop. She knew, now that she was here, she wouldn't be able to even get near Dell, at least not without great risk to them both. She wished she had pushed him more to run away with her, she could tell he wanted to. She tried to tell herself not to look at the handsome soldier when she stepped from the carriage, it would be too painful, but she couldn't stop herself. She felt her heart clench and stop beating as she watched him stiffen up. She wondered if he had only been toying with her while he was away and now, back at the castle, would no longer be interested in her – too busy with his duties and trying to become a knight. She looked at her feet for a moment, fighting back tears and the lump in her throat, then up to the queen.

She stiffened when she saw who was standing beside her aunt. She had been so preoccupied that she hadn't noticed Faelan was there. She had hoped to have a few days at the castle without having to keep watch out for her virtue. She forced a smile to her lips as she climbed the steps ad stopped before her aunt.

****

"My parent's extend their gratitude to you for allowing me this opportunity, your grace," said the princess as she dropped into a deep curtsy.

"Rise, Niece. My castle is open and welcome to you and your companions. My lady-in-waiting, Linny, will escort you to your suite. If there is anything you require, let her know and she will see to it."

"Thank you, your grace," said the girl, curtsying again. She nodded to Faelan and put her hand out to him to take and kiss then. She fought the urge to cringe as his cold lips touched her skin and to pull her hand away when he didn't remove them right away. "Hello, cousin."

"Princess Anya," said the man, still holding her hand, which was pleasantly rose scented. His eyes roamed her body very slowly as he added, "You are looking lovely as ever."

"Thank you, Lord Faelan," she said, wishing she could slap him.

The queen could see how uncomfortable her niece was so she said, "I will expect you in the great hall for tea in an hour, Anya, for your first lesson. Until then I imagine you would like to relax in your room?"

"Yes, I would. Thank you, your grace," said the girl, very thankful for her well-timed interjection. She pulled her hand out of her cousin's sweaty grip and started into the castle.

****

Dell tried hard not to notice the princess as she climbed from the carriage but he couldn't stop himself from looking at her. She said she wanted them to be friends but he knew that was impossible, no matter how much either of them wished it. Now that she was at the castle, near people of her own station, she likely wouldn't even think about him again. She would likely laugh at how silly she'd let herself get – the thought of giving her heart and virtue to a serf and giving up a chance at the crown. He would soon be forgotten if he hadn't already been.

He would never forget her or the kiss they shared. He hoped that memory would keep his heart warm for years to come but he knew that was all it would ever be.

He wondered, for the briefest of moments, if she would tell the queen of his indiscretion. She had said she wasn't toying with him but what if she had been? He watched her turning her head and prayed he wouldn't see an evil and conniving smile on her face, like he had seen on her cousin's after trying to have his way with Cameron. Her eyes connected with his for only a split second. In them he saw that not only had she not lied but she did want him still. He felt a flash of hope. His mind began to run ways to see her again. He watched her look at her feet and shake her head slightly; telling him, he guessed, that it truly was over in her eyes. He knew, in his head, that there was no hope for them anyway but, in his heart, he had hoped.

Dell watched her approach the queen and the young man beside her, saw her stiffen under his gaze, and saw his gaze, which was obviously more than friendly. It reminded him of the way Acthiel looked at Cami. He guessed then this was the other cousin she had spoken of. He wanted to jump from his horse and run the man through with his sword but he didn't. He would not live long after. The princess would be safe from him then, though. He reminded himself of his place and that the man on the steps had a right to look at her this way. He forced himself to keep his eyes straight and his face stoic, not wanting any of his thoughts to show. The sergeant at arms motioned them away then.

Staying in their lines, they brought the horses to the stables and dismounted. He let the stable master take the reins of his and stumped toward the barracks with the others. He was glad Kyi wasn't the one who took them because he really didn't want to see his friend just then, he didn't even want to see Cami.

****

Sir Alyn was standing before the soldiers' barracks with the other half of the soldiers' commissions. He was smiling proudly at them all as he handed them out. "The king instructed me to give you all the afternoon off to do with as you please."

This made them all but one cheer heartily.

Alyn saw that Dell was tense and wasn't smiling. The older soldier followed the younger one inside, stopped behind him and waited for him to pull the coverlet and armor off. "Did you dislike your first assignment, Boy?"

Dell's eyes shot up and he quickly said, "Yes, sir, I liked it very much."

"Then why the long face? Did you not get to see your friend?"

"I did actually," he said as he pulled the sword the older soldier had lent him and held it out, "I have commissioned his master to forge me a sword, which he plans to have to me at the bazaar the end of next week. I just…"

"It can be hard to adjust to being back at the castle sometimes. We can send you out on another mission straight away if you like?"

A part of Dell wanted to say yes. He knew it would be better for him, and Anya, to put distance between them, but he would miss out on seeing Wayde if he left now. He wanted to see his best friend again and he needed to see the princess one more time first, for his own heart and peace of mind. "Thank you, my lord. Maybe in a few weeks, but I think I would like to remain here for a time."

"Very well. Since you are staying, there is to be a Feat of Arms tournament the last day of the bazaar, after the craftsmanship awards. There is a young knight from Castle Delmsley entered in it that I have been wanting to put in his place for many years. I might just could with you."

"Me?"

"We have very few who are as good at hitting targets from horseback as you."

"A tournament?"

"Aye, show your prowess on a horse and on foot with a sword. Be lots of young ladies in the audience… drooling," said the sergeant at arms winking.

There was only one young lady he wanted to watch him. "Does the king and queen and… any of their guests come to watch?"

Alyn's eyes lit. He wondered if Dell had taken a fancy to the princess' friend, Ashlynn. She was only slightly higher in society than he was and he was rising fast so the gap would close quickly enough. "Aye, they typically do."

"I would be interested then."

"Very well, we will start to run you through the games in the morning then."

"Might I be able to procure a bath after, sir?"

"Yes, I think we could arrange something for you."

"Thank you," said Dell.

The older man nodded then turned and left the barracks.

Kept to the Shadows

32

A Rose By
Any Other Name

The princess had thought about using the back halls of the castle to get to her aunt's room for their planned meeting to avoid her cousin but decided against it. She didn't want to run into him in any of them. Few wandered the back halls so there would be no one to come to her aid if she was to need it. So instead she walked along the main hall, hoping he had heard their aunt saying the time for her to be in her rooms so he wouldn't try to hold her up if she did see him on her way there.

She was going over the things her mother told her she would be learning and the skills she already knew and would be polishing in her mind as she approached the queen's chambers. She already knew most of what she needed to, her retinue and tutors had seen to that, but she needed to show the queen her skills to get approval to be introduced into society properly. She practiced her walk as she came upon the doors, being certain each foot completely met the floor before moving the next, keeping her posture straight, her head up and her eyes forward. She took a deep breath as she reached the door then gently tapped on it with the first knuckle of the index finger of her right hand.

The door opened to the face of a girl about the princess' age. She smiled, curtsied and said, "Hello, Princess Anya. I am Queen Vela's first lady-in-waiting, Kera. Please come in."

Anya nodded and stepped past the girl.

Vela was sitting in a mauve colored wingback chair by the grand fireplace; a small fire was burning inside it – giving off ample heat. Another chair was set beside it, which would be for the princess. An off-white linen towel, a bone hoop, many colors of thread and an embroidery needle were setting on a table between the chairs. This told the girl her first lessen was to be embroidery, which she didn't particularly like but was good enough at. Anya stepped up to the chair, dropped into a curtsy and said, graciously, "Queen Vela."

"Rise, Child," said the queen. "You may address me as aunt, Niece."

"Thank you Aunt Vela."

Vela motioned for the girl to take the empty chair then. "Was your trip here serene?"

"It was."

"And the soldiers were all courteous?" asked the queen.

Anya jumped at that, she wondered if Tish had spoken to the queen. "Yes, Aunt, they were all very courteous. The commander, Weatherby, was on top of all our needs and was very quick to see to anything that arose unexpectedly."

"Very good, I will report his affability to the king... And, the others?"

"The others?" asked Anya, swallowing hard. "I am unsure what exactly you are asking?"

"There were many new to the king's guard and this was their first assignment. I am only wondering how they handled themselves."

"They were as courteous as the commander. I have no complaints at all in them, Aunt Vela," said the girl.

Vela could tell, by how the girl jumped that there was more to her answer than she had verbalized. She didn't want to frighten her only make sure that she knew she could speak out if one or more of the soldiers had said or done anything to make her feel uncomfortable.

"I was young once, Niece. I had to go on trips without my parents before as well and can remember the hours of having nothing to entertain me except watching the soldiers in my escort party make fools of themselves. I am certain they did not realize how loud they had been at times or that I had heard some of the comments made in regards to my person. I know too that it was only said in jest but if a girl were insecure in her place it could be construed as… being said with intent or… with malice."

Anya stiffened her shoulders and said, "I heard nothing of the kind said about me, nor any member of my party, Aunt."

Vela was also trying to nip any possible attractions in the bud before they had a chance to sprout or grow any further. "I had more than a few that could turn the head of any warm blooded woman as well… the armor makes them look quite grand and stately… and they have been known to work out while on long trips, sometimes in very little attire. It is not unheard of for a young princess to find herself taken with their acts of valor which are most often only done in the course of their duty."

Anya could feel her face flushing a little. An image of Dell wearing very little flickered before her mind's eye. She had never lied to her aunt but she didn't want to get Dell into trouble. She looked at her feet.

"I do not need to remind you that you are to be promised to my son, Anya. I also do not need to remind you that it is essential for your virtue to remain until your wedding night."

"I promise my virtue is intact, Aunt."

"I never doubted that, Niece." Vela knew what she said next would surprise the girl but she wanted her to know no matter what she could always come to her if she needed a friendly ear and shoulder. "I'm not a fool, Anya. I know of my son's indiscretions, and I know they are likely well known to you as well... I know how difficult it can be when you feel you are being forced into a marriage you did not want with someone you would not have chosen on your own... I cannot say that life with my son will be easy but it is what you were born to do and it expected of you. You must resign yourself to this."

Anya wanted to tell her aunt she didn't want to marry her son but she didn't dare to – for the insult to her and the king of not wanting to be wed to their flesh and blood, nor at what it could mean for her family's name and her status in the court.

"I want you to know that you are free to say or tell me anything that ever causes you any ill. I want you to think of this castle as your home as long as you are inside it, and after..."

"Thank you, Aunt Vela," said the girl, hoping the woman would drop the issue.

"I know how attractive a chance to escape a fate you are anxious about may look... I never had the need or the desire, I grew to love my husband very quickly, and I am in no way condoning the act... but... if you were to find you have... desires that are not being met... it's not considered entirely inappropriate to request a certain soldier be assigned as your personal guard... I recommend it be done discretely though… and any acts done after be discrete as well."

Anya blushed a little at her aunt's obvious implication. The thought of being able to be with Dell, even if it was only as clandestine lovers, made her blood warm. She smiled a little in spite of herself.

Seeing how the girl blushed and the secret smile on her lips told Vela that anything said or done between her niece and the young handsome soldier had been mutual. She knew her niece would never risk her place in the kingdom and he very much wanted to impress her husband and wouldn't risk his future even for her niece – neither would want to risk the repercussions – so she decided to let the subject drop. She would let her niece think over what she had said and see if she came to her herself with anything that may have taken place. "Let us see how well you have been practicing your embroidery."

"Yes, Aunt Vela," said Anya. She took the towel, placed the hoop over it and clasped the inner and outer rings together to pull the cloth tight. She chose a soft pink thread and began to stitch a rough outline of a rose into the fabric.

It was about two hours later when the queen spoke again. She put her hand out to see the progress her niece was making. She was pleased to see an open rose blossom in three shades of pink with three green leaves bordering it on the fabric. It was done very well; she only found one place where the stitch was a little too tight. "Very nice, Niece," said Vela.

"Thank you, Aunt," said Anya, pleased that she had pleased the woman.

33

Espionage

The next morning came quickly for Dell. He had jumbled up dreams all night and jolted himself awake several times. A few of those times with tears streaming down his face. He managed to keep the other soldiers in the barracks from seeing this by being out in the field before the sun was up.

He was using one of the practice swords on the straw men constructed for this very thing. He was about to take a hearty swing, which likely would have taken the poor stand-in's head off, when he heard his name. He lowered the sword and turned around to find Alyn behind him.

"Why are you up so early, Boy?"

"Too full of energy, I suppose," said Dell.

"Hard to get used to the cots again, ain't it. They typically ain't so very comfortable but feel like heaven compared to the hard ground sometimes," said Alyn, speaking from personal experience.

This wasn't it at all but Dell only nodded and said, "Got that, sir."

"You got enough energy left to begin training for the Feat of Arms?"

"I do."

"Alright, go get your horse and I will get a few of the other men up to assist us."

Dell found the doors of the stable wide open but no sign of either of its hands or any of the horses. He guessed then they had them in the corral. He was just turning to find out when he was all but barreled over by a wheelbarrow so full of hay he couldn't see who was pushing it.

"Whoa!" he shouted before he was run over.

"Who's there?"

"It's me, Kyi."

"Dell?" asked the boy as he set down the handles of the barrow and stepped around the heaving pile of dried grass. "I didn't expect anyone to be here. You just got back… you don't have to go out already, do you?"

"No. Sir Alyn wants me to enter the Feat of Arms at the Mid-summer Bazaar so I wanted Sledge to do some training on."

Kyi got a weird look on his face for a second, then he said, "I have got to get this to the corral. Follow me."

Dell wanted to offer to take the wheelbarrow for Kyi, watching him struggling to keep it from tipping over, but he didn't for three reasons: first, he could get into trouble for doing the boy's work for him, second, the boy could get in trouble for not doing the work, and third, and the bigger reason, he knew his friend would take it as an insult. Kyi often got picked on and beaten up at the home, for being smaller than most of the boys his age. Dell and Wayde had both offered to defend him but he always refused, saying it would only make it worse. Dell guessed he was right but it had been hard to watch him getting hit so often only to stick to his convictions.

Finally, after the boy had to stop more than once to adjust his grip, the two reached the fencing that penned in the horses.

"Would you mind getting the latch on the gate for me?" Kyi asked Dell, not wanting to set the wheelbarrow down.

The soldier quickly went to it.

Kyi grunted a thank you and pushed the fast toppling barrow through it.

Dell closed the gate behind his friend and watched him fumbling the single wheeled cart to the trough on the far side of the field where he finally allowed it to tip so he could pull out its contents and put it in the feed bins. He was about to lean on the railings, to wait for Kyi to finish and get him his horse when he heard voices.

He turned and saw the stable master talking to the lord that had been on the castle steps when the princess arrived. He didn't know either of the men well enough to form an opinion of their character but the fact that they were behind a building in the far side of the castle grounds, away from most eyes, would imply they were up to something nefarious. He looked for a reason to get closer and found it as Sledge began to come toward him.

He walked toward the horse and met him half-way, which put him five feet closer to the clandestine meeting. He smiled as the horse nudged him and began to stroke his head but he was doing this unconsciously, listening intently to what was being said not far from him.

"... I only did what I could, my lord."

"Still, we are very pleased," said Faelan.

"You will remember this when you are..."

"Sssttt," barked Faelan, looking around quick.

The stable master nodded and said, "Yes, well, as long as my part is remembered."

"It will be, sir."

The stable master bowed deeply to the lord then.

The look on lord's his face implied he thought the stable master was no better than the horse dung they were standing beside but the stable master didn't see this, nearly bent in half bowing to him. It made Dell want to go over and ring the nobleman's neck. He may have a higher standing in society but inside he was no better than any of them. He wondered what it was the stable master had done that he wished to have remembered and what he had been about to say for when he wanted it to be remembered. Something told him neither was anything good.

"I see Sledge found you," said Kyi as he came up beside Dell.

"He did," said Dell, smiling at the horse as it nudged him for more attention.

"Did you want him tacked?"

"I would, yes."

Kyi nodded and put the bridle he had in his hands over the horse's eager head then led him toward the gate he had brought the hay through.

34

Training

Dell led the horse to the tournament field beside the castle; anxious to find out what this Feat of Arms was all about. He found Alyn, the king's advisor, Dulmuth, the lord he'd just been listening to behind the outbuilding and most of the soldiers waiting for him.

"Dell, my boy," said Alyn when he saw him.

"Yes, Sir Alyn," said Dell, dropping to his right knee.

Alyn waved him to stand up. "This is Lord Dulmuth, the king's personal advisor, and Lord Faelan, son of Lord Durbaith of Arrachsnow," said the sergeant at arms.

Dell dropped to his knee again and said, "It is my pleasure, my lords."

Dulmuth smiled at the sincerity of this greeting.

Faelan frowned.

"Rise, soldier," said Dulmuth. "Sir Alyn, here, says he thinks we can beat Lord Benner of Delmsley with you, what do you say to this?"

"I have never seen Lord Benner in action, my lord, so I cannot say, but I will try my best, in the name of the king."

Dulmuth and Alyn both looked impressed with this answer.

Faelan frowned deeper.

"The Feat of Arms consists of three parts. First is the rings, second a show of prowess with a sword and third the joust," said Dulmuth.

Dell nodded, he knew how to do the first and second well enough.

"Since you only need training in jousting, and to loosen up the horses, we will run them first," said the sergeant at arms, seeing that Dell's horse was picking up on some of the young soldier's anxiety and wanting to use it.

"Prince Faelan has offered to stand in for Benner. He has seen the man fight before and has said he will run the games as if he were the man. A warning to you, Young Dell, he has a tendency to not fight fair," said Dulmuth.

Faelan gave the advisor a sideways glance, wondering if the man had meant that intentionally as an insult to him as well as to Benner.

Dell hadn't missed the wording either. "If it would please you, my lords," said the boy bowing. He would enjoy getting to show the lord up, thinking again of how he had looked at Anya, and jealous that he could do it without having his eyes at risk of being plucked out.

Faelan let the statement drop. He was in too good a mood to let it drag him down; all his plans were falling neatly into place. Getting to show this up-start serf up before the sergeant at arms and the king's advisor would be very enjoyable. It would've been even more so if he could be doing it before the king, Acthiel and Princess Anya, but he would take what opportunities he was given.

"I promise to go easy on you, Boy."

"Pardon my speaking freely, my lord, but I would prefer you to come at me with all you have," said Dell

Dulmuth and Alyn looked surprised and pleased by this request.

Faelan frowned even deeper still.

****

Leb walked up to Dell with what looked like a one-sided armor breastplate. He motioned him to lift his right arm so he could attach the shoulder and neck guard to his chest under it.

"Have you ever seen a joust before, Boy?" asked Alyn.

"No, but I have read about them in books."

"Yes, well…" said Alyn. He was suddenly not so sure he wanted the soldier to do this, realizing he could get hurt.

"Has Prince Faelan ever fought in the Feat of Arms before?"

"No, he was a knight from birth so he has no need for the advancement one can get from winning the tournament."

"But he is an experienced jouster?"

"That he is."

"So, what do I need to know?"

"The object is to knock your opponent off his horse. You get a point if you flatten him to his horse's back and a point if you break your lance on his guard. If you can knock him from the horse entirely you will win the joust no matter how many points the other has."

"Are there any rules?"

"Only not to get knocked off yourself. Otherwise, anything goes. Most knights will not try to harm their opponents but Benner has a reputation for trying to do as much damage as he can before he finishes his off – wanting them humiliated as much as bested."

"Lord Dulmuth said Prince Faelan has seen the way Lord Benner fights?"

"On many occasions. I get the feeling he plans to reenact much of what he has seen of the other man's moves as well."

Dell suddenly wasn't so sure he wanted to be doing this but he had never been a quitter so he climbed into the jousting saddle Leb had just put on Sledge's back.

"Keep your shoulder stiff and your head down so your throat isn't exposed," said the other soldier.

"Thanks, Leb," said Dell. The soldier-serf turned his horse and started for the other side of the field.

Dell was just getting his horse into position when he heard intakes of breathe from the soldiers watching them. He turned in his saddle to see why. He too drew in a surprised breath as he watched Queen Vela, Princess Anya, her friend and her retinue walk up the stairs to the raised dais.

On any other day he would have been happy to see Anya watching him training, even though he wouldn't be able to speak to her, or kiss her, or hold her, but not this one. He was about to attempt a feat he hadn't mastered, against a man who obviously felt he needed to be reminded of his low station in life. He could not back out of it now – if he did he would be insulting Lord Faelen and he would be disappointing and embarrassing the captain of the guard. The former he could not care less about doing, he would die before he did the latter. He tried to ignore the princess but he could feel her eyes boring into him.

The sound of the trumpets calling their attention to the field of play made him jump and reminded him he had to do this whether he wanted to or not.

****

At the same time, Nox was assisting Faelan with his armor.

"Do you know much of this… soldier?" Faelan asked the guard, indicating his opponent, as the man tightened the strap of his armor.

Nox wasn't sure what exactly the lord was asking. "Not well, my lord. He is only a few weeks into the king's service."

"Sir Alyn seems quite taken with him."

"He has made a name for himself by way of having good skills with a sword, my lord," Nox couldn't help but say this with much admiration. He truly liked Dell.

Faelan picked up on this as well. "Sir Alyn did not say to which city he is from. Who is his father?"

"He has none, my lord. He is one of the turnouts."

"An orphan?"

"Yes, my lord."

This made Faelen smile. This soldier boy was truly no real threat to him them. Still, he would show him what it got him to aspire to being an equal.

* * * * * * * * * * * * * * * * * * *

The two men climbed onto their horses and took the long wooden pole weapons the men handed them. Faelan, already knowing what to do, hoisted his lance into his armpit, turned his horse and started for the far end of the field. Dell was trying hard to find the balance point of the long pole and get a decent grip on the handle of it.

The men were about fifty feet from each other and their animals were trotting in place, anxious to be moving. Both looked to the sergeant at arms and king's advisor for the signal to begin.

Alyn said a silent prayer Dell wasn't injured then raised his arm and slowly lowered it.

Faelan lowered the shield of his helmet and kicked his horse hard in the flanks with the sharp heels of his boots. The animal screamed out then reared up and bolted forward.

Dell lowered his face guard as well but he didn't need to abuse Sledge to get him moving. The boy and horse had been training together so much that a simple squeeze of his thighs told his mount what he wanted. He clutched the wood pole tight in his armpit, tried to brace his chest and lock his shoulder.

They met about the center of the field.

Dell had no way to know how it was going to feel when the blunted end of his opponents weapon collided with him so, needless to say, he wasn't ready for the piercing pain that shook him all the way through the thick plate armor covering the part of his chest it had hit. The pain continued through the rest or his chest muscles, his ribs, shoulder blade and spine, which felt a bit like someone was playing it like a xylophone at that moment. He had no idea how powerful a hit it was going to be either. His left hand released the lance, which fell to the ground, almost tripping Sledge up and his left arm flew up and back – almost pulling it from its socket. His right hand, which had been twisted in the pommel of the saddle, clamped tight, trying to keep him in the saddle.

His brain was screaming that he would lose if he fell from his saddle. This kept him from being on his face in the mud of the field below his horse but it didn't keep him sitting up in the saddle. He was lying over on his back in a position that threatened to rip his right arm from its socket and made it hard to breathe. He tried to pull himself back up but the weight of the armor was preventing it.

Leb and Nox ran over to Dell.

****

Leb managed to avoid the still dancing horse and picked up the lance while Nox grabbed the reins, pulled them to get the horse to stand still and helped Dell back up.

"Uhhh, Gah... I... I ca... I can't breathe," cried Dell, pounding on the armor plating that was dented into his chest from the hit. As the men helped him off the horse his eyes went to the queen and Princess – the pain in his chest was back with a vengeance when he saw that both looked less than happy. He wanted to run away in shame then.

Nox loosened the strap of the armor and lifted it off enough to allow Dell to take a breath.

"Do you wish to call this off?"

Dell looked over at Prince Faelan then. He had a pompous smile on his face that said he was expecting him to want to call this off. He saw the prince's lance tip, which was supposed to be kept up if he was staying in play, was hovering over a fresh pile of horse dung before him. He watched the man stick the end of it into the excrement and twist it back and forth so it got well coated, letting him know he intended it to be transferred to him with the next hit, thus muddying him. Then, if that wasn't enough, he watched him walk his horse over to the queen and princess and put his hand out to take Anya's.

Dell watched him lean forward, kiss her hand and hold his lips on her skin longer than was appropriate, unless the two were betrothed. He knew she was required to comply but it looked to him like she wanted to as well. He saw her eyes start to come up, perhaps to look at him, to see if he was watching her, then drop to her feet.

Feeling a heat light in his belly, Dell looked at Leb and said, "*Give me the blasted lance.*"

"You don't want to go into this angry, Dell," said Nox.

"Tighten the strap," Dell demanded through clenched teeth.

****

Faelan was smiling sickly as he watched the boy fighting to get himself back up from the hard hit he had given him. He stepped his horse around a pile of fresh droppings, not wanting it to get on the horse's hoof and cause the animal to slip, then smiled even bigger as he stuck the tip of the lance into the steaming pile and twisted it around to coat it well. He knew this was an insult that could get even him punished but he doubted the king's advisor would dare and knew for certain the sergeant at arms wouldn't. He looked around to be sure no one was going to point out his indiscretion and saw the queen and princess were in the dais. He hadn't noticed them arriving as the first run started. He couldn't believe his luck this day.

Faelan lifted the lance quickly, knowing the queen was one that would very much love to punish him for this intended insult against the other soldier. She had never tried to hide how little she liked him.

He walked his horse over to greet the ladies. "Good day "Aunt Vela, Cousin Anya, I am pleased you have come out to watch me," said the lord arrogantly. He was doing this partly out of custom but mostly to remind the upstart soldier that he would never be anything but a serf, which meant he would never be allowed to openly speak to the ladies himself. This was almost as much fun as the intended smearing would be.

"We heard Sir Alyn was running some of the men through training for the upcoming Feat of Arms and thought a show of support to the soldiers in training would be appreciated. The king certainly would've been here if he was in the castle," said the queen.

She was surprised to see the young solder, the same one she had been discussing, in a roundabout way, with her niece just a few hours before was on a horse across from them, trying to get a feel for the lance.

"Indeed, I am certain you are correct, Aunt Vela," said the prince. He shifted his eyes to his cousin then but not to her face, as was proper, they were boring holes in the bodice of her dress. Faelan removed his glove and stuck his hand out to her, knowing that she couldn't refuse the gesture. He took her delicate hand in his and leaned forward to kiss it when she did. He left his lips against her silky skin, smelling the rose scented soap she used in her morning bath and the soft perfume she was wearing. He could feel her tensing up in his grip but he didn't release her hand. In doing this he was also reminding her of her place, which was beside him and the queen not in the arms of an orphaned soldier serf.

He did finally remove his lips and release her hand, but only because he could see the queen about to speak about his ill manners. He sat up straight in his saddle, put his glove back on and said, "Wish me luck on this pass, my lady, Princess?"

Anya only grunted in response.

Faelan was in too good a mood to let her insult bother him just then. He glanced over at the soldier boy, expecting to see him all but in tears from the hit he'd just given him, physically and metaphorically. He was a little annoyed and surprised to see him take the lance from the soldier beside him brusquely and watched the other tightening the strap on his armor telling him the boy thought he was ready to try again. He smiled; he would enjoy ramming the dung-covered end of his lance into the soldier-serf's face on this next pass.

****

Anya felt her heart leap into her throat and do many flips when she saw Dell sitting on his horse on the other side of the field. She hadn't expected to see him. Her heart stopped when she saw him and her cousin both being outfitted in jousting armor. She wondered why the sergeant at arms was having them do this instead of the usually horse training. She heard one of the soldiers standing at the railing before her say Dell should feel honored Sir Alyn had asked him to train for the Feat of Arms and got her answer. She had little doubt Faelan was looking to do more than just assist in training though.

She wanted to tell the queen of her cousin's improper acts to her, hoping her aunt would be appalled enough to have him taken away in chains right then. She didn't want to embarrass Dell though. She could see how determined he was to run this joust in how stiff he was sitting in the saddle. She guessed he was doing this partly to feel like more than an indentured soldier-serf. She couldn't take the moment away from him.

She saw him notice her and saw the look of joy on his face turn to fear. She wanted badly to smile and wave to him to let him know he had no reason to be ashamed but knew she couldn't. She forced herself to keep her eyes down until the run began again.

She was leaning forward, clutching the railing with white knuckles as the two men began to move toward each other. She couldn't stop the squeal, grunt and whimper of pain coming out when she saw the tip of the lance hit Dell's chest. Luckily Ashlynn and Tish had made the same sound. She felt her heart squeeze painfully as she heard him cry out in pain and saw him drop the lance. She watched him struggling to get back up and didn't let herself breathe again until the armor had been loosened and she saw him take a breath. She saw him look over at her again then and saw only shame on his face. She wished she could tell him he had no reason to be.

She was just regaining her calm when she realized Faelan was moving toward her and her aunt. She tried to keep her face stoic as he made his snide comments to their aunt then saw his hand come out to her, asking her to offer him hers to kiss. She wanted to tell him not if her life depended on it but didn't. She let him have the customary gesture and tried to keep from cringing as his cold and far too wet lips came into contact with her skin.

"Wish me luck on this next pass, my lady, Princess?" he asked her.

She wanted to say she hoped he was knocked from his horse, right into the pile of horse dung she saw at his horse's feet but instead she only grunted.

****

"I don't like this," said Alyn. He jumped and cringed as if it was him that got hit instead of Dell. He could see the boy was struggling to sit himself back up in the saddle, the weight and stiffness of the armor making it all but impossible. He started to step forward, to go to his aid, when he saw Leb and Nox going to him.

"The boy needs to be able to handle worse than this if he is to be expected to protect the King, Alyn," said Dulmuth. He didn't like seeing Faelan abusing the soldier either but he knew the sergeant at arms had a soft spot for the boy and was letting that affection cloud his judgment. "He will get just as abused by Benner if he is to face him."

"He will have had more serious training by then, Dulmuth," snapped Alyn. "Faelan isn't looking to show him how to joust, he is looking to completely humiliate him," he said, pointing at what the prince was doing with his lance tip then watching him go over to the queen and princess, no doubt to rub in the fact that he was much higher in status than the boy, who would get hanged for even thinking of doing the same.

Dulmuth didn't like the statement Faelan was making by either act either but he didn't think it enough to stop the practice. He watched the boy soldier taking the lance back from the soldiers beside him and could see he wanted this to continue. "Dell seems ready for another try."

Alyn could have overruled the king's advisor and called the match off but he didn't want to embarrass the boy or grant the other man any accolades for his detestable actions. He settled himself back against the railing and prayed Dell would find his stride. He knew the boy had it in him he just had to have faith in him.

35

Tournament Etiquette

Dell was repeating *hold your shoulder stiff and keep your head down* in his head over and over. He knew the latter bit of advice was what he truly needed to remember, knowing the other man intended the dirtied lance to be rammed into his face if possible for the most possible insult.

He motioned to his opponent he was ready and saw him do the same. He watched the lord again kick his mount hard and painfully and squeezed his own thighs together only slightly to get Sledge to move. He was moving with the horse this time as they barreled toward the other man and horse. This time he had a trick up his sleeve.

Dell leaned to the side just as the brown stained lance tip was about to take him in the face shield of his helmet. He could feel the wind off the tip of it and smell the excrement dried onto it as it passed him by but it didn't make contact with him at all. A split second later he sat straight, tightened the grip on his own lance and pushed it forward slightly, it connected with the other man, surprising them both.

He was aiming for the guard over Faelan's right pectoral muscle, the same place as he had been hit the first run, but his aim was off. The man's head was up higher than it should've been, likely not figuring the soldier-serf would get near enough to him to hit him there, so his chin and throat were fully exposed. It was squarely on the end of the prince's chin that the tip connected. The lord fell back on his horse, dropped his lance and was struggling to get himself back up in his saddle now.

Faelan was spewing swears at the top of his lungs as he fought to right himself. Nox and Leb did go to him to assist but they took their time.

The prince grabbed the edge of his face guard, ripped it off his head and spit blood onto the ground just before the soldiers that were only there to try to help him. His ripped his glove off and his hand went to his jaw, finding the skin peeled raw.

"That insolent little bastard!" he growled.

He ignored the soldier that was holding his lance out to him and kneed his horse to go to Dulmuth and Sir Alyn.

"The boy struck me with malice and intention. He has no principles and is not following joisting etiquette," spat the lord.

"I myself saw only a fine move on his part, Lord Faelan. You know the stance, your neck was unprotected," said Dulmuth.

"He was trying to murder me," said the man, holding his bleeding chin up, showing that only a few inches lower and he likely would have had the lance tip through his throat.

"As you yourself pointed out, my lord Faelan, the boy is inexperienced. He was likely aiming for your chest," said Alyn.

Faelan wanted to argue further but knew he really had no argument so he turned back, took the lance Nox was still holding to him and moved up for the final pass.

****

Dell wanted to laugh when he saw Faelan go immediately to Alyn and the king's advisor, like a whiney little baby, but he held it back. He wasn't certain they wouldn't take the lord's side. He relaxed when he saw Faelan huff and turn his mount then the sergeant at arms wink at him.

"The score is tied, one each," said Leb as he handed Dell a new lance, the shaft of the one he had just hit Faelan with was now too unbalanced due to the force of the hit. "If you can get another hit or knock him over you will take the match."

Dell very much wanted to but he knew the lord was already very upset and would take even more unkindly to that so he would let the prince take the match, taking the man's intended hit without trying to avoid it. No matter what his opinion of the man was he was a lord by right and the king's nephew. He wasn't looking to gain any favors, except he didn't want to lose the king's respect. He didn't want to lose the queen's either or be further humiliated before Anya but he feared Faelan's wrath more. It mattered little to him who won this match, being as it was only a practice match.

He took the lance from Leb and started Sledge to the edge of the field again.

Faelan mouthed the words, 'Your dead!' before he lowered his face guard.

Dell didn't react; he had been threatened idly before.

The two men and their animals sped toward each other.

The soldier-serf waited until the man's lance was just about upon him then he laid back, letting the tip of the weapon only slide over the outer casing of his armor. This time he was more limber so he needed no assistance sitting back up. He slowed Sledge down and turned to face the opponent and the two men watching them.

****

Faelan was sitting slightly forward in his saddle, his head well down, not intending to let the idiot have another try at him there. His lance was aimed for the idiot's head, intended to not only knock him off his horse but also to knock his head off.

He was surprised and angered when he watched the serf lay back on his horse just as the lance was reaching him, essentially throwing the run. He looked over his shoulder in time to see him stop his horse and turn it to face him in defiance, not dropping from his saddle and bowing to him as winner.

He pulled his face guard up and again went to the elder soldiers, this time boiling with rage.

"He has *openly* insulted me this time. He did not even attempt to joust and he did not go to his knee to show respect for my win," spat the spoiled lord.

Alyn was having a hard time keeping a straight face, he knew he had to reprimand Dell for this insult but he also knew the boy well enough by now to know he'd take the punishment with pleasure for having gotten to embarrass the insolent lord this way – before the queen and princess.

"Again, my lord, Price Faelan, he is not trained in the manners of a knight. We will inform him of his error in judgment to be certain he does not offend and insult any of the knights he will be facing at the *actual* Feat in a few weeks," said Dulmuth, thoroughly enjoying it himself.

"But… he…" there was nothing Faelan could do, this was nothing but a practice run so the rules and manners of a tournament didn't actually apply. He huffed again and moved aside.

Alyn was still having a hard time containing himself as he waved Dell in.

The boy could tell his master was trying hard not to laugh and smiled as he nudged the horse to go to him. He kept his eyes lowered, as was proper as he came up beside the lords.

Faelan waited for Dell to remove his helmet then he said, "You stupid upstart…"

"Dell," said Alyn over Faelan.

"Yes, my lord," said Dell, he really didn't want to get his tongue lashing right in front of the lord, or within hearing range of Anya, even though he knew he deserved it.

"We are aware that you are unfamiliar with the ways of the tournament, Dell. Please take note in the future, if this were an actual tournament, like the Feat of Arms, what you did that last round would have lost you all your points up to that moment or gotten you disqualified entirely."

Dell had not known this. He was surprised he wasn't more upset with himself for the unintended insult. "Yes, my lord," said Dell, trying to sound humbled.

"And not dropping from his steed to bow to the winner," spat Faelan, seeing Alyn about to start a new discussion point.

"Yes, Lord Faelan. Dell, you also must remember that in the case you should lose at the actual Feat of Arms you are to immediately drop from your mount and go down on your right knee. You remain in that stance until the lord has made his round of the field to allow the audience to congratulate their victor and has returned to your side and released you," said Dulmuth.

"Yes, my lords. Please forgive my lack of manners, Prince Faelan. I will make certain, if you and I ever joust again, that I do all exactly as the rules and protocols require," said Dell, as he dropped from his horse then and went down on his right knee before them.

Faelan was angered by the soldier-serf's obvious mocking and again by the other lords' lack of concern of his feelings but he didn't dare say anything more on the subject or he would look like he was a sore winner.

"Alright, now let us see how you do with the rings," Alyn said to Dell with excitement, he knew the boy would be hard to beat in this action if he rode as he knew he could.

"Would Lord Faelan like to stay and challenge the soldier or should we choose another?" asked Dulmuth.

"I will stay in."

36

A Natural

Alyn motioned for Leb to set up the poles holding the largest size targets, then he looked at Dell. "You run the length of the field collecting as many rings as you can then a size smaller is put up and you run again, then one final run with the smallest size, the one who collects the most rings is the winner. Do you wish to go first, Lord Faelan?"

Faelan could do this in his sleep so he simply nodded, moved his horse to the far end of the field and waited for the signal to begin.

The prince raced his horse tight along the wall and brought the tip of the lance down just as he reached the first ring, he took it in the center with no effort, he missed the next two because the horse stumbled in the mud their jousting had created but got the fourth, fifth and sixth easily enough.

It wasn't his best run but he was pleased with it.

Dulmuth looked that way as well.

He waited for the soldier to set the next size down and started off again. This time he got all six.

The final set was put in place and Faelan kicked his horse into action, he missed the first two because the animal was caught off guard, but got the last four easily.

He was feeling quite proud, there were few who could get any of the last and smallest set of rings, and to have gotten fourteen rings in all was excellent. He had little doubt the insolent soldier-serf would be lucky to get half that. He rode over to the queen and princess, intending to point out each and every tiny flaw in the other man's riding ability, timing, and aim.

"That was a fine run, Lord Faelan," said Queen Vela, for all she didn't like her nephew it was actually. She was willing the soldier boy to get at least one more ring than he had though.

Princess Anya was also willing Dell as much luck as she could.

Dell didn't need any of their willed luck. He and his horse were like one, easily moving down the field. The mud beneath his feet didn't bother Sledge at all; he simply coasted over it. He took all six of the first round, all but one of the second, and that was because the sun going down flashed in his eyes, temporarily blinding him, and all six of the final and hardest set.

Faelan was beyond flabbergasted, the queen, Dulmuth, Anya and Alyn were all beaming.

Dell knew what he had just done had been an even bigger personal affront to Faelan than throwing the final round of the joust but he wasn't going to disappoint Alyn by downplaying his prowess in this Feat. He knew the sergeant at arms knew he should have no problem with it. He slowly trotted Sledge over to the lords, lady and queen and bowed to them from atop his horse.

"Fine show, Soldier," said Dulmuth.
Alyn was only smiling proudly.
"You and your horse ride as if you are one," said Queen Vela.
Anya was blushing deeply then, wishing she were Dell's horse.
"Thank you my lady, Queen," said Dell, bowing again.

His eyes quickly went to Anya then left her just as. His heart leapt in his chest when he saw the sweet smile on her face and the slight pinkness to her cheeks. He remembered some of what he had overheard the female castle workers saying while they were watching him in his training, how arousing it was to see him and the horse moving so in-sync, and felt a heat rising in his belly at the thought that he might have aroused her watching him just now.

"It is getting late. I think we can forego the swordplay this day. I am already confident in the boy's ability in that feat. He obviously can do the rings well enough. So we need only to focus on the jousting – perfect his skills there. What say you, Lord Dulmuth?"

"I say, I think King Vianor could not have chosen better himself and I have little doubt he would approve of him as the representative of the castle at the games."

Dell felt himself blushing to this.

"Take your steed and Lord Faelan's back to the stable and meet me at the barracks," said Alyn.

"Aye, my lord," said Dell quickly. He could see the look of hatred in Faelan's eyes as he dropped from his horse and held the reins out to him. Dell was in too high of spirits to let him bring him down. He took them, thanked the lord, bowed again to the others then turned his animal and led the other away.

****

Dell was still feeling giddy as he walked from the stables to the barracks. When he saw the sergeant at arms standing before it with his hands on his hips and his jaw set he knew he hadn't gotten out of insulted the lord quite so easily.

"I do not need to remind you of what insulting a lord will get you, do I Dell?" asked Alyn through the smile he was trying desperately to hide as Dell walked toward him.

"No, my lord," said Dell humbly. He had known he was going to get a lecture and was ready to take it, pleased it was being done in private.

"Faelan is the worst possible lord to insult as well, Boy. He is next in line for the throne if, the gods forbid, anything was to happen to King Vianor and Prince Acthiel." Alyn had to keep from saying the prince's name with distaste, knowing there wouldn't be all that much difference if Faelan took the throne in place of the current crown prince.

Dell had not known this. He grumbled to himself at how stupid he had been. "I did not. I really didn't mean to…"

Alyn gave him a hard look and said, "I understand your reasons, Dell. I was not always a knight. I had to cater to and kowtow to men like Faelan to get where I am. I am not saying he did not have it coming, I'm only saying to choose whom and how you insult high-bloods carefully."

Dell nodded, knowing that was very sound and well-meaning advice.

"Now, you asked for a bath after the training earlier, you still up for that?"

"Yes, sir, I would like one still."

"Very good, go on to the bathhouse then and tell the attendant I gave you permission," said the older knight, patting the younger one on the shoulder.

"Yes, sir, thank you," said Dell. He turned then and jogged toward the door the man had indicated.

Kept to the Shadows

37

Principles and Breeding

Dell was working his pectoral and shoulder muscles where the lance tip hit him under the hot water. He was surprised he didn't have a bruise, or at least not on the outside. He guessed he was bruised deep in his muscle by the tightness of it though. The heat in the tub was helping it and to relieve the built up tension. He couldn't relax the way he really wanted to because he could smell the scent of roses wafting in through the open window of the chamber.

He was trying hard not to let the smell conjure the thoughts it was giving him but it was hard not to. It had been four days since he and Anya had kissed yet it was still so vivid to him, every time he closed his eyes and licked his lips. He felt tears welling up and splashed some of the very warm water into his face to stop them.

He decided the bath wasn't helping him as much as he had hoped it would.

Dell was getting out of the tub when the water boy stepped in with a fresh bucket of hot water.

"Pardon me, sir, are you finished?"

"Yes, I think I am."

The boy set down the bucket, took the towel from the stool beside the door and passed it to the soldier.

Dell thanked him and began to dry off.

The boy emptied the bucket down a chute that would empty into the troughs beside the kitchen then went to close the window. "Lovely evening outside, sir. What with the full moon, it's almost like daytime."

"Yes, it appears to be," said Dell. "The garden beyond, is it for royal use only?"

"No, sir, they are open to the public. Not many use them though, which is a pity."

"Thank you."

Dell laid the towel on the stool beside the tub then pulled on his trousers and his tunic, the top garment left untucked. He ran his hands through his disheveled hair as he went down the back stairs and stepped out into the garden.

He followed the gravel path a little ways then stopped on a bit of a knoll. He could see most of the garden from the high point; it was nearly five times the size of the one at the inn in Pemberley and close to fifty times bigger than the one he had started at Abbeydrew.

He could still remember how surprised the wardkeepers at the home had been when he asked if he could start the small garden patch. Many thought he would be interested in nothing but causing pain because of his size and how well he did with the sword in the competitions they had held between the homes.

That garden had only one rose bush, two azaleas, some perennial flowers and a lopsided bench he built out of leftover and spare lumber and was actually more just an oversized flower-bed – still, it had made him feel good. He wondered who was tending to it now. He knew Sister Jessa thought it was nice as well since he had happened on her on the bench reading a book more than once when he went out to weed or trim the shrubs.

If he hadn't gotten to be a soldier he thought he likely would have asked for something in gardening.

He took a deep breath and was hit with the smell of fresh cut grass and an even stronger scent of roses, as well as that of magnolias, which made his heart hurt worse.

He slowly walked along the gravel path in awe, looking at all the different colors of roses. He saw several shades of reds, pinks and yellows, even a purple one – that one he had to stop and look closer at. He had never imagined there were so many different colors.

He was starting into a set of archways that had been created from dried grape vines with pale yellow climbing roses clinging to them when he heard the gravel ahead of him shifting. His heart skipped a beat as he thought it might be Anya then it sank, hoping it wasn't. He didn't think he could stand to see her again knowing he couldn't be with her.

He had been so happy earlier when he caught her looking at him, smiling and blushing after showing so well in the practice tournament, now he was only remembering again how far apart they were.

He could tell Faelan had enjoyed rubbing in that he could speak to her, hold her hand and kiss it without fear. He wondered if the man was just innately a bastard or if he knew of their attraction to each other. He hoped it was the former for Anya's sake.

He was about to turn around and go, not wanting to get either of them in trouble – it would be just his luck that Faelan or the queen herself would decide this evening to get some fresh air as well. The queen was likely not as easy to fool as Weatherby. The thought of getting to see Anya again was too much though.

He felt his heart sink even further than he thought it already was when he saw it was only her friend, Ashlynn, walking toward him. He hoped he hadn't grunted and sighed as loudly as it sounded like he had to himself.

He started to turn away when the girl called for him to stop. She was only a lesser noble's daughter but she was still above him, meaning he was at her beck and call as well. It was his duty as a soldier to find out what she wanted. He turned to her, lowered his eyes to the gravel and asked, "How may I be of service, my lady?"

"Are you the soldier named Dell?" she asked.

Dell wasn't sure if he should say yes or not. If she knew what he and Anya had done she was well within her rights to turn him in. He had never liked lying, even when it was to save his own neck. "Yes, my lady."

"I wasn't sure how I was going to do this," she said more to herself, looking around to be sure she wasn't being seen. "Princess Anya asked me to get this to you," she said as she took a piece of paper that had been folded up out of her scrip and held it out to him.

Dell gingerly took it from her. He wasn't sure how to respond. He was about to ask her if she knew what it said but she turned and walked away, back in the direction she had come from like it was something bad and she didn't want to be there to see his reaction or to wait for his response.

He watched her disappear then looked back at the piece of folded parchment. He wasn't sure if he wanted to know what it said. What if it was telling him it had all been a silly joke, or worse – that she felt he had violated her trust and was going to be telling her uncle, the king, upon his return so he should be ready to explain his actions, or, possibly even worse still – she *wasn't* joking, she had no intention of telling her uncle and still wanted him to take her away?

How would he handle any of those scenarios?

He was about to tear up the note without ever seeing, deciding it was better not to know, when he heard raised voices coming from the direction of the castle's inner bailey. He wasn't sure if there was a way from there to the gardens but guessed he could jump a wall if needed. As it turned out there was a gate, which brought him out just beyond the smokehouse.

He walked further into the yard and saw the king's advisor, Faelan and several soldiers talking to Alyn in front of the barracks. He quickly tucked his tunic in, stuffed the note under his belt, ran his fingers through his still damp hair and jogged over to them.

****

"What is it, sir?" asked Dell as he came up beside Alyn.

"Reports of bandits on the road through Bywood forest," said Alyn.

"Isn't that the route..."

"Aye, the king, prince and their party took," said Alyn.

"I want a group men made ready to depart in an hour," said the king's advisor.

"Aye, sir, I will have them before the steps," said Alyn, bowing to the man.

"I volunteer to go?" asked Dell, anxiously. He noticed the queen and princess had come to the steps behind him and could feel the younger woman's eyes on him, which warmed his heart and made it break at the same time.

"You only just returned, Young Dell, and you just tired yourself out in training earlier this very day. If we are to continue your jousting training in the morning, you will need to be rested," said Alyn.

"I am sworn to the king and prince's safety, if they could be in danger it is my duty to assist them not play at jousting, and no matter how rested I am, Sir Alyn."

Alyn smiled at the boy's determination. He was still going to say no when Faelan spoke.

"If the soldier wishes to go, then let him," said Faelan. "He was good enough in his joust with me that he will give Benner a good enough run for the award."

Both Alyn and Dulmuth looked at the prince oddly.

Faelan wasn't doing this on the boy's behalf, of course, he was doing it to get him out of the castle and away from the princess.

Alyn couldn't openly dispute this prince as more than he could have Acthiel. He said, though obviously distressed, "Very well, get suited up and be back out here in ten minutes."

Dell put his right fist over his heart and ran into the barracks. He was pulling the tunic off as he was going through the door.

****

Dell and nine others were waiting with Alyn ten minutes later, standing before the steps of the castle. Dulmuth, Faelan, the queen and the princess were there as well. The women both were looking worried, as was Dulmuth, Faelan only had a slight smirk on his face. In the king's absence it was Dulmuth and Faelan's place to approve of the choice.

The latter did so quickly, not especially caring who went.

The former looked them over closely before nodding.

"Godspeed to you and luck in finding the king and his entourage in good health," said Dulmuth to the men.

Dell's eyes went to the princess' as Dulmuth said this. He was surprised to see she was looking directly at him. He wanted to smile at her but he knew it wasn't appropriate, especially with the queen, Faelan and Dulmuth beside her, and since he had no idea what her note said. He thought his heart had stopped when he saw her mouth the words, 'please be careful' and watched her wiping tears from her eyes.

He wanted badly to see what the note said then but he couldn't.

He dropped to his right knee with the other soldiers then followed them and Alyn to the stable yard where the stable master and Kyi were waiting with their horses.

****

Anya wasn't sure what to do with herself; she was supposed to be meeting with her aunt for some lessons in managing the finances of a castle but worry of what the soldiers would find in the forest had upset her aunt too greatly and she had taken to her bed. Anya wasn't terribly upset by this; her mind wasn't really ready for anything that required mathematical skills just then herself. Worry for her uncle as well as what Dell might be riding into keeping her on edge.

She had gone out to the garden hoping it would help get her mind off things but it was only making them more profound.

She was leaning on the wall that surrounded it looking out at the castle courtyard all a bustle with activity. It was still being made ready for the king and his party's return – expecting Alyn and the soldiers with him only to act as escorts to keep them from being threatened by the bandits if they were about. She watched two people hugging in the yard beside the kitchen and felt an unusual desire to go and slap them. She really didn't wish them harm she was only jealous of them. They had no need for proper decorum, no need to keep their emotions in check so that no one saw they were a real person, no need to put on airs.

She had no idea who they were, other than obviously both castle workers. She could tell it was only a friendly hug but it still made her heart ache. Even her best friend, whom she had known since she was barely five, wouldn't hug her that way – in a way that they didn't expect anything in return except the show of affection. Only Dell had hugged her in that way, even knowing it could never go any further. He was the only one she really wanted to as well.

He had said he would never wish her less than what she was but she truly would give all this up to be just like the pretty blonde girl she was watching running for the kitchen door.

She turned from the view of the courtyard and began to walk along the path again, barely paying any attention to where she was going. She was out more for the fresh air than the gardens. She found the gazebo and started to step inside then stopped, it made her think of Dell and their far-too-short kiss. She wished he would appear before her now and do it again.

She placed one hand on her stomach, which was all of a sudden doing flips, the other she placed over her mouth, trying to stop the whimper of pain, fear and worry she wanted to let out. She hoped he wasn't riding into danger. She wasn't sure what she would do if anything were to happen to him. She turned from the wooden structure and started toward the fishpond instead. She caught her breath as she passed the last of the rose covered arches.

A man was standing in front of the small pond with his back to her, his wavy brown hair was blowing loosely in the gentle breeze and his cloak was pulled tight around him, showing a large build. She thought her heart was going to stop. She had Dell's name on her lips, about to ask if he had come back to the castle and was here to meet her as her note had asked. The man must have heard the gravel shifting beneath her feet because he looked up and turned to face her. It wasn't Dell.

****

"Hello, Princess Anya," said Faelan. His eyes traced her body; much as they had the day she arrived. This time they lingered on the areas that weren't covered with as much fabric as they had been then. He was enjoying the way the thinner fabric clung to her new shape.

The look he was giving her made Anya feel dirty. She wished she had the thick cloak her retinue thought she should wear no matter where she was or what the outdoor temperature was then instead of only the thin dress.

"May I say, I think your beauty has increased in the hours since we last saw each other?"

Anya fought the urge to sigh at how smarmy he was. "Thank you, my lord, but I am sure it is only the change in the light."

"Ever modest, as you should be," he teased. "We have not had time to speak, with all the excitement since you arrived. How was your trip here, Cousin? Must have been horrible for you to have no one but the soldiers to keep your attention," he said sneakily.

"I had my retinue and my friend with me," she reminded him, sounding more snide than she probably should have, given who he was.

"Oh, yes, I had forgotten them. I am pleased your parents thought to allow you the companions. I have had to travel with no one of my good acquaintance with me before; it's so tiring trying to be gracious to the soldiers who have no idea of anything but blood and swords."

Anya jumped a little, wondering if he knew about her and Dell. She tried to tell herself he was only trying to make polite conversation but knew he wasn't the kind for that and the look in his eyes was more like one that said he knew she had spoken to, and been spoken to by, someone that was beneath her. She prayed he didn't know, or hadn't figured it out, that she had also kissed and begged one of them to take her away and would have willingly done more. She guessed now the man hadn't only been trying to show up a serf in the training for the Feat of Arms. This man before her was one that would certainly string Dell up without any thought if he found a way to expose him. "I know nothing of their lives, my lord," she said curtly.

"As it should be. Death is something none of us should have to deal with but... if it is to keep us all safe and in our lives then it must be endured. I'm very pleased to see that the king has such a fine and loyal group of soldiers here to offer us protection from having to even think on the ugly subjects."

Anya tried to smile at the backhanded compliment her cousin had just given the king and his soldiers.

"There are quite a few new ones since last I was here. Some of them not much older than ourselves, yes?"

"I am sure that is true, I didn't particularly notice," said the girl, getting stiff again. She knew he was playing with her now.

"It is right that you didn't. I have often found it better not to speak to them any more than is necessary. It gives them thoughts and notions they can never hope to aspire to… No, it's better to let the serfs stay as what they are meant to be. I have tried to tell my father that it isn't fair to them to let them think they have anything more than they do."

"They have as much right as we do to be happy," said Anya.

"But they are, in their humble lives, don't you think? They have not the capacity to deal with the things we must, nor principles or breeding," said Faelan, enjoying this game.

"I have met some who have better principles than many of the lords I know, Lord Faelan," said Anya. She knew she was getting dangerously close to angering him and of confirming his accusations.

"Are we speaking of a specific serf or in generalities?" asked Faelan, getting a curious look on his face. "Perhaps a dark haired soldier that recently joined? Perhaps one that was part of your escort party? One that I noticed turned your cheeks a bit red when his eyes stopped on you briefly earlier at the tourney field, and again a few hours ago when he was preparing to go out after our uncle?"

"Pardon me?" asked Anya. She was angry that he would have the gall to ask her that question so directly, whether true or not it wasn't his place to even imply it. "I'm surprised you didn't wish to ride out with them, to greet our uncle and cousin. To be sure they are truly safe," she said snidely, thinking *and to take some of the glory from the young handsome soldier.*

"I would have only gotten in the way. No, it's better for Uncle Vianor to see how his new soldiers handle themselves. Give them a chance to make themselves better than their breeding, yes?"

Anya was tired of his teasing, she looked around quickly, hoping to see someone about, even one of the castle workers, whom she might could go and speak to, to get away from him.

"Tell me, Cousin," said Faelan as he stepped closer to her, seeing her starting to move away and not ready to end his game. "It's only the two of us here, no one else to hear what you say... That soldier-serf boy... he is quite well built, isn't he... I imagine a woman would find him very pleasing to look upon. Might there be some longing there? Have you found it hard to be so near to such a fine, young, handsome man?"

"Lord Faelan, I am sure I do not understand your question." Anya understood it perfectly, actually.

"It is only natural for you to get such urges... thoughts... and needs. Your body is coming alive, you are becoming a woman. You are no doubt getting desires you have never had before, perhaps, even now, as you stand so close to me? I would hate to see you learning of them with one that isn't worthy of you... Not only because of what it will do to your position but what it would do to the poor serf, who would certainly lose his commission if not his head for it."

"I assure you I am having no such feelings, Lord Faelan, and I would appreciate it if you would not discuss this further. I would rather not have to inform my aunt that I am not feeling so completely comfortable here as she wishes me to be," said the princess.

This didn't deter Faelan at all; in fact it only confirmed his thoughts. He didn't need her telling her aunt of this conversation though, for all they were the same class it wasn't appropriate for him to be asking her of her feelings and desires. "I'm sorry if I have offended you, my lady," he said as he bowed to her. He reached into the rose bush closest to him, snapped a bud from it and held it out to her. "I am only trying to see to your comfort and safety, the same as our aunt and the soldier boy."

"The same as *all* the soldiers in our uncle's service," said Anya quickly. She didn't want to take the flower from him, partly because she knew it would encourage him but mostly because it made her think of Dell and the one he gave her in the garden in Pemberley. She did take it only because she didn't want to offend him either.

"Yes, well, if there was ever a case when this was not so I only wish you to know that I will not back down from a need to fight for your virtue."

"Thank you, my lord," said the girl. She curtsied then turned from him and added, "I am beginning to feel a little chilled; I am going back into the castle to see about some warm tea."

"Good day to you then, Cousin," said Faelan as he watched her walk away.

He enjoyed watching her walk away as much as toward him, her hips had filled out since he had last seen her as well. He would enjoy getting to do much more than only look at her. He only had to play his cards right and she would be promised to him instead of his cousin.

He looked into the darkness of the forest beyond the garden wall and wondered what the soldiers would find when they arrived at Bywood Forest.

38

Bandits in Bywood

The soldiers rode hard to reach the edge of Bywood forest, making it in eighteen hours instead of the twenty-four it normally took. They knew they were risking their horses by doing this but if they were riding toward what they thought they were that would be the least of their worries.

It had seemed such a pleasant place when Dell rode through it on his way to getting the princess, a cool and inviting respite from the warm summer sun. It was early morning when they were entering it that time, now it was just reaching dusk and it was cold and eerie. Shadows hid much of it, giving plenty of places for bandits to be hiding in wait. It was less than comforting not to see any sign of recent passage, telling them the king and his men had never left its darkness.

Alyn led them himself this time. He ordered five of them to light torches and the others to have their swords at the ready. He made sure Dell was one with his sword in his hand, for all he was not even a month in the position he was one of the best swordsmen the king had.

They rode single file into the darkness, every other man with a torch, and moved slowly along the road, looking from side to side, hoping to be able to give warning if they saw anything that didn't belong.

The light from the front-most torch was being reflected back at them by the broken shards of the carriage windows and the exposed blades of swords lying on the ground beside bodies. Some they didn't recognize, those would be the bandits the soldiers had managed to kill.

"Look for life, find the king and prince," shouted Alyn as he dropped from his horse and ran over to the one closest to him.

The others fanned out, keeping a lookout around them as they went. The freshness of the blood told them it had happened not too long before, meaning the bandits that had survived were likely not far from them.

The first two men Dell came to were slain and dead. He went on to the next, who was bleeding from a belly wound but was still alive. "Here. One alive, here," he shouted.

Alyn was beside him in a flash. "We haven't found the king or prince yet," said the man, waving him to go on.

Dell came to the castle steward next. He had many injuries, showing that he had fought equally as long and hard as the true soldiers had. A slice to his throat had finished him. The boy quickly crossed himself and said a silent prayer.

He felt oddly detached as he stood back up and started to move toward the carriage. He didn't see anything moving in or around it. He was just about upon it when he stopped dead and thought his heart had stopped. His eyes took in a body lying face down. His throat constricted so tightly that he couldn't shout out. He wasn't sure who had ordered his muscles to move but they did. He stumbled over, fell to his knees, pulled the body over and cradled it in his arms.

Vianor's eyes fluttered open and he opened his mouth. He was about to tell the bandit who had him to roast in the fires of hell then he saw the face before him. "De... Dell?" he asked.

"It is, my lord," said the boy. The tears that had been just waiting, flooded from Dell's eyes. He saw the man had a wound in his right shoulder, the cut going all the way through the leather armor, woven jerkin and thick tunic the man was wearing, denoting something extremely sharp having been used. The fabric over his left thigh was covered with blood, the edges of it were imbedded in the wound he had there, which was acting as a bandage of sorts. It looked like he had another in his stomach but Dell didn't dare find out. "Don't move, King Vianor, please," Dell managed. He swallowing down the huge lump in his throat then he shouted. "OVER HERE, I FOUND THE KING."

Alyn was by his side again in an instant.

The sergeant at arms could see the king was in great pain by the way he was clinging to the boy holding him. He started to tell Dell to move away but seeing all the wounds beginning to bleed again from being moved the first time he didn't dare to. "Hold him, Dell. Hold still, my lord. Men, get the loose horses harnessed to the carriage so we can get the king home."

Vianor shouted out in anguish as Nox and Clem started to take him from Dell's arms.

The king was clinging to him like he didn't want him to release him, and Dell wasn't sure he wanted to either. "I got him," he said. He motioned them away with a twist of his head then got his knees under him and hoisted the king up in his arms. He followed the soldiers to the carriage and climbed inside. He more fell onto the seat than sat, the king still clutched tightly to him.

The other soldiers gathered around the carriage; some were helping the other men they had found alive, all were wanting to know of their king's status.

"Where is the prince," asked Alyn, seeing he wasn't among those survivors.

"He isn't here," said Clem, they had checked all the men there but none was the prince.

"Could they have taken him to hold for ransom?" asked Alyn.

"He was last seen on one of the horses, riding that direction," said one of the soldiers that had ridden with the king and prince, pointing to the west. He had an arrow shaft protruding from his thigh and had been knocked unconscious but neither was mortal.

Alyn nodded and said, "Nox, Clem, take a torch and check in that direction for any sign of the prince. Dell, go with them…"

"No," said Vianor, not wanting to release the boy.

"Alright, Dell, stay there. Leb, go with them. The rest of you men, take up positions around the carriage," said Alyn. "Keep an eye out for more bandits."

****

The ride inside the carriage was less than comfortable for either man inside, they weren't moving at as slow a pace as one normally did in a carriage, they were riding hard, to get it back to the castle before the king bled out. Dell tried to give the man as much cushion against the rough ride as he could but it really didn't help much. He cringed every time the man moaned painfully.

"I'm sorry, King Vianor, hold on," said Dell, fighting to keep his voice steady.

"I… I should have… I should have waited for you…" said Vianor slowly and painfully.

Dell wasn't sure what he meant so he only nodded.

"My son didn't even try to fight…" said the king, coughing and bringing up blood with it. "He is a coward… You would have never left like that… Barely in my guard and already a good soldier," he coughed up more blood then.

"Please, my lord, just lie still," said Dell, thinking the man must be going into shock or he was in the deliriums of death.

"I wish you had been my son, Dell," said the king very clearly.

Dell's heart leapt into his throat then, he wasn't sure what to say to that. "Please, my lord, you will be alright."

The king coughed one final time then went silent.

Dell waited to see if he spoke again. He began to panic when he felt the man's body going limp in his arms. "King Vianor? Ki… My lord? Stop the carriage," he shouted out the window. "STOP THE CARRIAGE… Alyn! ALLYYNN!"

Alyn trotted his horse over, jumped from the saddle, ran to the door and threw it open,

"What is it, Boy?"

Dell couldn't bring himself to say the words.

Alyn saw the look on the boy's face and all the color drained from his own in an instant. He reached in and put his first two fingers against the king's throat, holding his breath as he did.

He breathed out and shook his head, "It's alright, Boy, he's only unconscious."

"Thank the Gods," said Dell, not even trying to fight the tears streaming freely down his face.

****

It took three men and the physician to prize the king out of Dell's arms, and then only after he had carried him all the way to his chamber and placed him into his bed. The boy stumbled into the corner of the room and watched as the physician worked the fabric of the king's trousers out of the deep cut to expose the man's thigh. A deep gash that was filled with bits of dirt and moss now showed. The man released the sword belt from the king's middle then cut up through the thick jerkin and tunic to expose the man's chest.

All could see the true seriousness of his injuries now.

The shoulder wound was clean through and luckily hadn't harmed anything but muscle and tissue; the one in his belly was deep, as was the one to his thigh. He had lost a lot of blood and was now going in and out of consciousness. They didn't need the look on the physician's face to tell them it wasn't good.

39

Wishes, Hopes and Dreams

Dell staggered from the King's room, about to be sick. He had no idea where he was going he only knew he needed to be away from there. He wasn't looking where he was going so didn't see there was someone in the hall until he had run headlong into them. "Oh, sorry," he muttered. He didn't realize whom he had run into until he heard the intake of breathe and a scream.

"Dell?"

His eyes focused on the face of the woman he loved and his heart did a funny fluttering thing, happiness and pain making it beat erratically.

The princess had heard the men return while she was in the gardens. By the time she made it to the front courtyard everyone was inside the castle. She had gone inside it herself to find out what was happening.

"Anya? I mean... my la..." Dell had suddenly forgotten how to breathe, or stand – his knees collapsed under him and he fell to the floor.

"Dell," said the princess. She saw the blood coating the front of him then. "Oh my God, are you hurt... Dell? Dell?" She looked around her quickly and started to shout.

"I... I am not hurt."

Anya couldn't imagine how he could not be with the amount of blood covering him. She thought he either didn't know he was or was trying not to frighten her. She put his arm over her shoulder then and helped him stand.

Dell wasn't paying attention to where Anya was taking him, still in a daze. When he saw the inside of the room he realized this was her private suite. "Lady, no, we can't... you will get into trouble..."

"Shush and get off your tunic," said the princess as she helped him sit on the stool of her vanity. She went to the pitcher and bowl on the stand by her bureau and grabbed a cloth from the rod beside it.

Dell complied, still in too much of a daze to argue.

Anya turned around and froze for a second. She had never been before a man without his tunic on before; she doubted many of them looked as good as this one did this way. She thought for a moment of the conversation she had with Faelan in the garden, of urges and desires; there was no denying she was having a few of both at that moment. Seeing blood caked on his right collarbone and the side of his face reminded her what she was supposed to be doing. She sat down beside him, dipped the cloth into the water and began to wipe that blood off him, trying not to look at him or his muscled chest as she did.

Dell was trying not to enjoy her doing this, or the smell of her hair that was tickling his other shoulder blade. His heart was doing a funny double beat then skipping a beat over and over in his chest and his skin was tingling. He felt a strange feeling in his innards, he was twisted up in pain thinking about the king but he was also fluttery and warm at being so close to the woman before him. It took all his energy to remind himself to breathe.

"What happened to you?" asked the princess, she couldn't find any injuries on him, other than the bruises he sustained in the training the day before. "Whose blood is this?"

"We... Bywood Forest... the king... we..."

"The king? You found him then? Is... is he..."

"He... his belly... and... and his thigh..." said Dell, his voice gave out as he brought his hand to his shoulder, intending to tell her of the wound the king had there. Tears began to fall from his eyes again. "I... I couldn't... Nothing I could..."

"This is the king's blood?"

"I... I left as the physician was... was looking him over," said Dell. He started shaking then, the reality of what was likely happening in the king's chamber hitting him full at that moment. "He said he wished... his son... I never..."

"The prince? Is Acthiel hurt as well?"

"I... I don't... We never... We never found him... I didn't... I... never wanted this..." Dell's voice was coming in hitches, not even trying to hold back the tears now.

Anya threw her arms around him then and held him as he cried, making her cry as well.

It was only a matter of moments before they were kissing and then he was lifting her into his arms and carrying her to her bed.

As they reached it, reason returned to the boy.

Dell knew he could have her then if he wanted to, and he very much did, but he couldn't do that to her. Their moment of pleasure would be the absolute definition of heaven but it would ruin her future as well as his own. He appreciated that she thought she was willing to give it up to be with him but she would be disgraced, as would her parents, and thus, the king. He couldn't do that no matter how much he wanted her.

"Dell?" asked Anya, feeling him tense up.

"I can't do this to you, Anya."

"Yes, you can, I *want* you to make love to me, Dell," said the girl, starting to unbutton the front of the thin dress she was wearing.

Seeing her milky white skin and the sides of her perfect breasts as she was doing this stunned him for a moment and made him start to rethink his convictions. He forced himself to look at her eyes and saw fear mingled with desire in them; he guessed she was a little frightened since this was her first time. "I would love to make love to you, Anya," he said as he stopped her hands before she got the dress fully open. He kissed them then shook his head. "But, I will not be the ruin of you."

"I will not be ruined…"

"If I take you out of wedlock it will be seen as raping you."

"Not if I want it as well," said the girl desperately.

"Even then. I am a serf, Anya. I should not even think of speaking to you... to think of kissing you and touching you..." he paused then, closing his eyes as images of having done that and wanting desperately to do it again, flooded his very confused and fevered brain. "If it was known that I had not only thought of those things but... It would be seen as an open act against the king. He would resign me from his guard then and, if he didn't have me flogged and hanged, I would be left with nothing. I would end up like one of the bandits in Bywood."

"You would never have to be one of them, Dell; I have a large enough dowry."

"You honestly think your father would let me have it?" asked Dell.

"We don't need anything but each other," said Anya, leaning forward and kissing his hands that were still holding hers.

"Only one who has always had everything would think that," said Dell under his breath. "You would find life as a serf not to your liking."

"If I am with you I will love it, Dell."

"It's easy to say that right now but... for how long? I offer you nothing but poverty and hardship, Anya."

"You also offer me love and protection."

"I can do that from afar." He saw her about to speak and placed a finger to her lips then brushed her cheek as he said, "You are a princess, Anya; your father and King Vianor would never allow you to be with someone of my class."

"I heard some of the other soldiers talking. They say they would be surprised if you aren't a knight within two years."

"I pray that is true but even then... I will still be too far beneath you and I cannot ask you to wait long enough for me to gain status enough."

"My aunt said it is not uncommon for a noblewoman to take a lover after she is wed… If we were discreet we can…"

"No, Anya," said Dell, shaking his head.

"But it is a way to be together," said the girl.

"How long would we be able to stand sneaking around and risking getting caught, always looking over our shoulders… I don't want it that way. It would make our love feel sullied…" said Dell. He was aching inside at having caused the woman any kind of hurt, even for the right reasons.

"I don't understand, Dell." Tears were welling up in her eyes, "Don't you want me?"

"More than anything, I do, Anya. More than I have ever wanted anything. I would do anything for you, anything but this… In a few years you will forget me and, I hope, forgive me," said Dell as he climbed off the bed, grabbed his tunic and left the room.

Anya started to cry then stopped herself; she knew Dell was trying to do what was best for her, which only made her love and want him even more. She watched him stumble out of the room. Her heart stopped beating for a moment then she began to cry. She wished there was some way they could be together.

****

Dell was in tears again, though now it was for what he'd just done rather than the king's condition. He wasn't sure how his heart was still beating, he could feel it in his chest but it felt like he had ripped it out and left it behind with the woman he had just left.

He knew he had just ruined his chances of ever being with Anya by turning her down just now. She would never allow herself in that vulnerable a position again. He knew that he would not be able to say no if they came that close again so he wouldn't allow himself to put her there.

He didn't know just where he was going, having never been in the guest side of the castle before, he hadn't been fully aware when Anya took him from just outside the king's chamber so he didn't know which way would take him back to the main hall. He went down a set of spiral stairs hoping to find a door to get out to the yard; from there he thought he would climb onto a horse and just disappear.

He heard loud voices and crying when he reached the bottom. He started in the direction of those sounds and found himself in the doorway to the great hall. He watched several people moving around a table in the center that had a body on it then he saw Nox and Clem standing off to the side, looking like they had been in a war. He walked over to them and asked, "Is that... is that the prince?"

Neither man could speak.

Dell's face drained of its color as every wish he had made to see the prince come to harm replayed in his mind. He wondered if he was being punished for thinking he could one day be more than he was, if his being so vane was being visited on everyone around him. He stumbled away from them, sure now that he was going to be sick.

He was leaning against a marble post in the hall, letting its coolness comfort him, trying to catch his breath, when he saw the physician, looking in almost the same condition as he, walk by fast, heading away from the king's room. Again Dell thought his heart had stopped. He pushed himself off the post and started to walk up the hall, toward the king's suite. He knew he shouldn't be in this part of the castle without permission but he needed to see him. The man's words to him in the carriage, that he wished he was his son, were making him do this. He would give anything for that desire to be true and not only because he could then be with Anya without fear.

****

Dell stopped in front of the double doors. He took a deep breath, slowly opened one a crack and peered inside. The king was lying in his bed, the sheets pulled up to his chest and his arms folded over it, looking very peaceful, as if sleeping or…

The boy stepped into the room further and took a step toward the bed. He inched a little closer then stopped in the center of the room. He knew he should turn and go but he couldn't. He needed to see, to know, if the king was alive. He couldn't tell if the man was breathing from where he was so he took the last steps and stopped at the bottom of the bed. He jumped as the king took a sudden breath. He thought then that he woken him and was about to beg his forgiveness. He bit back the words and relaxed when the king didn't open his eyes. He stayed frozen where he was, just staring at the man who had been so kind to him, even though he was less than dirt to him.

"I wish… I wish you were my father too," his voice catching in the back of his throat. He jumped when the king's eyes opened. He watched them scanning the room then stop and focus on him before he reacted. "I... I'm sorry, my lord, I..." He turned to go, knowing he had just doomed himself to death. He was just about back to the door when he heard the man say his name.

"Dell?" asked the king, his usually strong sounding voice was weak and shaky.

"It is, my lord," said Dell. He prayed the man wouldn't shout out for the guards. "I am sorry to have disturbed you... I... I wanted to..."

"Come closer," said the king.

Dell looked at the doors, afraid someone would come in and find him where he shouldn't be. He couldn't refuse to do as his king asked. He went to the hand that was outstretched and took it in his. "What do you need, my lord, King."

"Acthiel..." said the king.

Dell didn't know if the king knew his son's fate yet so he only swallowed hard.

"I am sorry he was so cruel to you," said the man. "It was my fault... I gave you too much attention..."

"No, my lord, I did my share of instigating," said Dell.

Vianor's eyes closed again then and his hand went limp.

Dell panicked, unsure what to do. If he was the last one in the room when the king died would they say it was his fault? Would he be put to death for causing it? He couldn't shout for help but he couldn't risk not getting him help if it would save him. He leaned over, hoping to hear breaths being inhaled. He jumped when the king did, coming awake again. "Forgive me, my lord," said Dell, jumping back. "I was only..."

"I am so tired..." said Vianor.

"Uh... I will go... I did not mean to disturb you."

The king said nothing more, only closed his eyes.

Dell could see his chest rising and falling so he knew, this time, he was only asleep. He gently laid his hand back on his chest and walked out of the room quickly.

****

Faelan stepped from his room, intent on finding out what all the noise was. He stood in the hall, looking up and down it, waiting to see if anyone came through he could ask. When no one did he started toward the stairs to the great hall. He took two steps and realized the king's bedchamber door was open a crack.

His first thought was one of the servants was inside, intending to take something valuable to sell off while he was away. He peered inside and saw the soldier Anya had been drooling over standing at the bottom of his uncle's bed and smiled. How perfect, not only would he get him for having messed with the princess but also for stealing from the king.

He started to draw his sword and step in then stopped when he heard the king's voice. He heard him telling this boy that he had given him too much attention and thought then that the boy must be trying to force his uncle into something, threatening him to get favors. He again started to step in then, intent on freeing his uncle from this leach-like burden, then saw the boy turning to leave the room and that his face was covered with tears and his front was covered with blood. He thought then the boy must have slain the king.

He stepped back, intending to call for the guard, when he saw the king's advisor and the physician appear at the top of the stairs.

"Lord Dulmuth," said the spiteful prince, walking over to him quickly.

"Lord Faelan?" asked Dulmuth, seeing him coming from the king's chamber.

"The king is…" started Faelan.

"He is suffering a fever," said the physician, anticipating the man's question.

Faelan turned, intending to finish what he was about to say. He saw the serf boy's back disappearing down the hall. There was no way he could accuse the idiot upstart of anything if he was no longer in the room, there would be no way to prove he had been there. He would have to find another way to make sure the boy got his. He turned back and said, "Is my uncle alright?"

"He's very ill. We are trying to keep him comfortable."

"And, my cousin?" asked Faelan.

Both men looked at the tops of their shoes.

"They just brought him in… He is in the great hall now… I'm sorry… Lord Faelan… the prince… His chances are not good," said the physician.

Faelan felt odd. He would be upset if his cousin died, he truly did like Acthiel, but he also felt a jolt of pleasure. This would mean he was no longer in competition for Anya's hand. Even if Vianor survived he wouldn't be fit to rule for quite some time, if ever again. If he could have himself appointed regent, *to allow his uncle to fully recover*, it would be hard for anyone to remove him. He almost hoped the boy soldier had just killed his uncle then he wouldn't seem to be a usurper when he claimed his birthright.

"Do you need assistance?" asked the physician, seeing the odd look on the lord's face.

"I... I think I need some fresh air," he said, stumbling down the stairs.

40

Sad Happenings

Dulmuth stepped into the king's chamber and walked to the side of the bed. Vianor was fighting a high fever and the wound he took to his left thigh was infected but the physician was loath to amputate. The king had lost a lot of blood and he feared the infection had already spread throughout his system so giving him more wouldn't help him either. The king's advisor watched a servant girl gently pat the king's forehead with a cloth then dampen it again and place it over his fevered brow again.

"Is there anything more I can do, my lord?" asked the frightened girl.

The man couldn't think of anything so he waved her away.

She curtsied then took the pan with the pinkish stained water in her arms and left the room quickly, closing the door behind her.

The king's advisor was just about to sit down when a loud commotion came from beyond those doors. He didn't want to leave Vianor's side but he didn't want it to awaken the king so he went to see what it was and have it stopped immediately.

****

The queen had been in hysterics since she got word her husband had been found and was even worse when they said Acthiel had not been. She was about to order the sergeant at arms to call all the soldiers the king had in and begin a search when two of them came through the castle gate with him.

She nearly broke her own neck running down the stairs when she got word her son had been brought into the great hall. Those two soldiers held her back, refusing to let her enter the room. She tried to find the words to order them out of her way but she couldn't. She had no idea if he was alive and Vianor was only holding on by the thinnest of threads. What was she to do?

Several of the guards and her ladies-in-waiting tried to calm her down but she wouldn't let them. The queen tried again to get past them as she watched two nurses and the physician, the same one that delivered the boy, sixteen years before, working on her son at a feverish pace.

She watched the physician walk away from the table, over to Alyn, and strained to hear what he was saying.

"The arrow that pierced him nicked his heart and has gone through his left lung making his breathing shallow at best."

"Can you perform surgery on him?"

The man only shook his head.

"NNOOOO!" screamed the queen, shaking her head as her legs gave out.

Father Anaith was sent for as soon as the king was brought in. He had left on his pilgrimage to the Lichland monastery earlier in the week so it took a few days to reach him and get him back. He was the only one that might be able to calm the queen.

He came through the main doors at the very moment the queens was falling. He ran over and caught her just before she reached the floor. "My queen, please come to the chapel with me," said the priest, "We will pray for his recovery."
The queen was so numb that she didn't fight him.

****

The chapel was smaller than most castles had but it was intimate. The alter was all white marble and a statue of the virgin mother stood with arms spread out in welcome to all. Five rows of oak pews filled the rest of the chamber and warm candles burned in sconces along the walls, lighting the room pleasantly.
It was empty, allowing the priest and queen were alone and could speak openly.

Father Anaith had just gotten the queen to the first pew when she cried out, "What will I do if Acthiel dies? I should not have allowed Vianor to take him... It is my fault!"

"My lady… my lady… Vela," pleaded the priest, trying to stop her crying. "You had no way to know this would happen. The bandits' attacks had subsided in the last weeks. All thought the roads were safe."

"We are being punished, aren't we?" she burst. Admitting a fear she had since the day the boy was born.

"Punished? For what, my lady?"

"For taking the people's children from them."

"No, my lady, it was the drought that did that."

"What will I do if he doesn't live? The physician said I would never conceive again… If there is no heir… Vianor must have an heir."

"Please, my lady," begged the priest but she was deep in hysterics again. He just held her, knowing she would hear no more of his comforts until she had cried herself out.

Anaith was about to go to the alter to get the wine hidden inside the podium when one of the nurses appeared in the doorway. The look on her face told him all he needed to know. He started to shack his head, to tell the woman to go back away, when the queen looked up.

Vela knew the look as well. She wailed again but this time no tears came.

****

The scullery maid, Sally, managed to walk out the doors of the king's chamber. As soon as she was through them she began to run. The blood stained water in the bowl clutched tightly to her was sloshing over the sides and she was in full tears as she burst through the doors into the kitchen. Her eyes were so clouded over that she didn't see Gerti in front of her.

The fat girl screamed out as the bowl of pinkish water splashed over her front, seeing it quickly turning her white apron the same color.

Clara, who had been about to enter the pantry, ran over and grabbed the still balling girl, pulling her further into the room. She brought her hand back to slap the girl but stopped in mid-swing when she saw the look of horror on her face. Seeing it wasn't her causing it. She brought that hand down to grab the girl's other shoulder and began to shake her violently, "What in the heavens is wrong with you, Child?"

It took Sally a moment to catch her breath enough to speak and then it came in hitches so it was hard to understand. "The... pr... is... de..."

"What? What are you saying?" said Clara more forcefully.

Sally's sister, Kathy, ran over to the two then. "Please Miss Clara," she said.

Clara looked ready to slap Kathy then. She did release Sally, seeing all the others looking as if they might not take kindly to it. One, or even two, she could bully but if the lot decided they didn't want to be bullied she might find herself in a lot more pain than she would like to be in.

Kathy put her arms around her sister and began to stroke her hair, "Ssshhh, it's alright... now tell us what happened."

"The king is bare... barely alive and... the prince..." said Sally, bursting into tears again.

"*The prince is what,* Child," screamed Clara.

"THE PRINCE IS DEAD!"

****

The queen was just getting herself back into a bit of decorum when Dulmuth appeared in the doorway.

The look on his face was even worse than the look the nurse had.

Father Anaith saw the man and quickly tried to motion him away, figuring he was there to tell the queen her son was dead as well.

He shook his head.

"Please, Lord Dulmuth," said the priest as he came up to him, stopping him from entering any further, "the queen already knows..."

"The king," said the man.

Vela's head shot up then, "What... what about Vianor?"

"He is... he is asking for you."

The queen pushed past both men and ran up the hallway to her husband's bedchamber.

Vela threw open the doors of her husband's bedchamber when she arrived without even knocking. "Vianor?" she asked hesitantly. He was lying still with his eyes closed and his hands clasped over his chest. "My darling?" she asked, stepping closer.

His eyes opened slowly. He tried to smile but he couldn't do it, "Vela..." he said as tears burst from his eyes.

"My darling," Vela cried as she ran to his side and laid her head down on his arm.

He cringed but he didn't want her to leave his side. "Please forgive me," he said.

"There is nothing to forgive," said the queen.

"If I hadn't taken him with me…" said the king as he began to cough, blood shining on his lips when he was finished.

Dulmuth stepped into the room and quickly went to the queen, about to pull her off Vianor so the physician, who was right behind him, could reach the man.

The physician motioned Dulmuth away and slowly stepped to the other side of the bed. He placed the backside of his hand on the king's forehead and grasped his wrist with his other, counting the number beats.

Anaith arrived seconds later.

The physician motioned the priest to him and whispered for him to take the queen away.

Anaith went to Vela's side and started to place his hands on her arms as Vianor's eyes fluttered open again.

"Father Anaith? Is that you?"

"It is, my lord, King."

"Please tell me I am forgiven."

"My lord, you are in no way responsible for the happenings of this day. Your soul is clean," said the priest. He kissed the top of the king's hand and held it to his chest.

They all got stiff when that hand went limp and slid from the priest's grip.

Anaith looked at the physician, suddenly unable to speak or breathe.

Vela looked up as she heard an extended breath leave her husband. "Vianor? Vianor?"

The physician lifted each eyelid then held his hand under the man's nose. "He is only asleep again. He will be in and out of consciousness until I can get his fever broken."

Anaith put his hands on the queen's arms then, again with the intention of lifting her up; he was surprised when she let him. He directed her to the balcony and set her in the chair set out for the king to get fresh air. He knew now was the time to tell her the secret he had been keeping for so many years.

41

Broken Proclamation

Vela was stunned, she couldn't imagine how she was able to breathe. She had lost her son and it looked like she might lose her husband. What was she to do now? She asked the same question aloud.

Father Anaith knew he had to tell the queen the secret he had kept from her for sixteen years then. "My queen... I have something I must tell you."

Vela couldn't imagine him saying anything that could make her feel any more numb than she was at that moment. She looked at him through her red and swollen eyes and waited; seeing that he was trying hard to find the words he wanted to say.

"The day Acthiel was born..."

Vela shuddered, although she wasn't awake for most of it what she could remember was not anything she wished to relive just then, or ever again. "Please, Anaith, not now," she begged.

"I must now, Vela... It must now be known... for the good of the people... That day... you gave birth to more than one that day," said Anaith.

It took Vela a moment to understand what he had said. She hadn't thought she could find any more tears but she did then. Why would this man, whom she had thought was her friend, whom she had thought cared for her, need to tell her that she had actually had a second child that day, a child that would've been destroyed according to the proclamation? Why would he feel the need to tell her this now of all times? "I do not want to hear this, Anaith," cried the queen.

"Yes you do, Vela. I could not follow the proclamation…"

"You what?" asked Vela, no longer comprehending what he was saying.

"I could not… I did not…"

"What are you saying, Anaith?" asked Vela. Her heart suddenly began to beat faster, hoping she was hearing what she thought she was hearing.

"I could not destroy part of you and Vianor, my queen. I know it was wrong… I know I should be hanged for going against the proclamation… I have watched others being punished for having done this and said nothing… I bade one of the servants... told her one of my parishioner's had given birth… that the mother had died in childbirth… bade her go to the nearest orphanage."

"What?"

"There may still be a living heir."

****

Clara was pacing the courtyard as she waited for Queen Vela to appear. Her entire female staff was lined up against the stone wall behind her. All were shaking, partly from being unsure what was going on themselves.

The queen had never asked for such a display before, usually she made her judgments of the staff's capabilities in private. She wondered if it was her or one of them that caused whatever this was about, if she found out it was one of her staff, claiming some unnecessary or excessive abuse, she would personally string them up. Why would she be doing it now, when her dead son was still lying on the table in the great hall and her husband wasn't far from it?

The head kitchen servant's eyes went instantly to Cami. She had been seen speaking to the prince and king both. Perhaps the girl had decided to use her fine attributes to win the favors either of both men. She remembered her asking for a sweater recently... perhaps to hide a growing bulge in her middle? If the girl was pregnant with either man's child she would be the mother of the heir to the throne. Clara knew that would mean she would be out on her ass soon after then, she hadn't been exactly kind to the girl and she had a feeling she could be quite vindictive.

She was about to go to the girl and ask her just what she thought she could get away with doing to her when the doors behind her opened and the priest, Father Anaith, stepped out. Followed closely by the queen, who was looking quite pale.

****

Cami saw that Clara was looking hardest at her. She tried to remember if she had done anything that would upset her so. Maybe it was because she wasn't crying like the others? She was sorry the prince was dead but she was also relieved. She did feel horrible for this thought.

She knew it would take hours and a lot of elbow breaking scrubbing to get all of the prince's blood off the floor of the great hall and she guessed the table he was laid on would be beyond cleaning, the blood having soaked too deep into the wood grains. It would likely be burned in the furnaces. She hoped they did the same to the prince's body.

She jumped when Clara's eyes stopped on her again then. She looked disgusted, like she might have read her mind. Could she be put to death for having hateful thoughts? She jumped again when the doors behind Clara opened then. She watched the priest, Father Anaith, and the queen step through them. She felt her knees going weak then, wondering if she was about to be called out as a heretic for wishing this on the prince and burned at the stake as a witch.

****

Anaith walked the line of frightened girls, disregarding any who were under thirty. Those wouldn't have been alive at the time of the prince's birthing let alone working at the castle.

"Anyone under the age of thirty may go," said the queen.

Clara's heart leapt then, it wasn't as bad as she thought then. She snapped her fingers and told the girls to go to their room and wait there.

That left only five, including Clara.

The queen looked at Anaith. She could tell he didn't recognize anyone.

"How many of you were serving here on the night the queen went into labor sixteen years ago?" asked the priest.

Only two raised their hands, Clara being one of them.

"The rest of you may go," said the priest.

Anaith looked at the two woman before him, neither looked like the one he remembered but a hard life might have made them age faster. "What I am about to say is not to be repeated," said the priest cryptically.

Clara watched the queen's face drain of all its color and put her hands on her stomach.

"The day of the prince's birth, I brought something to a girl that was new to the castle. Something I told her was to be kept a secret. I need to know if it was one of the two of you."

One woman had a look to say she had no idea what he was talking about, the other, the head kitchen maid, had lost all the color in her face now.

"Was it you?" he asked Anaith.

Clara swallowed hard and nodded.

The other woman was waved away, leaving only Clara.

"Where did you take the bundle I handed you?" asked the priest.

Vela's heart was in her throat.

Clara was racking her brain for what to say. The man before her had told her one of his parishioners' that had died in childbirth. She hadn't known, had never put two and two together, that it was at the same day and the same hour as the queen was in the middle of giving birth. He had made her swear, on her life, that she would never tell, no matter who asked her. He was above her and a priest besides so she had no choice but to obey, she couldn't be punished for that could she? "I... I..." she started.

Vela was before her then, "Acthiel... my son, is dead... Anaith says you... if you know where..." said the queen, tears coming to her eyes.

"You... you said... one of your parishes'... you said I was never to speak of it..." Clara cried out, looking at the priest.

"I promise you, no matter your oath of that day, I will not have you punished," said the queen, "I must know if I have another male child alive."

"I don't know where they were taken," said Clara.

"They?" asked Vela, looking at Anaith, "How many were there?"

"Two, my lady," said Clara.

"I had triplets that day?" the queen said. She looked from the kitchen maid to Anaith and back. "Boys or girls?"

"I do not know, I... I never looked," said Clara.

The queen fell back.

"I took them to the head kitchen maid... she cleaned them up and... and took them..."

"Where is she now?"

"She... she died many years ago now," said Clara.

"How are we going to find them, Anaith? We don't know if they lived or even if they are sons or not."

"My... my lady?" said Clara hesitantly.

The queen and priest looked at her.

"They were put in... we put cloths on them, on their bottoms, for their... for their messes."

The two looked at her harder, not understanding.

"They were castle linens… with the king's crest on them."

"Your oath to keep this a secret is still in place, do you understand?" asked the queen.

"I do, my lady," said Clara, bowing low.

The queen waved her away.

Once she was gone Anaith turned to vela and said, "My queen, I most humbly suggest we find out if either survived before we say anything to the king. He needs to focus all his efforts on healing."

"You are supposed to be sworn never to lie, Father Anaith," said the queen. "How can I ever trust you again?"

"I did it for the sake of the kingdom, Vela. I could not destroy your blood."

She wanted to be angry with him, she wanted to punish him for breaking the edict and for lying to her all these years but she couldn't be. "You are right. Vianor does not need to know this now. How is best to proceed? It must be done without it drawing attention," said the queen.

"I can make some discreet inquiries," said the priest. "Most of the city's attentions will be on the upcoming festival. I will visit the housemothers of each home and see what I can learn of them."

"I will trust you in this, Anaith, but only because I believe you were thinking only of the kingdom. You will report your findings only to me."

"Of course, my Queen."

****

Vela managed to make it to the stone wall beside the garden. She slowly sat down on it. A wave of grief, anger, regret, relief and hope washed over her suddenly, making her feel dizzy. She was glad she was sitting down still or she would have fallen. She was feeling very strange at that moment. She was aching inside but also strangely at peace.

She would have never admitted it to anyone aloud but she often wished she had never had Acthiel. In many ways the kingdom would be better off without him as its heir. Now she learned she could potentially have two others sons...

She ached inside for the lives those two children must have had to live. How they had suffered having to fight for every morsel, bit of food and piece clothing, and the lack of attention they would have gotten with only the few staff at each home. She had heard tales of the wards being physically and emotionally abused and becoming cruel adults due to this treatment, what if they were no better than Acthiel?

Could she allow one who had been raised in that way to take her kind-hearted husband's place on the throne if he didn't recover? She really had no choice. She had to hope they wouldn't be beyond changing... having not been spoiled from the beginning as Acthiel had been.

What of Faelan? He most certainly knew of his cousin's demise by now. He must be just beside himself with joy at the thought of being moved to crown prince. Would he be so willing to relinquish that position, even though not truly his, for a child she could not truly prove was hers? One that, by all rights, should have been destroyed the day he came into the world?

How could she make the people accept that?

What if her other two children were girls?

What if… Life in the homes was harsh. Each home had its own plot in the cemetery, all three were nearly full. What if neither had survived? The queen began to cry silently then – she wasn't crying for herself, she was crying for her dead son, for her unknown children, for her dying husband and for her people.

Read the exciting conclusion in part 2
Cast into the Light

Made in the USA
Middletown, DE
30 September 2023

39729040R00224